From Across the Divide

by

K. Victoria Chase

FROM ACROSS THE DIVIDE
3rd Edition

ISBN 978-0-9890651-5-3
Edited by Faith Williams

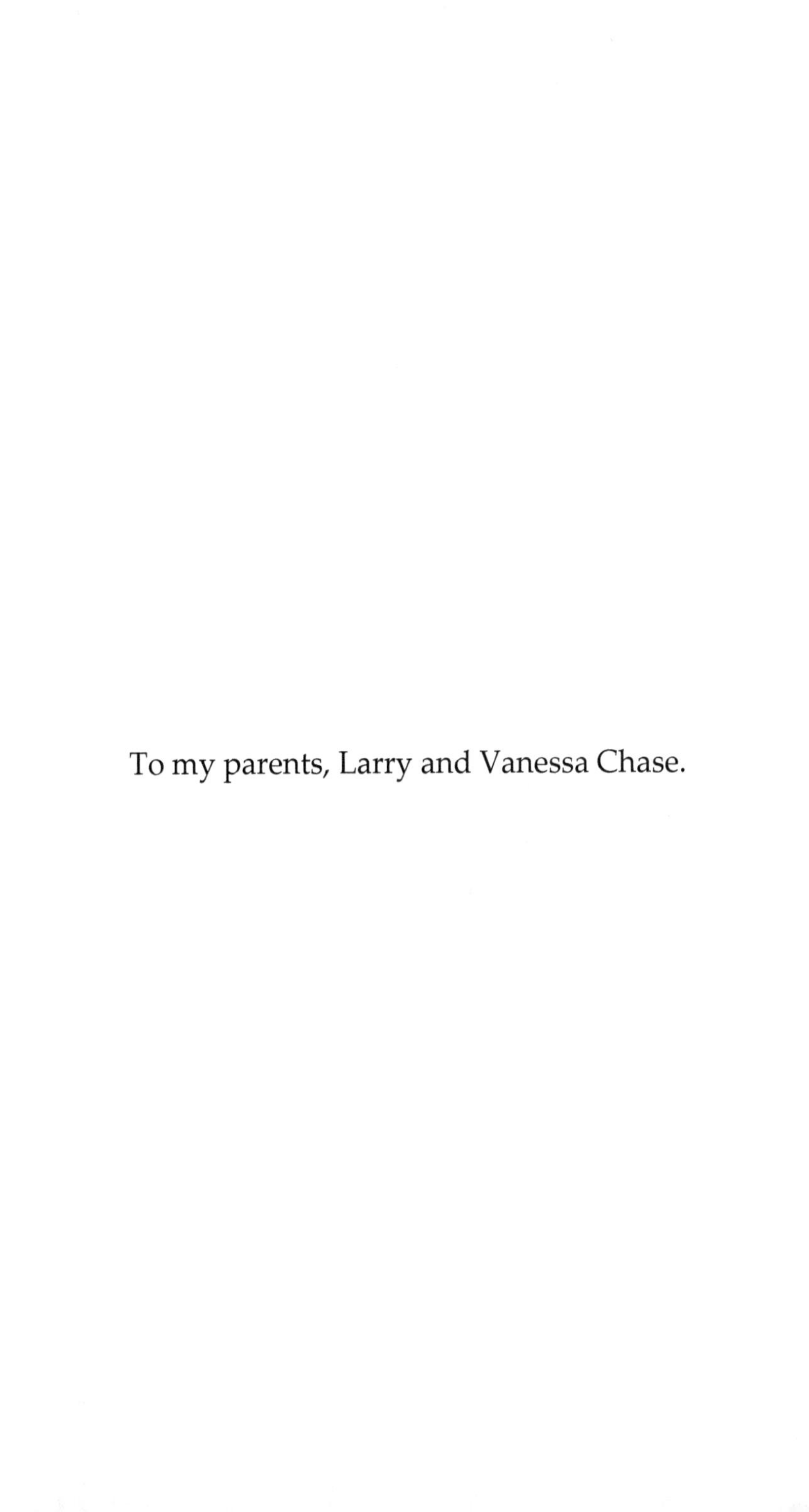

To my parents, Larry and Vanessa Chase.

Chapter One

PRODIGAL

Freeman, Alabama

Summer 1963

Elie Brown strolled alongside the bank of a familiar river, a book in one hand and a juicy red apple in the other. Her teeth sank into the sweet treat, a trickle of juice lining the outside of her lip. Her eyes never left the page as she wiped the sticky nectar on the back of her hand.

A branch snapped, halting her step and dragging her from fantasy into the real world.

Her mother often warned her of the dangers of walking alone, yet the sun still lingered high in the sky, keeping most white men at their jobs…Lord willing. From the deep recesses of her mind came the image of Leonard, his body bloody, beaten, and hanging from a tree a few miles up the road. Elie shuddered, forcing the gruesome vision of her friend's broken body—his lifeless eyes—from her mind.

Leonard's murder had been the first attack in several months, and a fear that more bodies would follow gripped the black residents of Freeman, but night lynchings did little to shake her confidence in the Lord's protection. She never quite feared her solitary time on this particular spot of the lane so close to the Montgomery estate, a place she'd been acquainted with since birth. Isolation energized her, allowing her to dream. Not a soul had ever bothered her here, her old haunt, in her twenty years of life.

Many black youths were never bothered until they were found floating face down in county streams.

Elie scanned her surroundings, shivering in the warm wind. Overgrown brush and solid oak trees, with branches thick enough to hang rope, surrounded her. Glancing over her shoulder, her gaze collided with the man behind her and the scream in her throat evaporated.

Hands in pockets and a foot propped against the trunk of an oak, the man was dressed in a crisp white shirt and a waist-length jacket the color of his chocolate slacks. A wide-brimmed hat was tucked under one arm.

Elie's breath hitched.

Tall, lean but powerfully built, his wavy, dark blond hair curling at the nape of his neck contrasted with the sophistication of his wrinkle-free attire. Her gaze locked on his eyes—a hypnotic green as deep as the color of moss beneath riverbed rocks. His mouth dropped open, a flicker of recognition in his gaze.

"Elie…" His deep timbre, nearly lost in the rustling of the leaves in the wind, warmed her heart with familiarity.

Eric Montgomery.

Elie squealed in delight. "Eric!" Dropping both book and apple on her picnic blanket nearby, she left the edge of the creek, running up the slight hill, and into his outstretched arms. He laughed, twirling her around, her white dress billowing in the breeze. After setting her feet on the ground, he gripped her shoulders, his gaze holding hers.

"Elie?" he asked in almost a whisper, his eyes betraying

his disbelief.

She raised a teasing brow. "Oh, so you greet every woman this way?"

Eric gave her a heart-stopping grin, and she blinked with sudden awareness. In her mind, she saw the boy she'd known years earlier, but the defined jaw, the size of his hands on her arms, and the heat from his nearness, formed the undeniable image of a man.

"It's been a really long time…" His voice trailed off, his gaze still lingering on her face as if trying to recognize the girl he hadn't seen in years.

Elie laughed heartily at the amazement she read in his warm eyes, but goose bumps rippled on her arms. "How long has it been?" Eric glanced down as color flushed in his cheeks. "You didn't even come home after college." She tried to keep the hurt from her voice, but his actions had stung. After his sophomore year, Eric had chosen to remain on campus grounds and rent an apartment near school during the summer. Every day she'd awake with the hope he'd return and every day she was disappointed.

He released her arms. Turning his back, he walked to the tree he'd been leaning on moments earlier. A hand on the bark, he leaned heavily against it, and then rotated his neck, his sullen gaze taking in the calm river.

"That was a very long time ago," he murmured.

Elie's heart constricted. Whether the wistfulness of his voice was for his mother or her, she didn't know. Growing up the last few years without her best friend had left her with a sizable loss of her own. Who was the man before her? How much had he changed from their youth? They'd been inseparable since her birth but, for almost five years, she'd come to know a silence louder than the laughter that had always followed whatever prank he'd succeeded in pulling on her.

Elie took a hesitant step forward. "We didn't know you

were comin'. Your father will be so happy," she said softly, wondering whether Eric believed her. Correspondence from Eric to his father, Morgan Montgomery, had trickled over the last year and a half…even though Morgan faithfully mailed his monthly letter.

The corners of Eric's lips tweaked upwards. "You remember when we used to play here as kids?" He faced her, a glimmer of good times sparkling in his eyes. "We'd come out here and run around, skip through the water, get all dirty and fight like cats and dogs." Another smile—this time with deep dimples—and her heart fluttered in a strange way. "I recall you got the best of me on several occasions as we rumbled in the jungle here." He gestured around at the trees and overgrowth.

"Well, at least you have the humility to admit it." Smugness filled her and she smiled, the memories of her victories, however few, giving her pleasure. "You'd never let me forget that not only was I three years younger than you, but also quite a bit smaller." Elie raised her chin, crossing her arms over her chest. "I'm not so puny now."

His full mouth slowly eased up into half a grin. His eyes roamed freely over her form, one brow lifting, considering her challenge. "I wouldn't dream of punishing you on my first day back."

Elie laughed nervously, his appraisal drawing heat to her cheeks. She retrieved her blanket from the earth, hiding her face from his study. Very much the self-assured Eric she remembered, yet something about him told her he was…experienced. After folding the cloth and tucking it under one arm, she picked up her book and placed it in her hobo, and then tossed her half-eaten apple into a nearby bush.

Eric frowned. "You have to be somewhere?"

"As a matter of fact, I'm going to be late for work if I don't leave now." She walked toward the road. When she didn't hear his footsteps, she faced him. He stared after her, uncertainty in his eyes. "Are you going to walk with me or not?"

Eric gave her a quizzical look but started forward. He placed his hat on his head and then snatched up his tattered brown luggage before matching her stride.

"Is that all you have?" She expected more than one bag. He'd lived away from home for several years. Did he not own books, or at least more clothes?

"All that I own, yes. Where do you work?"

"I work for your father at your home." She curved her lips up at him, before continuing on to the road. "I've been workin' there ever since I was fifteen. Remember?" Out of the corner of her eye, she noticed his tight jaw, a fist lost in a pocket, and his eyes on the dirt. She sensed an uncomfortable tension building. If he wouldn't make conversation, then she would. "I heard you were in France for a while. Was it beautiful?"

Elie was eager to hear about the years of his life she'd missed. When Eric obliged to write the family, Morgan had allowed her to read the letters. Eric had kept the correspondence brief, affirming his location and the state of his health, never divulging intimate details of his affairs.

Eric matched her pace, his eyes on the ground. Noting the pensive look on his face, she waited patiently for him to answer. They walked along in tense silence. Eric glanced at her blanket, plucked it from under her arm, and secured it beneath one of his own. Startled, Elie stared at him, hoping to catch his eyes, but the earth seemed to hold more of his interest. Unable to endure the wordlessness any longer, she reached up with one hand and put a finger beneath his chin, guiding it until he locked eyes with her. She lifted a brow and repeated her question about France.

"Yes, it was..." he said, his eyes warming as she smiled at him.

"I hope you enjoyed your time there."

"I did."

Elie wished she could believe him, but he had run. Run from home, from the people who loved him…from her. They all shared the same pain, and together they'd come through the last few years a stronger unit. All except Eric. He'd chosen the company of strangers, the distance of half a globe, over the fellowship and comforts of family and home. She doubted he'd truly enjoyed himself. She wanted to challenge him on the truthfulness of his declaration, but kept silent, refusing to ask the more pressing question burning on her tongue…why?

Elie fingered a loose thread on her hobo. "Your father would have met you at the airport."

"I didn't want to trouble him."

"Eric, you're his son—"

"Not for the last five years."

Biting her lip at his clipped response, Elie pondered her answer as she stole a glance at him. A hardened jawline, back ramrod straight, and green eyes now zeroed in on some imaginary spot ahead of them. He oozed anger, not grief. Yet, he'd made the decision to leave. And now he was angry?

Elie lifted her heavy braid off her neck, hoping the warm wind might dry some of the sudden perspiration. When the sun baked her moist skin instead, she replaced the braid, sighing. She and Eric were no more than strangers.

Eric flicked her braid, just like he used to when she was a child. He offered a small, apologetic smile. "Forgive me, I'm…a little overwhelmed."

Grinning, she nodded, ready to forgive. "Well, the prodigal son returns." She looped an arm through his. "Welcome home."

Did he just cringe?

****

Eric's heart pounded in trepidation as his home came into

view. A massive three-story with white columns and a wrap-around veranda, popular with Southern homes. In the distance, stables held more than a dozen thoroughbreds—one claim to the Montgomery fame. A smaller barn was situated much closer to the house and with it, the familiar hayloft he and Elie had frequented when they were younger.

The memories of time past flooded his mind. His last supper in the dining room, the horses tended by Elie's father, Emmett Brown; the smell of fresh baked cookies by Miss Hattie—their pleasantly plump housekeeper—and his mother; his mother decorating the Christmas tree, her laughter filling the room. A new fissure ripped through his hemorrhaging heart.

Elie gently squeezed his arm but it did little to release the acid in his muscles. "Your father will love that you're home. He's missed you so much."

His discomfort eased slightly. All these years, guilt that he'd somehow failed his father had caramelized over the pain still cooking within him.

Elie giggled. "Just wait until Miss Hattie sees you. She'll make such a fuss over you! Better think of the meal you missed the most while off in Europe. Miss Hattie will probably die if she doesn't fix it for you."

Eric glanced at Elie, her smile bright as her gaze flitted to the Montgomery home. His nerves settled as he thought of Miss Hattie. "Fried chicken," he mumbled.

"What? They don't eat fried chicken in France?"

Eric laughed, squeezing the hand still resting around his biceps. "They don't make it like the South. Fried chicken, potato salad, hot rolls, collard greens…"

"So now you admit you missed home?" She pressed closer to him.

Eric's gaze lingered on her round, brown eyes, full of…hope. Hope for him? Did she sense what his soul gave up on long ago? "I missed you." The soft answer was past his lips before he knew it. She flushed a soft, reddish hue and then hid her eyes from his view.

"Mistah Montgomery!"

They strode toward the horse track built in a field a short distance from the house. Emmett Brown stood in the center of another patch of land, separated from the track by a fence. The horse he guided around a training circle stopped running after Emmett moved to the part of the fence nearest the pair. Eric slipped from Elie's grasp and jogged to the fence.

Eric grinned, his heart warming at the sight of his childhood mentor, Emmett Brown. Like a second father to him, Emmett had taught Eric everything he knew about raising horses—even how to ride. The man's receding hairline was dark and peppered with gray, as was his thick, well-groomed mustache. A stocky man, Emmett possessed broad shoulders, thick legs, and now a pooch hung slightly over his belt. All in all, he hadn't aged much.

Eric reached over and gripped Emmett's outstretched hand. "Mr. Brown, it's really good to see you again."

"Oh, Mistah Montgomery, you sure have grown. Yes, sir, you are lookin' like a fine young man." He returned the hearty handshake with a white-toothed grin.

"Thank you, Mr. Brown, but the real shock is seeing Elie."

She walked up to the fence and met his gaze, her lips quivering in an uncharacteristically shy smile.

"I've looked the same for a while now but," he said, shaking his head in amazement, "she's completely changed." Her smile turned affectionate.

At the clearing of Emmett's throat, Eric broke his connection with Elie. Emmett glanced from his daughter back to him, and Eric could have sworn displeasure had sparked in the eyes of his old friend. Had he said something wrong? Worse yet, was the relationship between Emmett and Elie strained?

Emmett cast a glance over his shoulder at the young

equine. "I've got to get back to this one here. He's a rebellious one." Eric inwardly flinched at the hardened stare Emmett gave him. "Your father…" Emmett produced a melancholy smile. "Your father will be grateful you've returned home." Emmett pinched his daughter's cheek before calling out to the horse and resuming the training regimen.

Grateful? His father? *Try furious.* He'd be forever grateful if his father allowed him to walk through the front door again.

With his feet cemented in the dirt, Eric stared at Emmett's back while contemplating the uncomfortable churn in his stomach. "I see your father is still training horses. Does he still board some at your farm?"

Elie followed his gaze. "Yes, he does. He has a great reputation for the care of the horses. Some of them have owners who live hours away. They board them here at our farm just because of Daddy's service." Shifting, Elie put her elbow on the highest rung of the fence, laying the side of her face against her fist. "You stallin'?"

Eric smirked. "A little. You always knew how to read me." An image of time past emerged—the number of hands he lost in cards due to an ineffective poker face—and the sudden thought she could see into him caused him to steel his emotions.

"Nervous?"

She did it again. "Do you read minds?" he asked sarcastically. Elie's frown pricked his conscience. Strange, his conscience rarely made an appearance. "I'm sorry. Yes, I'm a bit nervous. 'The Prodigal Son returns' as you said." He scuffed the dirt with his boot, the layer of dust on his shoe drawing his groan. Eric snatched a handkerchief out of his front right pocket and leaning over, he wiped clean the grime. After replacing the cloth, he flattened his hands on his chest and smoothed down the already ironed fabric of his shirt. Even though his clothes were wrinkle-free, his life was not—and he was growing tired of the facade. "I'm unsure about the reception awaiting me."

"Along with my address, did you forget the Bible as well while you were away? The Prodigal Son was thrown a party. I wouldn't expect anything less from your own father."

Eric held her gaze, reading the slight chastisement despite her grin. Maturity had tamed her sharp tongue, but only a bit. She was right, however, and when her eyes continued to hold fast to his, he smiled out of respect for her. She mirrored his grin and turned toward the house.

Begrudgingly, he followed her, but soon stopped short. Morgan Montgomery ran toward them, followed by a huffing Miss Hattie.

Morgan's strides slowed until he ceased moving. A blend of emotions crossed his features—shock, love, joy—but not fury. Tears welled in the older Montgomery's eyes, and a chasm tore through Eric's fragile heart. Long minutes ticked by—neither man advancing to the other.

Eric's jaw rattled with uncertainty. He was the prodigal, not his father. Regardless of the felicitous welcome Elie assured him of, it fell upon him to make amends. With a sharp inhale, he traipsed forward, stopping a few feet from the man who had sired him. Eric swallowed the lump of rejection in his throat.

"Hello, Father."

Chapter Two

CHANGE

Eric awoke early the next morning, exhausted from a restless night. Dream-induced tension racked his frayed nerves. His father had cried tears of joy into his shoulder yesterday, extolling God for Eric's safe return. Even Miss Hattie had raised her chubby hands to the sky and danced, her swollen feet lighter than air. Seeing a pink-cheeked Elie grinning at his embarrassment made the reunion all the more uncomfortable. Did he expect a full pardon? If it had been granted, why did weight remain tied to his soul? This morning had been just like all the others over the years, and Eric questioned the logic of returning home. The cure wasn't here.

I need to get out. After a quick shower, he dressed and made his way to the kitchen. Spying wrapped leftover cookies on the kitchen island, he snuck a few of the sweets and ducked out of the house. A hazy, early morning fog rose off the ground over the estate. Eric breathed in the fresh dewy air of his home. Crows gawked at the knocking of the yellow-hammer woodpeckers. Here, time had stood still.

Eric eyed his father's full-sized sedan, the top retracted, on the gravel driveway. His lips snaked upward. Where would his father keep the keys? He didn't wonder for long. Slipping back into the house through the kitchen's back door, he spied the keys in a small wicker basket on a decorative table in the front foyer, swiped them, and exited through the front door.

The drive past adjacent farms and through familiar neighborhoods was so uneventful he wondered whether life in the small city had changed. When he turned onto Main, he got his answer.

Eric remembered segregation existed in Alabama, but the years of living abroad where the races were integrated didn't prepare him for the shocking reality. Signs reading Colored Only hung over business entrances, public restrooms, water fountains, even bus stops. Adherence to this code was clearly mandatory. The white population avoided those isolated areas, and blacks never strayed toward locations not specifically marked for their presence.

Across the street, a middle-aged black man in a crisp, white shirt and a white apron tied around his waist stood at the window of a small bakery. He flipped over a hanging sign on the window to show the public the shop was open for business. At the barbershop next door, a young man stood inside, sweeping the floor and preparing for the day's customers. The red, white, and blue cane swirled over the doorframe. Eric didn't recall blacks owning many businesses—at least not on Main Street. Integration seemed to be phasing into the heart of Alabama.

A short distance down the road—positioned predominantly on the corner of Main and First Street—sat the Montgomery Bank, a business his father had opened at the age of twenty-four. Eric eyed the building across from the bank. The city's administrative headquarters towered over the other buildings on the block and all others across from it. He hoped to obtain a driver's license at the Driver's License Bureau prior to a cop stopping him and issuing a ticket.

A barking dog arrested his attention. Near the barbershop, an old black man walked by a parked police cruiser. The officer leaned lazily against the back of the vehicle, holding the leash of a hound. The old man paid no mind to the dog's vicious bark. The policeman, however, sneered at the man, apparently not interested in how fiercely his dog tugged the leash.

An unexpected jolt of apprehension for the elderly man hit Eric, followed by heated relief. How long had it been since he cared for anyone but himself? He'd believed the concept as foreign to him as his travels abroad. Much of his time had been spent wallowing in self-pity.

The old man continued his quest, drawing the attention of three men in dusty overalls and soiled shirts, lounging on a rusty-colored truck outside of a small pub. Two sat on the back bumper. The other stood on the truck bed, leaning on the outside of the cab. Eric wondered what three men would be doing at this hour in the morning, in the city, relaxing on a truck.

The man standing in the truck bed had a youthful appearance with hair dark as midnight, and a slight build. His stance, however, arms crossed and legs apart, dared to be confronted. The man closest to the sidewalk also sported dark hair cut short to the scalp. More muscled than the younger-looking man, he had a firm countenance, yet his stance was the most relaxed of the three. At times, he glanced around the city with a pensive look on his face. The third man was the complete opposite of the other two. He shifted his bottom on the bumper every few seconds, shaking his scraggly blond hair and spitting tobacco into the street. He also possessed a strong build, but a round face, unlike the angular lines of the other two; the gentlest looking of the three—and the most restless.

The dog continued to bark while the policeman watched the old man's progress. The aged man halted, his sight on an object to his right.

A water fountain.

His head tilted back. A white sign with the words White Only in large black letters was clearly posted above. The man ambled toward the fountain.

The marked fountain for the colored was positioned at the end of the block.

Eric kneaded the back of his neck, the tight muscles unyielding beneath his treatment. The two men on the truck bumper eased into a standing position and the officer shifted his right hand to rest on the butt of his gun.

"Hey, old man!" the younger man in the cab shouted. The elderly gentleman didn't respond, but leaned against the fountain, dipping his head down until his lips tasted the drink. The young man leapt out of the truck bed, the other two on his heels.

"Get 'im, Shane," the blond one yelled.

Fists clenched at his sides, his youthful face twisted into fury. "Hey, old man!"

Water sprung from the fountainhead, splashing into a dark-skinned mouth.

In two strides, Shane had a hand on the senior's shoulder, whirling him around. "I'm talkin' to you!"

Startled, confusion crossed the face of the dodderer. His widened eyes dodged from one man to the other, to yet another. He made an effort to shrink back, but the white-knuckle grip of his detainer imprisoned him.

The blond huffed, a growl emanating from his chest. "Yeah, you pay attention when my brother's talkin' to you." He cursed, calling him a foul name, one Eric remembered hearing when he was a little boy. Its use was forbidden in the Montgomery household.

The old man sputtered, putting a shaky hand behind his

right ear.

Shane slapped the man's hand into his ear. "What? You deaf?"

The man frowned, his gaze downcast.

Hands on the old man's chest, the blond shoved hard, and the already hunched back slammed into the metal water fountain.

The elderly man let out a painful yelp and slumped to the ground, his face twisting into a look of intense pain and fear.

Eric sprinted to the scene. "Hey!" He slowed to stop a few paces from the men. The blond and the short-haired man faced Eric, while Shane kept his glaring eyes on his prey. "Can't you see the man is old and hard of hearing? He's probably half blind."

With raised brows, the short-haired man crossed his arms over his chest, his stance nonchalant. "What's it to you?" Still as relaxed as ever, a man not easily riled. The blond, however, sounded close to hyperventilating, as though trying to keep himself from flying off the handle.

The blond hacked and spit onto the sidewalk. "Yeah, this ain't your affair," he let out in a dangerous rasp.

Shane yelled a slur before kicking the downed pedestrian in the stomach.

Eric heard a moan as the man rolled onto his side, clutching his stomach. "I'm making it my affair. Back off," he ordered through clenched teeth.

The blond laughed. "Make us."

Eric ran back toward the officer who'd been watching the scene with interest. The officer arched his brows at Eric's approach.

"Why are you just standing there?" Eric chastised the officer. The uniform's lashes narrowed into slits. "You see they're beating an old man—"

"Who was drinking from a white fountain. I could arrest him for that. You wanna see him in jail?"

Eric blasted a frustrated breath. "The man is old, probably near blind. Beating someone without personal provocation, isn't that a crime as well?" Eric reasoned. The officer glanced past Eric toward the old man, whose shirt gathered the spit of the three bullies. Eric's hands balled into fists at the display. He glared at the officer, growing more impatient by the second. The officer touched the cap on his head absent-mindedly, opened the cruiser door, and placed the dog inside. He then strode toward the group.

"Now, come on off him, Shane," the officer spoke. Without acknowledging the officer, Shane landed another foot into the old man's stomach. Looks of shock crossed the faces of the blond and the tranquil man.

The blond spoke. "You're oversteppin' your authority, sir. This darkie drank from our fountain."

The officer shook his head slowly and placed his hands on his hips. "Now, I saw that, Chase, but you want your daddy to be embarrassed when I have to arrest you for assault?"

"You gonna arrest the old man?" the calm man beside Chase asked.

The officer shook his head. "No, no I ain't, Edward. Figured he got what was comin' to him, but y'all have yourselves a witness." He pointed back toward Eric.

Eric braced for the stern looks Chase and Edward cast him. Shane's head snapped up in Eric's direction, his eyes narrowed and teeth bared. "Let's not have any more trouble. Just move along." The officer glared at the senior, who struggled to crawl away. "Move along, old man!"

The injured man floundered.

"You know someone is gonna have to sanitize that fountain."

"Yeah, I'll get someone on it, Edward," the officer sighed in response to Edward, who pointed at the fountain.

Edward slapped Chase on the back and moved toward

the driver's side of the truck. "Come on, Shane," he commanded, not looking back. Chase hopped into the truck bed. Shane didn't move, but continued to stare, the threat from his glower not reaching Eric.

"Shane!" Edward shouted.

Eric grinned slowly. "Run along."

Shane spat on the ground and climbed into the front passenger seat of the vehicle. The truck moved across the street and parked. Shane got out of the truck and hopped into the back with Chase. Edward hung is head outside of the window. All three kept their eyes on Eric.

Eric rolled his own eyes and sprinted to the old man's side. Stooping, Eric placed his hands underneath the man's arms, and gently lifted him off the ground. The man whimpered in pain and Eric winced, hoping he hadn't made the man's injuries worse. "Are you all right?"

The man's tired, aged eyes brimmed red and were moist with tears. "Yessa," he choked. He attempted to pull away, rejecting Eric's assistance. "No sir, you better not…" He squeezed his eyes shut and a hand clutched his stomach.

"Let me help you to the other fountain…It's a little ways down."

With a resigned nod, he hobbled alongside Eric as they moved at a snail's pace down the block toward the colored fountain.

From across the street, the baker came running.

"Tobias!" he said breathlessly as he reached them. "Tobias, what happened?" He took Tobias's other arm.

"Those three over there in the red truck," Eric explained, nodding his head in their direction. "They beat him for drinking from a white fountain."

"Ah, now Tobias, I told you to come to my shop if you needed a drink." The baker caught Eric's eyes, and then immediately returned his gaze to his hunched friend. "Thank you, sir." Keeping his eyes down, the baker offered a shaky smile. "Tobias here is old, and he can barely see." He bent toward Tobias' ear. "Or hear!" he shouted with a smidgen of sarcasm. The old man chuckled, nodding his head, his weathered face easing into an expression of gratitude. Eric cast a glance over his shoulder, noting the three men in the truck and the officer leaning on his police cruiser—all watched with keen interest.

At the fountain, the baker placed a hand on Eric's arm. "You had better go, young man. I can handle Tobias from here."

Eric's brows knitted, unsure how safe the two men would be if he left them alone. "It's no trouble, sir."

The baker shook his head and pulled the old man to himself. "No trouble for you, sir, but this is a colored fountain. You already being watched by those brothers." He nodded in the direction of the red truck. Eric protested again but the baker put up a hand. "No sir, I thank you, but we don't want no more trouble."

Eric clamped his lips shut.

"You helpin' could be trouble for *us*." The baker shifted Tobias to the fountain where the battered man took long sips of water. With a resigned nod, Eric turned away. His back to the three brothers, he marched the opposite way down the street, toward his father's car.

Edward, Chase, and Shane.

Eric rammed his hands in his pockets in frustration. *Coming back to this place was a mistake.* He couldn't believe anyone would beat on an old man, black or white. *And the law enforcement here is no help,* he thought glumly. The behavior he'd witnessed earlier added to his discomfort at returning home. He could still feel eyes burning into his back. When he reached the car, exhaustion struck him, and it was still early. Turning the key in the ignition, Eric slammed on the accelerator and started his return to the Montgomery estate.

Chapter Three

DINNER

Eric arrived at the estate, still mulling over the changes that had come over the city. When he was little, he'd noticed the races didn't consort, but most of his time was spent on the estate where his family and Elie's had socialized as equals. Eric exited the car and walked toward the stables. A headache had formed during his drive back, and upon spying Emmett tending to one of the mares, it edged away.

"You're here early, Mr. Brown."

"And you're up early, Mistah Montgomery." He brushed the back of the horse. "Already been out?" He continued rubbing the horse's neck, guiding it to the second stall.

Eric leaned against the beam supporting the stall door and glanced around the massive stables. Many prized horses had been born here thanks to his mother's love of breeding. "I went into town to see how it had changed."

"Ahh, couldn't sleep I see. I s'pose it will take you a little while to get used to being home. You've been away for a long while."

"Everything is so different."

Mr. Brown gave one last pat on the horse's neck and came out of the stall to stand near Eric. "Different yes, but it's gettin' better."

Eric shot him a skeptical look. After what he'd witnessed today, how could it have been any worse?

Mr. Brown responded with a confident smile. "Oh, you'll see. In our lifetime, we'll see." Emmett started toward the stall across the way. A chocolate brown stallion neighed a greeting. "Alabama is tryin' to hold out on integratin' but equality will come to blacks. In fact, I think sooner than we 'spect."

"Mr. Brown, I witnessed some violence in town today. Three men were mercilessly beating on an elderly black man for drinking at a white fountain."

Mr. Brown stopped brushing the stallion.

Eric absent-mindedly moved a few stray pieces of hay around on the ground with his boot. "This change you feel coming, it won't be easy." His tone was grim. "It will be met with strong resistance."

Emmett continued his brushing. "Well, my boy, I will agree with you there. We're already experiencin' unthinkable assaults. Lynchin's, murders, and I suppose now beatings in broad daylight. Usually the attack you described would've taken place at night, where those cowards could hide their deeds." Emmett's voice was low with a touch of sadness.

Eric's gaze found the main house through a window in the stables. "Is Elie here yet?" A sudden need for her company overcame him. When they were children, they'd been safe—protected from the acts of violence Emmett described. Some of his happiest memories were of the two of them laughing and discussing their dreams for the future, minus any of the racial hurdles.

"No, not yet." He heard Mr. Brown strain, as he was bent low looking underneath the horse's belly. "She'll be up at the house a little later, maybe early this afternoon."

Eric nodded. A second wave of exhaustion struck. His eyelids drooped. Straightening from the beam, he stretched fatigued muscles. "I'm going back to the house and—" He yawned. Mr. Brown laughed. Eric grinned lopsidedly. "Sleep."

"Sweet dreams, son."

****

The house's main library was a source of pure joy for Elie. She fingered through Mr. Montgomery's selection of fiction, the decision on what to read eluding her. He kindly let her borrow whichever books she chose, and she always returned the treasured items to their rightful place.

"I didn't know you could read." The tease came from behind. Elie countered with a rueful grin. Eric leaned in the doorway, his eyes sparkling with interest. His clothes seemed slept in, his hair disheveled, and lips curved into a smile that rocketed shivers up and down her spine.

"You're late gettin' up," she said casually, ignoring the heat in her spine. "Europeans don't start the day until it's halfway over?"

"Actually, I was up at the crack of dawn. I went downtown to sightsee, I guess you could say." He walked to a nearby settee and proceeded to settle into a comfortable lounging position.

"And how did your tour go?" She sat in an overstuffed armchair across from him.

A dark cloud came over his face. "The city is different from what I remember…especially the people."

Elie's interest was piqued. "Which people in particular?"

Eric placed his elbows on his knees, fixing his deep green eyes on Elie. "Do you know three guys named Edward, Chase, and Shane?"

Elie sighed. Where would she begin? They were only the worst lot she'd ever encountered in her short life. *Parasites.*

Eric lifted a brow. "What?"

Had she spoken out loud? "The McDougal brothers are, I suppose, the town bullies. Their father, Asa McDougal, is the city mayor, so I guess they think they can throw their weight around. They're always harassin' black businesses, and even people on the street!"

Eric nodded, looking at the floor. "I was a witness today to said harassment."

Despite her skin crawling at the thought, Elie leaned forward, hands gripping her knees. "What happened?" she asked, impatient for the story.

He met her gaze and let out a long breath. "There was this old man, um—Mr. Tobias—and, well, he's practically blind because he drank from a white-only fountain."

Elie gasped, her hands going to her mouth.

With solemn eyes, Eric held her gaze. "The black-only fountain was a bit farther down the block."

Elie moistened her lips, waiting for Eric to continue. Instead, he dragged his hands through his hair, releasing a loud grunt. "And? Eric, stop leaving me in suspense."

He gave her a half-grin. "Still impatient, are we?" Glaring at him, Elie ignored the statement alluding to how, as a child, she used to beg for Ms. Hattie's biscuits before the dough had risen, or when she'd stomp her foot while waiting for Eric to teach her how to ride with her actually *on* the horse. He raised two hands in defeat. "Well, the McDougal brothers just happened to be near the fountain and they immediately attacked him."

"Attacked him?"

"The blond one, um…"

"Chase."

"Yeah, that one," he grumbled. "He shoved him to the ground, and Shane kicked him and spat on him. It was disgusting."

Elie closed her eyes and put a hand to her temple, her

head spinning at the mental picture. *Poor Mr. Tobias!*

"To make matters worse, there was this officer standing nearby, intent on letting those boys get away with the attack."

Worry for Mr. Tobias and rage against the McDougal brothers coursed through her veins. An old blind man, beaten over a simple mistake. She always adhered to the signs for her people; the threat of jail loomed if she or any others broke the law.

"I practically threatened the officer to get him to stop them," Eric ground out.

Elie took comfort in Eric's disdain for the mistreatment of Mr. Tobias. She silently said a prayer of thanks, grateful Eric had happened upon the situation and intervened. "Is Mr. Tobias all right?" she asked, her voice shaking.

Eric sighed. "He is. A baker came by and helped me get him to the right fount—the fountain." He averted his gaze, tunneling his fingers through his hair.

Humiliating heat seared her cheeks. She swallowed a lump of discomfort, and raised her chin. "You don't have to be embarrassed. You're right. You got him to the *right* fountain."

Eric focused his gaze on her, a lingering trace of an apology in his eyes. She smiled briefly before turning the conversation back to the object of her ire. Grinding her teeth, she crossed her arms over her chest. "The McDougal brothers don't do anything except whatever their father wants. Usually, it's botherin' people."

"Well, it'll be too soon if I see them again. They watched me help the poor man, and I could tell they were thinking of ways to kill me." He leaned back with a sigh, eyes up at the ceiling.

Elie sat silent, buffing the sudden goose bumps marking her flesh. "Um, Eric?" She steeled herself for his response.

His gaze flickered to her. A sudden bout of nerves struck and she fidgeted. His eyes narrowed. Could he guess what she would say next?

"Wh-a-a-t?" He exaggerated every syllable.

"Your father has sent out invitations to a dinner party welcoming you home."

"O-k-a-y…" he said just as slowly.

"Well, the mayor has been invited, and wherever he goes—" She paused, biting her lip. He returned an even look. She swallowed.

"Don't say it."

"They go." Elie crouched back a little, not knowing how he'd respond. "Ever since Asa McDougal became mayor, his sons have been livin' like the privileged."

Eric groaned, leaning forward until he fell off the settee. His silly action made her giggle. She got on her knees, putting an arm around his shoulder as he knelt, face to the floor, head in his hands. "You'll be fine. I doubt you'll have to make conversation with them. Civilized discussion isn't exactly their talent," she said dryly.

Eric's gaze sought hers. She stuck her lower lip out at him playfully. He gave her a wide, sheepish grin. "Are you going to be at the dinner?" he asked, hope in his voice.

Elie gave him a slightly annoyed look. "Now, how would that look, Eric? Dining with the help?"

Eric offered her the same look. "You're not the help, Elie, and you know it."

"Yeah, well, they don't know that." She crossed her arms. "Besides, like you said, it wouldn't be…right."

"Elnora, that's not at all how I meant it to sound," he said in a raw voice, his eyes smarting.

Elie nodded. "I know," she answered softly. Even if she wanted to attend, the difference in their skin would separate them. It'd be untenable for her to sit at the same table as the mayor and his sons, no matter how detestable they were to their hosts. "I'm sorry, Eric." Elie blinked back tears of frustration. She, a black woman, shouldn't have to apologize for the restrictive and imposing culture of the white man. She longed for freedom…could almost taste it.

Eric groaned and rolled his eyes upward. "You're my best friend, Elie. I need you there." He stared at her intently. "I might lose it if I see them again."

*You're my best friend…*How odd he'd say that now after so many years of non-communication. She doubted the truthfulness of the statement—merely an exaggeration—and instead Elie released a fake laugh, to lighten the atmosphere.

Eric's hooded stare assessed her. "You find this humorous?"

Shrugging her shoulders, she obliged him with a smirk. He inclined toward her in a crouching position. Her breath caught. The look in his eyes…A slow mischievous grin spread across his angled features.

"You wouldn't dare," she breathed. "I'm a woman now!" He lunged for her, pinning her to the floor. "Get off me, you brute!" she cried half serious, half laughing.

"Stop laughing at me 'cause this is serious," he ordered.

She couldn't help herself; her laughter continued.

"What am I supposed to do when they get here?" he pleaded with her. "I can't just leave the party." He sat back on his heels, and gazed upwards as though summoning some sort of divine intervention.

Elie laughed at his discomfort. "Get off me!" She crunched and punched him in the stomach. He doubled over and landed to the side of her, laughing. They both sighed, hands on their stomachs, grins on their faces. Settled on their backs, they stared at the ceiling. He reached a hand over and fingered a curl that had loosened from the bun during their scuffle. She felt his gaze on the side of her face and those pesky goose bumps marked her flesh.

She shifted to her side to meet his eyes. He didn't so much stare at her as through her. He still threaded a few strands of her hair with his fingers but his focus wasn't on her. "What are you thinking about?"

He blinked from wherever he was and released her hair. "When's the dinner party?"

Where did he go? *How little I know him now, after knowing everything.* "This Saturday."

Eric returned his gaze to the ceiling, pinning his hands beneath his head. "Two days..."

****

Morgan Montgomery took one last look at the guest list to the dinner party. He would make apologies again for the last-minute notice, but Eric had given him no indication of his return. Still, Eric's decision to journey home satisfied Morgan, and he was eager to introduce his accomplished son.

But what *had* he accomplished? There'd been no mention of employment in the letters Eric sent, nor had his son spoken to him about positions he may have held in Europe. All he could extract from Eric was he'd left his job and sold everything he had to pay for the trip home. Although his son's appearance was impeccable, how was his life in Europe? Did his job provide him with a decent salary? His insides twisted at the thought of his son destitute.

Morgan frowned as he glanced at the ornate invitation. Elie had chosen the design, her excitement over Eric matching his own. She'd always seemed a bit forlorn while Eric was away but, now, the radiant light in her eyes convinced him the void in her life had been filled once again. But with who? *Eric is still so distant...*

Morgan's eyes strayed to the framed picture of Evelyn. He reached across his desk and fingered the glass pane in front of his wife's face. He sighed, leaning into the high back of his leather chair as the memory of golden hair caressing a perfectly round face made luminous by her cheerful smile filled his mind. *How did I make it this far without you?* He, too, had known a void he once believed could never be filled. But his faith in God had truly sustained him, as promised in the Good Book.

"Oh, Evelyn, our son is so lost and I can't seem to guide him," he whispered to her image. "I'm thankful you're not here to see..." The mixed look of defiance and dread in his son's eyes on the lawn the other day haunted Morgan's waking thoughts. Eric must have struggled with the decision to return to Alabama. Did he want to come home? Morgan had hoped he had, but perhaps not...

A knock on the study's door interrupted his musings.

"Come in. Ah, Miss Hattie. How are things?"

"Very good, sir. Everythin' is ready. Dinner will be prompt at seven."

"Thank you, dear. Um, where is Elie?"

"Elie's upstairs with your son, sir. Said the guests will be arrivin' in half an hour. I've appetizers set up in the parlor." Miss Hattie exited the room.

"Thank you, Miss Hattie!" he called after her as she left. Morgan stood, smoothed his jacket, and headed to the foyer to receive his guests. Apprehension came over him.

The mayor and his sons had confirmed their attendance.

****

Eric stood in front of his mirror, trying in vain to tie his tie. Leaning in the doorway watching him, Elie fought hard to suppress a smile. He sighed in frustration as his fifth attempt failed. She moved to stand in front of him and, with steady fingers, deftly tied the cloth. "How did you ever dress yourself without me?" she teased, straightening the knot.

"If I'd known you wanted to dress me, I'd have paid for you to join me in France," he replied smoothly.

Elie placed her hands on her hips in mock annoyance. Had he ever thought of her? Her mind had strayed to him often, so much so she'd dreamed of their times together at the lake and even had mock conversations with him on her walks home from school. What did he do for money? If he had any, he sure didn't write to invite her for a visit.

"Are you certain you won't stay?" he asked again, smoothing the collar on his jacket. Elie watched him in the mirror.

"I can't. I'll be helpin' Miss Hattie in the kitchen for a little while and then I'll be headin' home."

He faced her for approval. She smiled and nodded. He did indeed look handsome. His blond hair was slicked back with ample product, and the pale blue dress shirt somehow managed to make his jade eyes even greener. "You'd better hurry. The guests will be arrivin' any minute now."

He dropped a swift kiss on her cheek. Astonished, Elie placed a hand where his lips had touched. "Thanks for the help with the tie." Then he raced out of the room. He smelled of fresh soap mixed with a bit of cologne.

The warmth of his lips left a tingly sensation on her skin. The corners of her mouth tweaked upward. He might not have wanted her in France, but he needed her now, and that suited her just fine.

****

Eric stood beside his father on the front steps as the chief of police made his way up the circular driveway. A long black car pulled around the drive and both men tensed at the sight of Asa McDougal stepping out of the passenger door. Eric suppressed a groan.

"I'm sorry about this. I didn't know you had trouble with the McDougal boys, or I would have—"

"Not invited the mayor?" Eric interrupted, amused.

Morgan smirked.

They received Police Chief Wilcox, shaking his hand before Morgan directed him inside. Asa's three sons followed their father out of the vehicle. Instead of dusty jeans and stained white T-shirts, they'd exchanged their country attire for dark suits and plain ties. Asa hefted up the steps, his hand extended.

"Morgan Montgomery! Good to see you this evening." Out of breath, he pulled a handkerchief from his front lapel and wiped his shiny brow. He shot Eric a penetrating gaze. "You must be Eric. I'm sure your father is pleased to have you home after so long an absence."

Instant dislike coursed through Eric as they shook hands. From the scowl on the mayor's face, Eric guessed the feeling to be mutual.

"Mayor McDougal, it's a pleasure to have you grace my home this evening," Morgan said.

"Well, when I received your invitation I couldn't say no! I'm not sure I've ever been to this estate." He glanced around, taking in the columns and the porch, followed by a look over his shoulder to view the modest front grounds.

Morgan cleared his throat. "Please, sir, make your way into the parlor." He gestured inside. "Dinner will be served shortly."

Edward, Chase, and Shane—standing mute behind their father—now made their way forward to shake the hand of their host. Morgan politely greeted each one. Eric gripped the hand of a sneering Chase while Shane glared at Eric—eyes bulging, wild—even while greeting Morgan.

Eric could still feel Shane's gaze even as the three moved past him and continued into the house. He fixed his stare on the sky and expelled a loud breath.

Morgan slapped a hand on his back. "Look at it this way, son—when dinner starts, their mouths will be too full to speak."

Eric offered his father a scornful smirk.

"Have I said I'm sorry yet?"

Eric's smirk turned rueful. "The sooner we eat, the sooner

they go home."

****

Silverware clanged against plates and sounds of satisfaction at the taste of food surrounded Eric. The evening had been progressing well, despite the McDougals' icy greetings. He'd easily conversed with the other gentlemen and ladies in attendance, and his earlier anxieties digested away with Miss Hattie's buttery yeast rolls.

His father had given him permission to state he'd be joining the family business as a partner in the bank. Eric welcomed the chance for work. While away in France, he had drowned himself in it, a familiar comfort.

"Many states have already adopted integration," Morgan stated. "It's only a matter of time until Alabama follows suit."

Chase snorted.

"Mr. Montgomery, as mayor of the city, I have an ear to Governor George Wallace and his wishes on policy in this matter. And I can assure you, segregation will hold in this state," Asa responded firmly.

Morgan didn't back down. "With no disrespect, Mayor, the decision might not be up to the governor. There's talk of federal legislation, which will—"

"It don't matter what the government says. They won't be integratin' with us," Shane interrupted with a spat.

Silence ensued.

Eric gripped his fork, color draining from his knuckles. Elie, Mr. and Mrs. Brown, Miss Hattie—they were family to him and the insult struck deep.

The mayor cleared his throat. "What my son has failed to communicate delicately," his stern look at Shane brought a twitch to the young man's upper lip as he concentrated on his plate, "is that it's the governor's intention to maintain a state's right to choose policy for its people. The people voted him into office, and that includes the Negroes."

Unhurried, Morgan chewed his food. After swallowing, he took a sip of his wine. "I understand the governor may wish to uphold state rights, but if it's for the good of the people that integration be law, then the governor couldn't possibly object."

"The good of the people?" the police chief scoffed. "The majority of people wish for separation and, from what I've heard, there are an increasing number of advocates that will see their choice upheld." He cast a knowing look to Asa, who seemed triumphant.

"You're referring to the Klan."

Eric took in his father's hard stare, his tight jaw. He'd only heard vague third-hand accounts of the Klan's activities while traveling Europe. His blood chilled at the thought their members were close to home, perhaps sitting at this very table. Elie had been right not to stay. How she would have suffered to sit through the defamation of her people, to know advocates of those who personally sought the demise of her race surrounded her. Meeting his father's intense gaze, he marveled at the man's restraint. If he were the host, he'd have long demanded their leave.

"Their membership numbers have increased. That should say somethin' 'bout the people's wishes," Edward offered victoriously.

"Surely, not everyone shares their sentiment. Especially when they use violence to convey their point," Eric answered with almost a hiss in his voice.

Chase shot from his chair, his face red with anger. Asa put a restraining hand on his arm, his eyes warning him to settle down. Chase eased into his chair, undeniable animosity burning in his eyes.

Asa glanced around the room at the somber guests, his face flushed with embarrassment, apparently tired of having to referee his son's insolent behavior. "I apologize again. My son meant no disrespect." A glint of detest reached Eric. "And to you, Mr. Montgomery, we forgive your ignorance, seeing how you haven't been here for a few years."

"Ignorance?" Eric asked, raising his eyebrows and feigning innocence at the suggestion. Out the corner of his eye, he caught his father's cautious gaze.

"Violence is always provoked by dissention."

"You mean the civil rights group," Morgan offered.

"They picket and cause disorder and chaos. Sometimes the only way to bring order is through the strong hand of the law." Asa exchanged a glance with the police chief, who nodded in agreement.

Disgusted, Eric settled his gaze on the bubbles in his champagne. He'd witnessed the "strong hand of the law" earlier.

"Well, this is all very interesting, but I'm afraid this good food won't sit well in my stomach if this discussion lasts any longer," said Mrs. Emmeline James, the wife of a prominent city attorney.

Eric had already lost his appetite.

Emmeline asked Morgan if any new mares showed promise to race in national derbies. Morgan seemed grateful for the change of subject, and went into a lengthy discourse about prospective riders and their mounts. The dinner passed without further disagreements but the tension in the air continued to suffocate Eric, and he longed for the freedom of the French countryside.

****

Elie sat on a stool in the Montgomery kitchen, nibbling on one of the cookies prepared for the party. The dinner servers were coming in and out of the kitchen, bringing dishes and taking desserts and fresh coffee to the table. Elie had planned to leave for home soon after the guests arrived, but decided to stay, hoping to hear stories of the night's events. Miss Hattie had left the kitchen a couple of minutes ago to oversee the deliverance of the desserts. Elie's eyes strayed for the tenth—possibly twentieth—time to the pile of hot chocolate chip cookies. Just there, in front of her, on the island. She argued with herself over taking another treat, and finally refused, blaming the late hour.

The kitchen door slammed open, crashing against the wall. Elie jumped, half a cookie in her mouth. Eric stormed in, face crimson and jaw rigid, walking briskly toward the table where she sat. He picked a stool opposite hers and thumped his fists on the table. The cookies claimed another victim as not long after Eric's gaze glanced their way, one was in his mouth.

Elie eyed Eric, her own jaw tensing with anxiety. He noticed her then and sighed. "Not going well?"

His green eyes darkened. "I thought you were going home," he snapped.

Her breath caught. He continued to chew, his gaze somewhere else. She hopped down from the stool and marched toward the door until she felt a hand grab hold of her arm, halting her progress.

"Stop, stop. I'm not mad at you, just a little surprised to see you're still here." His eyes full of contrition, his bottom lip puckered out. "I didn't think I'd have your support tonight," he said with more patience in his voice.

Elie returned to her stool. "I wanted to hear how it went—" An increasing warmth on her arm stole her thought and her eyes found his hand still resting there. The next moment—a chill from the loss of heat.

"I swear—those McDougal brothers." He slammed his fist on the table again. She placed a hand over it and gave it a gentle squeeze. His eyes held astonishment and fury. "They're adamant segregation will remain in Alabama."

Elie shrugged. "They fight for it." She took another cookie and this time didn't argue with herself.

"Fight?"

Did they still lurk in the house? Elie suppressed a shudder of fear. Leaning close, she whispered. "They are members of the Ku Klux Klan." More and more men wore the white coat of the Klan, and their efforts to procure support increased every day.

Eric stopped mid-chew, his brows dipping. He abruptly stood, swallowing the last of the cookie. "You wanna walk out back with me? It's a bit stuffy in here with all the heat and the—" His eyes shot to the main kitchen door. "McDougals," he ended in a low tone.

Elie nodded and followed him out the back kitchen door. Nightfall had settled on the land and the light from the stars shone bright in the clear sky. Elie inhaled the hazy night air and then turned her gaze on Eric, waiting for him to speak. "Anything else exciting?" she asked, hoping her lighthearted tone would tempt him to socialize.

"Nope."

"Are you sure?"

"Positive."

She shook her head, irritated at his indifferent tone. "I don't understand you, Eric. At times you're open, and at other times…" She blocked his path, forcing him to face her. "Like now, you're closed off to me."

"Were you expecting our friendship to be the same?" His pointed question stung as he sidestepped her and continued onward. "We're not children anymore, Elie." He stopped and with hands on hips, hung his head.

Why was he being deliberately rude? Did something occur at dinner? Elie tried not to take his attitude personally. "The only expectation I had was that you'd come back," she said softly, moving forward. She reached out a hand to touch his back, but let her arm drop without contact. "And now you're back."

He turned, regret in his eyes and, perhaps…exhaustion?

She immediately dismissed his sharp tone. She inched closer, hoping he'd see her smile in the night light. "I only want to know you again."

His eyes widened and he, too, edged forward. Convinced she'd broken through his armored exterior, Elie relaxed. She reached out both hands for him to take, but he backed away and turning around, continued on into the darkness, leaving her there, staring after him.

Chapter Four

DEFIANCE

I should apologize.

Eric strode toward the wooden fence that enclosed one of the training areas on the family estate. The summer sun was bright; fresh cut grass and honeysuckle scented the warm moist air, and the sky was a clear blue. Eric wiggled his toes in the grass as he walked along barefoot. He snapped the suspenders holding up his dated, calf-length trousers. The loose, old white buttoned-down shirt allowed his skin to breathe somewhat in the hot air. Emmett's deep voice carried from a distance as he busied himself with one of Morgan's thoroughbreds. Placing his hands in his pockets, Eric continued past the stables to the training ring.

Ever since his homecoming dinner, Morgan had insisted Eric invest as much time as he needed in himself. Perhaps his father suffered from guilt over hosting the event without Eric's approval. Eric was eager to work again, but his father never pressed the issue. He appreciated the distance granted him to make his own decisions.

Speaking of distance…

Even though she worked on the estate, Eric had barely laid an eye on Elie in the last several days. She had indeed stayed during the dinner, waiting patiently for him to report to her, and he frowned as he recalled how he'd spoken to her. Still fuming over the McDougals, he'd left her in the dark, not entirely in the mood to open his heart to, frankly, a woman he barely knew. Yes, they were practically raised together; yes, she was his best friend; no, he didn't want to relive the past. Too many painful memories.

Eric approached the ring and climbed the fence, sitting on the top beam of wood. Emmett waved. Eric raised his hand in a similar gesture. He remembered sitting on the fence as a boy, watching Emmett train horses. Tilting his head back to feel the sun's rays on his face, he breathed deeply the warm wind blowing his hair.

I've missed home.

The realization had grown steadily over the week, and he wondered at how little home had meant to him during his absence. How little family—and Elie—had weighed on his mind. Until he woke up one morning in the arms of a woman whose name he couldn't remember after meeting her at a party the night before. He'd allowed himself every pleasure until he was sick in the stomach from his overindulgence. Nothing about his life held meaningful purpose.

He told himself he'd returned to do his duty to his father—he'd serve in the family business. Not beg for forgiveness. The first day or so tested his ability to walk on eggshells, but no one asked for an apology and he was obliged not to give it.

But being home wasn't enough. Not even the grand size of the family home could fill the fathomless chasm in his heart. An old itch had flared the other day and he loved to scratch. For just a short while, he could take his mind off the pain and indulge.

Eric sighed, resting his head in his hands. He couldn't wait to begin work at the bank, hoping to lose himself in it as he'd done in the jobs he held overseas.

What about another muse?

Yes. This time he'd have something different to soothe the ache. A familiar comfort. A leggy blonde had attended the dinner party, but her name escaped him. His lips curved upward. His father had a copy of the guest list…

****

Elie arrived at the Montgomery estate, intent on remaining only as long as necessary. She avoided Eric, and he seemed only too happy to do the same. Whenever they were in each other's presence, she could toss a coin to guess his mood. Completely at ease at times, and during others, she'd run smack into his impenetrable wall. What was he hiding? What did he want to protect? Why wouldn't he let her in?

Making her way to the kitchen, she paused upon seeing the housekeeper exiting a pantry.

"Oh, Miss Regina, I'm lookin' for the order sheets I left on the desk in the front office. I didn't see them there. Did Mr. Montgomery perhaps move them?"

"Ma'am, your father took dem papers with him. He be outside with the horses."

Elie laid a hand on her shoulder. "Thank you, Miss Regina."

Glad to get out of the house—there would be less chance of encountering Eric there—Elie hurried out the kitchen's back door. The corner of her lips curved upward, the warm air comforting her. The sense of ease and relaxation died as she rounded the stables. Eric sat on the training fence, watching her father interact with one of the horses. Her heart sank before a pang of guilt struck. There was no reason she shouldn't reach out to a former friend struggling with an inner pain. She never shied away from a challenge, but there were complications. Eric's mood swings, for one. Two, whatever issue he kept bottled, he refused to unscrew the cork. Three, sometimes being near him gave her goose bumps, and she liked the feeling of them a bit too much.

****

Eric turned his head at the sound of soft footsteps approaching from behind. Elie rested her arms on the top rung, keeping her eyes on her father and the thoroughbred. His stare didn't induce her to give a greeting.

He refocused his gaze on her father, aware of the tension growing between himself and Elie. Her glee over his arrival had now died. Refusing to confide in her was clearly a source of frustration for her, but self-preservation was a necessity. Being vulnerable with a woman—this woman—held no obvious benefit. A woman he hadn't been connected to in a long time, despite the slight lingering feeling that perhaps they'd never parted.

Elie's soft voice broke the taut stillness. "I want to get past this…whatever is between us."

Never one to beat around the bush, it came as no surprise she initiated what they should've discussed days ago. He swallowed a bit of pride and offered her the words she wanted to hear. "I'm sorry about how I behaved at the dinner party."

"That's not what I mean."

He knew, but he wasn't ready to explore that territory with her. "It's not that easy, Elie."

"Why?"

"Because it just isn't," he responded, almost grumbling.

"You know whatever it is, you can tell me. I'm your friend, Eric. I've always been your friend. And I'll always be your friend."

Her quiet voice penetrated deep into his soul, shaking his

very core. She spoke the truth. Their eyes met and he held her even gaze. "Always? Through anything?"

"Yes."

"Anything?"

"Of course." She edged toward him, her eyes pleading—anticipating.

Eric broke their connection, his line of sight instead going to the thoroughbred. He hadn't seen or spoken to her in several years. What did they know of each other? She believed he was the old Eric she'd called friend, but that boy had died a long time ago. God had killed him in a cruel twist of fate. How could he make her understand?

He closed his eyes and put his hands to his temple before fanning his fingers through his hair. "What does one do when everything they've been taught to believe turns out to be a lie?" Out of the corner of his eye, he saw her mouth drop and her eyes widen in shock. Perhaps he'd made a mistake. She was too young, too naive to understand.

"What do you mean?"

He could hear the struggle to remain calm in her voice. Had she guessed his dilemma? Her persistence to live up to her promise earned his respect. God didn't, and He was…well, God. "Have you ever broken a vow to someone? Someone who meant more to you than life itself?" She neither nodded nor shook her head. He smirked. Neutrality was a safe place to be. "Well, how about telling someone you love them, then when they ask for something, you refuse with no explanation. Nothing."

She expelled a short breath. "Just say what you mean."

"I'm saying there's this void inside." He put a fist to his gut. "It's been growing like a cancer, and it won't stop. And your God caused it."

Elie's brows came together in angst. "You think God caused your void?" Elie reached to put a hand on his arm but he pulled away. "Am I a cancer, too?"

"You're certainly not the cure," he whispered, turning away from the swelling hurt in her eyes. He couldn't stand her touch right now. If she tried to console him—if he felt her touch, his skin would burn. What was it about her that made him recoil?

Her retreating steps caused him to rotate, taking in her form. Well, she lasted just about as long as he predicted. "You said anything."

She whirled, facing him, her eyes flashing with anger. "Anything having to do with you. You being plain nasty to me is not part of the deal. And I don't believe you're telling me everything." She once again trekked toward the house.

Did she really expect him to lay out everything all at once? He hadn't seen her in years. Who was she anymore? *If I couldn't talk to my own father...* Eric leaped off the fence. "You're walking away."

"You taught me how!"

Eric drew in a sharp breath. She had the audacity...

He sprinted after her, taking hold of her arm and rotating her back to face him. She yanked her arm from his grip. Instead of moving away, she stood toe to toe with him, her slitted stare holding him to his spot, piercing his soul—searching for the answer—and dragging his voice from him. "Okay, I'm sorry. You're right. I haven't said everything."

Elie released an exasperating sigh. "Why can't you just say what's wrong?"

"God."

She blinked, confusion crossing her features. "What?"

Blood rushed to his head, his heart pounding in fury. His fists clenched and the longer she stared at him, the more he saw his mother's beautiful smile, the cross she wore around her neck: a staunch believer in Jesus.

"I cursed Him. Cursed Him for not answering prayers, for taking my mother, and I curse Him today for how I feel."

Chapter Five

ICE CREAM

Eric casually strolled down Main Street. At midday, the streets were abuzz with traffic; car horns and fire truck sirens mingled with the voices of people and music being played from several of the shops. Curious to see his new work environment, he considered visiting his father at the office today. He also planned to stop by the theater house to catch a movie. Paul Newman's *Hud* was still in theaters, and at the moment, the story of a Western rebel youth really appealed to him.

At the sound of jazz music, he turned to look across the street. A young black boy in a dark brown cap, faded white shirt, and gray trousers held up by gray suspenders tap-danced on the sidewalk in front of a row of shoe-shining booths. A couple of old men sat in chairs clapping and smiling at the boy as he tapped and slid awkwardly across the concrete sidewalk in shiny black shoes. Eric smiled as he passed; the kid kept to the music, and jazz typically had no discernible rhythm.

Eric ambled on toward his father's bank, pulling his hat low to shade him from the scorching heat of the high sun. As a familiar water fountain came into view, he slowed his pace. *Poor Tobias.* He hoped the man had recovered from his injuries.

Past the water fountain, an oasis presented itself. From outside the window, the ice-cream parlor was alive with people trying to stay cool in the summer heat. Eric's mouth watered at the prospect of the chilled, smooth milky texture of his favorite ice-cream indulgence.

He stepped inside the parlor and scanned the shop. Couples eating banana splits, a jukebox playing an unfamiliar tune, and the lively conversations of customers enjoying their cool treats filled the parlor. The entire counter and most of the tables were dedicated to white patrons, and only a small section, toward the back, seated black customers. Eric swallowed, the walls of his throat tightening. Growing up, the Montgomerys and the Browns had eaten at the same table. Now, his place was with the white population.

Eric swallowed, wetting his throat and loosening the muscles. Taking a seat on one of the stools at the counter, he thanked the smiling waitress who offered him a menu. After choosing a banana split, he leaned back a little, smiling at the prospect of smooth ice cream and bananas.

The door chime drew his glance. In walked the blonde. He cursed silently, still unable to remember her name, but he knew she worked for his father at the bank. She casually glanced around and when her eyes rested on him, her red lips took on a sultry twist, her hips sashaying as she grew near. She was thinly built, but with legs traveling far up her knee-length red summer dress to a small waist cinched by a bright yellow belt. With each inhale, her breasts strained the fabric holding them back. She placed her clutch on the counter and eyed the empty seat beside him.

"Is this seat taken?"

"It is if you care to sit in it," he answered with a slow

grin. Gracefully, she slid onto the seat and crossed her legs, angling them toward his own. Her dress slipped back a bit toward her waist as her knees crossed, allowing him a pleasant view of a slender thigh. She flicked a curl over her shoulder and leaned in to look at his menu. He didn't bother handing it over, forcing her to shift a bit closer.

"It was just so hot outside, I thought a sundae would cool me off." She gazed up at him, her eyes a deep bluish-green much like the waters of the Mediterranean.

"You're not working at the bank today?"

"Oh, I am. I'm on my lunch break and needed something sweet." She shot him a demure smile.

Eric shifted closer, enjoying her wiles. "I ordered a banana split. How 'bout we share?"

"Oh, I wouldn't want to intrude," she hurried to explain, her slight Southern drawl feigning innocence. "I'm sure you're eager to satisfy your own sweet tooth."

"Your company satisfies more than enough. The banana split is just icing on the cake."

Pearly whites gleaming, her slender fingers splayed across his thigh, driving heat through his muscle and drawing his even gaze. She was no innocent. *Hello, muse…*

****

If I'm late, Jasmine is going to let me have it! How her friend would know that today of all days would be the hottest and the kids at school the rowdiest—the perfect time to suggest a frosty shake. After ushering the last of the rug rats out the door of the tiny schoolhouse on the back acreage of the Montgomery estate, Elie rushed downtown to meet her friend. She crossed the front of the parlor to the Black Only entrance and spotted Jasmine Harris, who waved her over to her table.

Jasmine greeted her with a chastising smile. "You're late."

Exasperated, Elie shook her head. "I know, I'm sorry. The

kids wouldn't let me leave." She slid into the chair, dropping her purse on the floor closest to the wall. "And it's so hot outside! How did you know today would be the perfect day for a milkshake?"

Jasmine used both hands to flick her hair to her back, revealing her smug grin. "I'm psychic!"

As they shared a laugh, Elie's eyes caught sight of a familiar blond head and a pair of green eyes. The laughter died in her throat.

Eric.

The sounds of the parlor faded and her breathing slowed as she continued to stare. His own gaze did not relent. They hadn't spoken since yesterday when he admitted to cursing God. She was impatient to know how to help her friend and until she had a plan, she intended to avoid him. Again.

"Don't you know it's impolite to stare?" Jasmine said and rotated in her chair to see what had captured so much of her friend's attention. Her head snapped back.

Elie's connection with Eric continued until a sharp pain in her shin caused her to jump. "Ow!" Irritated not only at the pain in her leg but because her focus had been diverted, she shot Jasmine a dirty look.

Jasmine leaned in, eyes wide, face contorted in confusion. "Who's that guy?"

Elie vigorously rubbed the space underneath her knee. "Eric Montgomery."

"Oh." Jasmine's mouth formed a small 'o' and her gaze shifted to the menu on the table. "Well, he sure looks, well, I'm not even sure." Jasmine discreetly glanced over her shoulder.

Elie, too, studied Eric—unable to look away from the broad grin he offered the woman on his left. Forcing her eyes back to the menu on the table, Elie sighed. She snatched the menu from the table and pretended to give her complete attention to choosing a shake. The choices of flavors were on the opposite side.

"You gonna tell me what *that* was all about?"

Elie glanced at her from over the top of the menu. Jasmine's sly smile put steel into her spine. "What what was about?"

"Do you want me to kick you again?"

Elie remained mute but shifted her legs away just to be safe.

"You two were staring at each other as if you were the only people in the parlor," she whispered insistently.

Eric was still casually conversing with the woman on his left. She *had* felt as if they were the only two in the parlor. Or was that just her imagination? Whatever he felt, his attentions had shifted to another woman. And fast. Heat rose to Elie's cheeks. She refocused on the menu.

"It's nothing."

Jasmine snorted. "Didn't look like nothin' to me."

Elie sighed again, placing the menu down and forcing herself to keep her eyes on Jasmine. "We were good friends growin' up. Best friends, actually. He's been away for a few years." She peered up at Eric, who instinctively looked her way again. She quickly severed their link. "Well, we don't see eye to eye anymore." She chose the view outside of the window instead of the one at the counter. She watched, uninterested, as people passed by. "It's awkward now. We don't…He's changed."

Jasmine frowned. When the waitress stopped by, they both ordered strawberry shakes. "I know you spent a lot of time growin' up at the Montgomery estate with your father trainin' their horses and everythin', but I didn't know you were so close with the family."

"I was born in their house," Elie said wistfully.

Jasmine's eyes grew wide. "Wow. And now…"

Elie inhaled deeply. "Now," she exhaled loudly, "I don't know. Sometimes we talk as if we've never been apart, and other times, we're strugglin' to find words." Her eyes found the blonde woman—in a stunningly tight sundress—inching ever so much closer to Eric. Elie squinted, trying to make out her features. "Is that Amanda Wilcox?"

Jasmine turned around. "Who?"

"She works at the Montgomery Bank." Elie leaned slightly to her right to get a better look. She grimaced. "I didn't know he was seeing her," she said to herself. Her eyes trailed from Amanda to the banana split between them. Two spoons. Elie's lips tipped downward.

"Cute pair. Both blonds."

Elie stuck her tongue out at her friend. Her eyes shifted back to Eric and Amanda. Jasmine was right; they were a handsome couple.

****

Eric's heart stopped when he noticed Elie sitting a few tables away from him. She had a look of surprise on her face, and he imagined his own exhibited the same. When their eyes met, for immeasurable moments he noticed no one but her in the crowd, and now his thoughts revolved around her. What was she thinking when she saw him? He had looked over his shoulder again and their eyes briefly locked. She sat in the section reserved for the blacks and he desperately wanted to say hello, but refrained, as she hadn't seemed eager to acknowledge him openly, either. Yesterday, outside near the training area, was the last time he saw her, when he'd made the foolish mistake of being vulnerable with her. Irritation bubbled in his stomach. Why couldn't he get away from her?

"Eric? Eric, where are you?" Amanda waved a small hand in front of his eyes, her eyes inquisitive. "You're not eating your split."

He'd completely forgotten Amanda sat beside him. He plunged a spoon into the dish and took a mouthful to keep himself from having to converse.

In the next moment, he was glancing over his shoulder again. Elie sipped from her shake before speaking to her friend. She smiled, looked out the window, around the parlor, anywhere but at him. *What does it matter?* Determined not to look at her again, he focused on the woman beside him, who was now sliding off her stool, obviously upset about something. He frowned, regretting his divided attention. "I'm sorry I kept you. I assume you have to get back to work." Amanda held his gaze longer than necessary. He gave her a slow, reassuring grin.

"No apology necessary, Mr. Montgomery, but I do have to return to work." With a satisfied smile, she extended her hand. "Thank you for the split, sir." He took her hand and held it. "Amanda Wilcox. Don't forget," she said, with a knowing look.

"How can I forget when I'll be working beside you every day?"

Her gaze dropped to their hands, still connected. "I look forward to it." Her eyes lifted slowly, enticing him. Slipping from his grasp, she slowly swayed out of the shop. He stared after her and decided not to visit the bank. One encounter with Amanda today was enough. He wanted to enjoy her and a little mystery would make things interesting.

Once Amanda was out of sight, thoughts of Elie immediately plagued him and he broke down, looking over to her seat. She was gone, and so was her friend. He rolled his eyes upward and attempted to work on finishing his split. A wave of exhaustion hit and his "sweet tooth" began to ache. Thinking of Elie was not only annoyingly aggravating, but physically draining as well.

He needed a nap.

Eric paid for the ice cream and headed out the door. Across the street, the McDougal brothers gathered around their beat-up truck with a couple of other men Eric didn't recognize. All had their eyes on him—all except Chase. Eric's brows knitted as he followed Chase's line of sight to see the last glimpse of Amanda as she entered the bank. Chase's eyes snapped back to Eric, who was only too willing to offer him a smug grin. Flushed red and eyes glaring, Chase started to leap from the truck bed but Edward held up his hands, impeding his brother.

Whistling, Eric made his way down the street, away from the McDougals.

Chapter Six

THE BATH

Eric wiped the sweat off his brow with his right forearm and squinted at the sun. Even in the late afternoon, the orb remained extremely bright, the summer heat scorching the earth, and the stables. He'd long since removed his shirt, and went about the task of bathing the family's horses. He stood beside Nessie now, a mare the color of dark chocolate, working from one large metal pail filled with clean water. She enjoyed her bath and his company, frequently nudging him with her wide white-striped nose. He laughed as she nestled her nose into his neck when he wasn't looking, causing him to lose his balance.

"How can you remember me, Nessie? It's been a few years and I've changed a lot," he said in a soothing tone, stroking her nose. Reaching down, he grabbed a large brush from the pail, and then gently glided it across Nessie's abdomen. Nessie's tail swished back and forth as he whistled a made-up tune. He came around the front of her to work the other side and Nessie once again dipped her head, nudging him playfully. He smiled widely at the horse who'd been a favorite of his ever since she was born a year before he'd left for college. Years later, the champion horse was still as fast as ever.

Elie.

He was sure an afternoon of bathing horses would keep his thoughts occupied, but too often did his mind stray to his former friend. She'd left the ice-cream shop without even acknowledging him, besides the couple of times they'd made eye contact. *Amanda might have had something to do with it.* As though that would stop Elie. Why she kept her distance from him, he wasn't certain. Was she suddenly tired of sticking her nose where it didn't belong and pointing out his flaws?

He was probably more to blame for her behavior than anyone. He'd made her uncomfortable with his confession and she didn't know how to approach him without risking another cold shoulder. *Well, she didn't have to ask.*

Eric hurled the brush into the bucket and threaded his hair with his hands. Nessie offered a comforting whinny, drawing his snicker and a shake of his head. Leaning against the wet beast, he stroked her long neck. "What should I do, girl?" Elie had only shown genuine concern for him, and although he wouldn't be regarded as some Christian charity case, his heart could trust her—of that he was certain. And there were few things in life he was sure of anymore. *You know what you have to do.* Unfortunately, that meant allowing this girl past his armor, and that was an inconceivable feat.

But first, he'd work to repair their friendship.

****

Elie stepped out of the main house, clipboard in hand, to check the amount of feed needed for the quarterly order. Technically, the order was due to the shop next month, but anything to keep her occupied and away from Eric—that is, until she figured out how to save him. She rounded the side of the barn and a familiar laugh halted her mid-stride.

Eric.

He wore nothing but faded jeans, his wavy hair slick with moisture and curling at the nape of his neck. Back and shoulder muscles flexed as he worked on Nessie's underbelly. His bare skin, wet from the bath water, glistened in the sunlight.

Heat coursed through her veins. Sheen beaded on her brow and tickled the crook in her neck. Remembering she wasn't breathing, she inhaled sharply. To keep from being noticed, she slid from view, putting her back to the side of the barn. She shook her head to clear the fog clouding her brain.

What's wrong with me?

Laying her head against the barn, she closed her eyes, allowing the shade to cool her hot skin. She breathed in and out, calming her pounding heart. Eric's image flashed in her mind again and her pulse increased. Her body's response to just a vision in her mind terrified her. An instinctive awareness of him sprouted…and grew…like nothing she'd ever felt before. Why now? Elie gulped, and not even the palatable moisture in the air could wet her parched throat.

You're being silly. And Eric's inconsiderate physical display would not keep her from her duties. She peeked around the corner…*Where did he go?*

"Looking for someone?"

Elie jumped. She whirled and faced her friend, hand on her chest, her heartbeat a runaway thud. "What are you doing sneaking up behind people and scaring them half to death?" Not waiting for his answer, she stalked toward Nessie.

Eric followed a step behind her. "What are you doing playing the peeping Tom?"

Elie halted and confronted her taunting accuser. She forgot, however, that Eric now stood a head and a half taller than she, and her eyes landed on his bare, muscled chest. Her blood simmered, and her heart rammed against her ribcage. Beads of sweat lined her spine. She closed her eyes and then lifted her head and only opened her lids when she was confident she'd be looking into green eyes. They sparkled with mischief. Elie steeled her resolve.

"I was *not* watching you. I was comin' to check the feed for the next order," she stated stiffly.

The edges of his mouth curved to his dimples, his eyes bright with tease. Elie's heart fluttered—to her immediate displeasure. *Why am I feeling this way?*

He folded his arms across his chest, his tone lighthearted. "You were standing on the side of the barn, peeking around like a spy."

She wouldn't let the movement of his arms to his well-formed pectorals distract her focus from his eyes. But she wanted another look. "I'm not a spy. I work here." A fact she didn't need to state.

"You wanna help me wash Nessie?" His tone changed into a friendly one, easing the tension. He looked over at his horse. "She's in quite a playful mood today." Eric returned his gaze to Elie and, scanning her form, produced a lopsided grin. "Anyway, you look a little hot, and the water is quite cool."

The burning sensation in her neck skyrocketed to her cheeks. Perhaps it was the sun, or the fact Eric had caught her snooping, or that she stood too close to him to remember her own name but either way, she needed to cool off fast, and a lemonade would be safer than cleaning Nessie with a half-naked Eric. "Um, I'm busy," she mumbled and started for the house, but not before catching Eric's knowing smile.

"Coward!"

"Put a shirt on!"

His laughter followed her all the way back to the house.

****

The laughter in his belly died as he watched the last of Elie's soft yellow cotton disappear from view. Something between them had shifted and the change had come in an instant. They were always playful with each other, and he remembered quite fondly how he used to pull at her braids when she was a child and trip her whenever they raced. Their wrestling matches near the lake for the biggest stick for fencing bouts nearly always ended in laughter.

Now things were different. They were no longer children, but man and woman. The look in her eyes before she'd closed them told him she, too, had detected the change. *She sees me as a man.* The lovely flush in her cheeks when they stood toe to toe proved it. Her discomfort gave him a strange yearning—a sensation of pleasure.

Plenty of women had ogled him before. Their behavior had been a source of great humor, knowing they'd given themselves away, but Elie was different. Her attraction to him had come as a surprise to her.

Then her eyes closed.

Closed to him.

Why that simple action displeased him, he couldn't quite articulate even to himself, but it did. Why didn't she keep her eyes on him? Why fight a natural feeling? *Does she prefer only black men?* The thought created a gnawing in the pit of his stomach he'd never experienced before and the denial cut him deep. *I can't help my skin color.*

She was always just his closest friend—nothing more. A girl. Never a woman. The image of her dress clinging to her skin, hugging her waist and falling over the curves of her hips launched a physical desire in him stronger than he'd ever known. He had to convince her he could satisfy as well as any black man.

He wet his lips, reflecting on the sensuous picture of her in his mind. He found her shape alluring. Her hair, pulled back at the front and cascading in waves around her shoulders, begged his touch. At the sight of his bare chest, the warm expression of approval in her deep chocolate eyes had sent a shot of lust right through him. Her lips...full, enticing, and he wondered how they'd taste.

Nessie nudged him but he refused the distraction. Elie's quick retreat bothered him. Perhaps he'd taken for granted the ease of securing women's affections over the years. Elie struck him as a woman who required much effort. Did he have the energy to spend? Did he even want her?

Eric sighed in response to Nessie's whinny, and returned to the now burdensome chore. He longed to go to the house and study Elie more—to discover how deep her attraction ran. He quickly finished Nessie's bath and led her to the fenced field where she could dry and play. He then picked up his shirt and hiked back to the main house.

Chapter Seven

A NEW DESIRE

Elie walked into the small office room down the hall from the kitchen and placed the clipboard on the desk. She took a sip of her lemonade and closed her eyes, sighing, the cool liquid erasing the heat of the outdoors…and Eric. She opened her eyes and placed the glass on her clipboard.

Walking to the window behind the desk, she stared out at the field behind the house. Nessie ran free, and the thought of her encounter with Eric caused her to tremble. Her heart had quickened at the sight of his slow grin. Embarrassment washed over her. Had he noticed the effect he had on her?

She reveled in the memory of his warm eyes, the way he placed his hair behind his ears, the confident stance he took before her. She lowered her lids to the image. *He's not the same.* The years away had altered him, and she chastised herself for being attracted to a man with no compass of morality. Why couldn't she just see him as her friend? He couldn't be more to her, and even now she considered perhaps he should be less.

"Elnora."

So engrossed in her thoughts, she didn't hear Miss Hattie enter the room and stand beside her. Elie continued to stare out the window.

"Elnora, is you all right?"

Elie's eyes faltered at the concerned tone and she left the window and took a seat on the brown sofa at the opposite end of the room. Miss Hattie sat next to her, placing a hand on Elie's back. "I don't know what's happening to me," Elie whispered.

"I think you do."

Her stern accusation jolted Elie from her introspective haze. She searched the housekeeper's eyes, finding disapproval.

Miss Hattie huffed. "You don't need to say it. But Elnora, he's white."

"What?" Elie leaned back, the words sounding foreign. "Miss Hattie—"

"You don't go thinkin' about him, Elnora," she interrupted. "He's Mistah Montgomery's son. He's a white man o' class, and you's jus' a black girl, the daughter of his employee. You can't be with him, ya' hear? He ain't right for you. You best stick with yo' own kind." She lifted her nose with an air of authority.

Elie stared incredulously at Miss Hattie during her speech. How had the woman guessed her partiality to Eric when it was still so new to her? The housekeeper was a dear friend to the family and Elie always appreciated her guidance, but the woman had jumped to conclusions.

Elie stood slowly, wrapping herself in a defensive shield. "I don't even know what I feel, Miss Hattie, but I certainly never said I wanted the man." She lifted her chin in defiance. "Even if I did, the color of his skin wouldn't matter. Haven't you been listenin' to anything Reverend King has been sayin'?"

Miss Hattie took in a sharp breath. Lips thinning, her

nostrils flared in anger. She kept her eyes downcast, but she squared her shoulders and stood. "I'm not ignorant to Reverend Martin Luther King's message. I ain't got nothin' against the man's skin color. I mean to warn you is all. Although we ain't slaves, we still don't live free." Her eyes challenged. "You do best to remember that."

Her last words were spoken in a heavy whisper, and Elie couldn't deny their truth. She wasn't free—not until she could sit in any section of her choosing at a restaurant. There was a division, no matter how much Elie tried to ignore it, and it existed not only in town, but also in the house she'd been born into.

The housekeeper barreled past her, her face hard with conviction, her eyes pained by inequality. Elie felt a pang of regret. "Miss Hattie, wait." The older woman halted at the door, refusing to face Elie. "I'm sorry. I just…I didn't 'spect this would happen. I never thought…" she trailed off.

She turned then, her eyes pleading. "Elnora, don't disappoint yo' family, yo' people. Let him be."

Long after Miss Hattie's departure, Elie continued contemplating her advice and decided she was right. The mixing of races would never be accepted by either side. Until she could safely drink from a white fountain, sit at a counter of an ice-cream parlor same as a white woman, reason dictated she keep her distance from Eric. Elie paced the rug in front of the sofa. Would her family be disappointed if she loved a white man? *Wait a minute…love?*

Eric entered the office. He'd changed into slacks and a white buttoned-down shirt. She could smell the soap from his shower. His wet hair slicked away from his face. What business could he have in this office? Perhaps he'd leave.

He closed the office door. No way of escape.

A dart of fear pricked her.

Eyes filled with concern, he walked up to her, placed his hands on her upper arms, and gave her a gentle squeeze. "Elie, are you all right?"

She'd have to work on her poker face. Did he struggle with the same feelings as she? If he did, he hid his efforts well. The lines of worry in his brow were for her, and not over some internal labor.

So these feelings are one-sided. Of course they're one-sided. She'd let Miss Hattie know her worrying was for naught. Eric did prefer a woman like Amanda.

"I'm just tired, Eric," she said, hanging her head, not wanting to stare into his eyes. He tilted her chin up, his gaze piercing. Only able to stand the assault for so long, she eventually dropped her eyes to the floor. He sighed and, taking her hand, led her to the couch.

"Elie, if this is about what I said this afternoon, I apologize."

She shook her head. "No, it's not—it's fine." She blushed, embarrassed over her fluster and her childish infatuation. She leaned back to put some distance between them, and the door handle creaked.

Morgan entered. "Am I interrupting anything?"

A flash of irritation crossed Eric's features before turning to his father. "No, Father, I was apologizing for distracting Elie from her work earlier today."

"Well, Miss Brown, it seems since my son has been home, he's spent a good amount of time not only not working, but keeping others from their work." Morgan strode over to the desk.

Eric grimaced. "Father, you know I'll be joining you in the office on Monday. I have no reservations about work."

Morgan's teasing caused her to grin, but her mouth slacked when Eric's eyes narrowed on her lips.

Morgan flashed his own set of dimples. "I'm proud to have you as an associate, son. I'm also glad the French didn't completely brainwash you into renaissancing all over Europe. Now, Elie," Morgan said, pointing a finger at her in mock command, "don't let my son be a negative influence on you." Eric tilted his head back and groaned audibly. Elie put a hand up to her mouth to cover her soft laugh. "You know she has plans for her life. She won't be working here forever."

Eric zeroed in on her face. Suddenly shy, she glanced away.

"Elie has been attending Selma University and will be graduating with her teacher's license next year. She's at the top of her class." Morgan beamed his approval.

"Selma." Eric eyed her with surprise. "The Bible college about an hour away, right?"

"That's correct. Elie has plans to teach at that primary school at the edge of town, when she graduates. She's been tutoring some of the children during the summer months."

"Sir, really." She rushed to put a stop to the praise.

The dilapidated primary school had been around for years. The poorest families sent their children to the school in hopes of giving them at least some of the education they'd never received. The nearby Baptist church took a collection every spring to pay for a teacher to give of her time to teach needy children. Morgan assisted with providing funds to purchase learning materials.

Surprise morphed into admiration and Elie could no longer stand the scrutiny of Eric's gaze. She stood. "I'll go help Miss Hattie in the kitchen."

"Feel free to join us for dinner, Elie," Morgan called after her.

"Thank you, sir." With one last look at Eric, whose curious gaze had followed her to the door, she escaped the room.

Chapter Eight

MIDNIGHT MEETING

Eric and his father galloped along the dirt road toward Wimbly Baptist. After dinner, Morgan had shocked Eric with an invitation to attend a civil rights meeting. He had no idea his father actively participated in the movement. Across the South, violence accompanied the organized desegregation marches. Very few marches were successful. Despite their lack of accomplishments, his father explained the congregation at Wimbly Baptist was considering orchestrating their own march in Freeman in response to the governor's stand against the admittance of two black students at the University of Alabama only a few weeks ago.

They are members of the Ku Klux Klan. Elie's words came to mind as he considered Freeman's own dissenters of integration. Morgan had called them "hoods," a description of the white hooded outfits they wore when committing violent acts against the black population. Eric had heard of the group's activities in Alabama while in France, and his father filled in the gaps of missing information concerning their acts and growth in membership.

The church came into view, and the Montgomery men slowed their horses' pace to a comfortable trot. The more distance they covered, the more anxious Eric became. He barely remembered any acts of violence in Freeman committed by the KKK when he was a child. Even as a teenager, he remained far removed from the brutality of the Klan by living on a horse farm.

A few people lingered outside the church, some in quiet conversation, and others armed with rifles. Did they expect hostility from other town residents? Details of the meeting were spread by word of mouth, and the late hour afforded the group some protection.

"Mr. Montgomery!" An elderly man holding a rifle came running to the side of Morgan's horse.

Morgan dismounted. "Ah, Mr. Wilson, good to see you. How is the turnout this evening?"

"Very good, sir. We have a guest speaker from Mississippi to give a report on what's happened since the shootin' of Mr. Evers."

"Excellent. Oh, I'm not sure if you remember, but this is my son, Eric." He gestured as Eric dismounted from his horse. Eric shook Wilson's hand. "He's just returned from his European travels, and I invited him to join us tonight."

Mr. Wilson appraised Eric with a toothy grin. "Yes, sir, I remember you! You were just a little boy but didn't you used to run lil' Elnora Brown home to her mama cryin' 'cause of some mischief you played on her?"

Eric smirked. "Yes, sir, Mr. Wilson, that was me."

"Well, she's gone and grown up now, and I 'spect you can't pull on her braids no more."

His body warmed at the thought of her being grown. "No, sir, I can't." He could have kicked himself for the huskiness in his own voice. Mr. Wilson's brows scrunched over his eyes. Had Mr. Wilson heard the sudden desire in his voice?

"You sure are lookin' grown up yourself, Mr. Montgomery." His gaze drifted over Eric from the dark riding boots to his untucked white shirt, the top three buttons open. "Yes, sir, quite the young man."

Eric regarded Mr. Wilson with a smile—and he cleared his throat before responding. "Thank you, sir."

"Elnora and her family are inside. You best hurry on in if you wanna get a seat. I'll tie up the horses on the side of the church."

Morgan patted Mr. Wilson on the back. "Thank you, Carl, we'll talk later."

The mention of Elie's name set Eric's heart pounding faster than Nellie's hooves in a full gallop. "How do you know Mr. Wilson?" he asked his father in an attempt to focus on something else.

"He owns the Wilson's General Store in town. I buy the horse feed from him. Good man. Knows everybody and almost everything about them."

****

Elie sat with her family in a pew near the pulpit. Her right leg bounced, eager for the meeting to begin as fear twisted her stomach into knots. She felt safer with the armed men watching for trouble outside, but danger was never far off. She let out a long breath, trying to calm her nerves when her college friend Maisy Wilson sat beside her.

Maisy's full lips broke into a sly grin. "Elie, Michael is here. And I've already heard him mention he wanted to talk with you tonight. 'Course, if I stepped any closer toward him, he would've known I was eavesdroppin' on his conversation. When are you gonna snatch him up?" Maisy fluffed her tightly coiled hair as if she expected to snatch someone up as well.

Elie shot her friend a confused look. "Snatch him up?

Maisy, I don't know what you are talkin' about. I—"

Maisy held up her hand. "You know he's sweet on you."

"Shhhh." Elie put a finger to her lips. She didn't want her mother to hear of them discussing Michael Jefferson. Her mother adored Michael and she'd hint of him being Elie's beau, but Elie never gave her reason to hope. He was handsome and intelligent, but she was too busy with work and school to even consider entering into a relationship.

Maisy giggled like a schoolgirl with a secret. She then straightened and surveyed the attendees in the room. "Is *that* Mr. Montgomery's son?"

Eric.

Elie's eyes quickly found the back door. There he stood, his gaze on her. He answered the slight uptick of her lips with a subdued smile of his own.

"You know him?" Maisy asked in amazement.

Elie desperately tried to break her gaze from Eric's. Their eyes were locked, even as he moved through the crowd to find a seat.

"Yes, his name is Eric." She successfully severed the tie and focused on Maisy. "He's just returned from Europe. We were childhood friends." Elie hoped her short answers would satisfy her friend's curiosity and temper the heat that had dusted her cheeks at the announcement of his arrival.

"He's um, well..." Maisy shrugged her thin shoulders, trying to find the words.

"He's what?" Elie braced for criticism—and was ready to come to his defense.

Maisy stared straight into Elie's eyes and she ignored how her cheeks burned, the collapse of her throat. "He's very handsome." Maisy zeroed in on him. "For a white man. And would you look at that hair?" Maisy asked, stroking her own. "I'm beginning to wonder what it would be like to run my fingers through it..." Elie nearly gasped for air. Grabbing Maisy's hand, she forced her friend back around.

"Would you stop staring!" she whispered fiercely, embarrassed by her friend's unabashed observation. "He'll know we're talking about him."

Maisy gave her a sideways grin. "*Very* wavy, and it does look soft."

Elie rolled her eyes and let out a noisy breath. Thankfully, a speaker came to the podium with a call for the room to come to order. She listened intently as he updated the crowd about the group's growing membership, and other administrative notes. He then introduced Melvin Hall, a civil rights activist from Mississippi who'd speak on behalf of the group he represented. The meeting would last at least an hour. *No need to turn around...*

****

Eric noticed Elie's skinny friend speaking to her and looking curiously in his direction. Elie wouldn't look at him, but he knew he was the topic of their conversation. Her friend openly stared at him—and didn't look displeased. He grinned to himself.

Mr. Hall stepped up to the podium. He thanked the group for allowing Michael Jefferson to speak at their last meeting in Jackson, Mississippi, stating Michael had stirred the hearts of many of the young college students living in town. A renewed sense of activism had taken place on the state's black college campuses, especially Jackson State University. He also spoke on the outpouring of support for Mr. Evers' family.

The police investigation of Medgar Evers' death was proceeding rather slowly. No arrests had been made, but everyone blamed his shooting on the local KKK chapter. Mr. Hall encouraged the group to continue in their fight against segregation. Mr. Evers' death was proof they were on the right course, for if their cause wasn't important, it wouldn't be worth killing over, or dying for. The attendants nodded in somber agreement.

Michael Jefferson spoke about their efforts for a march down Main Street in the following month. A number of his college friends would travel on the Friday before and needed places to spend the night. Jefferson thanked those who volunteered their houses and continued outlining the plans for the march. They'd walk down prominent streets and end at this church, for a potluck dinner and discussion. Several families would create signs, and T-shirts for the event had been ordered and were scheduled to arrive one week before the event. He closed the meeting with a prayer and an invitation to enjoy some refreshments by a few of the local matriarchs.

Several people gathered near the sweets, others sang hymns, and still others flocked around Mr. Hall to get more information. Morgan excused himself to speak to Mr. Hall, leaving Eric contently seated in the back, observing the crowd. A woman passed by him with a plate of brownies that smelled too good to resist, so he stood and made his way over to the food table.

Eric bit into a brownie and rested his gaze on Elie. She was in conversation with her skinny friend when Mr. Jefferson walked up and greeted them. After a moment or two, Elie's friend discreetly moved away, leaving Elie alone with Michael. Eric narrowed his eyes on the two. Michael did all the talking, but Elie's response to him ignited that gnawing feeling in the pit of his stomach. A sheepish grin appeared on the young man's face, followed by a shy smile on Elie's.

And the gnawing grew into outright carnage on his insides.

He didn't like the way she smiled at him or the brightness in his eyes as he spoke to her. Shoving the rest of the brownie in his mouth, he looked away. *I'm jealous. I'm jealous of a man I don't know, over a woman whose feelings about me I'm not sure of.*

Perfect, Eric. A tap on his shoulder had him turning to see Elie's friend smiling at him.

"Hi, my name is Maisy." She extended her hand. He shook it. "I'm a friend of Elnora's. She said you two were childhood friends. Eric, is it?"

Swallowing the last of the brownie, he mumbled, "It's a pleasure," keeping his lips as together as possible. He was sure his teeth were dark brown. "Is she well acquainted with Mr. Jefferson?" He hadn't meant to ask, but the question just—popped out.

"Why, yes she is. I think they're tryin' to keep their relationship a secret. We all expect them to announce their engagement soon."

Knots replaced the gnawing.

Maisy gave him a quizzical look. "Is something wrong?"

Eric met her gaze, forcing his jaw to remain loose. "No, I'm fine, thank you. Interesting meeting," he said, changing the subject to territory less damaging to his digestive tract.

"Yes, it was, as always. Isn't the upcomin' march excitin'? It will be our group's biggest event ever."

And quite an undertaking. The group had a respectable number; Eric counted at least fifty attendees tonight. But would they have an impact in Freeman? "So what work do you do, Maisy?"

"I attend Selma with Elie. We're both in the teacher's program. And my family owns Wilson's General Store in town. I work there during the summer."

"Really? I met Carl Wilson. A relation?"

"My great-uncle. He co-owns the store, thanks to your father," she said kindly.

"What about my father?"

She smiled, her eyes glowing with respect. "He gave our family a loan to expand the store and keep it in business. Most other banks wouldn't consider givin' us a dime. Your father has been very generous to our community."

Eric scanned the crowd and located his father's dark brown head. Morgan shook Mr. Wilson's hand and then ducked out of a door on the side of the church. A sudden burst of pride for his father detracted his attention from his stomach's discomfort.

Maisy scooted by him with a, "Nice meetin' you," leaving him alone. He searched the crowd for Elie, but she had disappeared—and so had Mr. Jefferson. Eric inwardly groaned and stomped outside to the horses. His father stood near the animals, preparing for the ride. "Did you get to speak with Mr. Hall?" Eric asked.

"Yes, I did. The bank is about to do business with him. But I'll brief you at the office." He gave his son a cautious look. "What did you think of the meeting?"

Eric detected the change in Morgan's voice, one of concern. Did he feel the need to protect these people from his own son? He might have been in Europe for a couple of years, but he hadn't forgotten how closely he was raised to this community. "Father, I'm honored you asked me to come. I'll be involved in any way I can."

Morgan expelled what Eric thought was a strained breath and nodded.

"Someone paid you a high compliment tonight. You're well respected in this community." Eric gestured at the people exiting the church. His father didn't ask him to repeat the compliment. He just humbly smiled. They mounted and eased their horses into a trot.

"I feel it's our God-given duty to help our fellow man and if I have the resources, then I'm willing."

Eric glanced over at his father. Back straight, eyes forward, his admiration for the man increased. He recalled what Maisy had said about his father providing her family a loan to keep the store in business. A white man purposely assisting black businesses. A risky venture.

Chapter Nine

MONDAY MORNING

Morgan Montgomery parked the family car behind the Montgomery Bank and he and Eric exited the vehicle. His father had briefly explained what he thought was God's calling on the family business. Although Morgan's political views would potentially drive away business, he saw their financial blessing as a tool to help those less fortunate.

The last time Eric stepped into the Montgomery Bank, he was a sophomore in college. The stately brick building showed little wear since its founding more than twenty years ago. The interior was updated with a fresh coat of a neutral-colored paint, healthy plants, and new furniture. A wave of anticipation ushered him forward. He'd always used work as an outlet for some of his frustrations, but he never really enjoyed the task. *This will be different.* Perhaps returning home was exactly what he needed to fill the void in his life.

As Eric listened to his father explain the number of loans the bank had secured, he turned, hearing the back door open. In walked the leggy blonde with her bright blue eyes and an equally radiant smile. *Amanda Wilcox.* Looking at her all day would be distracting.

She sashayed to the Montgomery men. "Good morning, bosses!"

"Good morning, Miss Wilcox. Hope you had a good weekend," Morgan answered politely.

Amanda nodded her head once, her grin cheerful. "Yes, sir, Mr. Montgomery, my weekend was wonderful, thank you for asking. I want to also thank you again for inviting me to dinner. I hope I will be able to join you again soon," she said, smoothly shifting her gaze to Eric, her smile coy.

He gave her a devilish grin in response.

"And you, um, should I call you…" Amanda pinned her plump bottom lip between two top teeth and raised a perfectly arched brow in question.

His eyes read through her innocence. "You may call me Eric, Miss Wilcox."

"And you may call me Amanda." Her gaze lowered but not before he caught a subtle look of pleasure. Her arm brushed his as she walked past him and continued on to her desk at the front of the office.

"Amanda works mainly as an assistant, but she's also a very capable teller," his father offered. "Whatever administrative tasks you need completed, Amanda will see to it."

Eric followed his father to a small office on the opposite side of the teller stations. The dark mahogany furnishings included a desk and padded chair, a bookcase filled with what Eric suspected were books financial in nature, and two cushioned seats in front of the desk. A semi-green plant in the corner starved for water.

Morgan straightened the desk calendar. "Well, this is your office." He sat on the front edge of the desk as Eric remained in the doorway, surveying the unimpressive mock paintings on the walls. "What we haven't gone over are your qualifications for this job." He smiled mischievously.

Eric smirked. "I think my academic references speak for themselves." He'd received his bachelors in economics from Duke University and his masters in finance at an accelerated program overseas.

Morgan nodded his head, considering. "But do you come highly recommended?" He laughed at seeing his son's look of boredom and stood up. "Well, don't just stand in the doorway, son. I want you in charge of home and vehicle loans, as well as the quarterly audits. If you find that you're not working enough, we'll add to your plate no problem."

Eric nodded in agreement and stepped into the small office.

Morgan met him at the door. "I'm going to see about getting you some office supplies, and when Mark Greene arrives, I'll introduce you. You'll be shadowing him this week to learn the ropes and get comfortable."

"Who's Mark Greene?"

"He's one of my associates. Mark handles bank transactions and a few personal loans. He's also been overseeing the quarterly audits, so I'm sure he'll be happy to get those off his hands."

He appraised Eric through slightly narrowed lids. Eric schooled his face to be unreadable. His father had to have his doubts about him. He still hadn't explained why he returned home, and his father respected him enough not to ask.

"Well, then, I'll let you get settled, and I'll go see about getting you some supplies."

"Thanks, Dad." They shook hands. Morgan took one last look around the office, a pleased grin on his face. He nodded to his son and left the room.

Eric took his place behind the desk. He twirled around in the seat and fingered the books on the shelves behind him. Beside a framed black-and-white photograph of his father standing in front of the bank as if it were the grand opening lay a book all too familiar and yet completely foreign. The Holy Bible. When he was a child, his mother had often read to him from their family Bible in the moments before he drifted off to sleep. She'd bought him a copy to take with him to college. Not long after her death, he'd returned home during the winter break of his sophomore year in college and tossed the book into the bottom drawer of his dresser. Was it still there?

He circled back around and Amanda stood at the door, her hands full of office supplies. He hoped she hadn't brought all the supplies—so she'd have to return again, and again. "Come in, Amanda."

"Your father said you needed some supplies, so I brought you some fresh pens, notepads, bank stamps, and I'll order you a personalized stamp as soon as you let me know how you want your name to appear on it."

Locking his hands behind his head, Eric leisurely studied his new assistant. Her blonde hair was pinned up in a professional manner, accentuating her high cheekbones. Her baby blue dress hung right at her knees, with a fitted belt sitting snugly around her small waist. The top two buttons of her dress were left unbuttoned, exposing the slightest mounds. Blood rushed to his brain—his pulse steadily increasing. "Please, come in, Amanda. You can lay those supplies on the desk, thank you."

She grinned, her rhythmic hips swaying until she rounded the desk and stood beside him. Her eyes locked with his as she placed the materials in front of him. "I see your plant in the corner needs watering," she said softly.

"It's parched," he answered with a raspy breath.

Amanda glanced up, considering. "It's not in my job description but if you want, I could water it for you."

His gaze captured her. "I would like that. It's on the verge of death, I'm afraid, and might need constant attention."

"My pleasure. As much as it needs."

"Come in at your discretion."

"I'll go get some water," she called over her shoulder, her seductive smile lingering in Eric's mind long after she left.

****

With the horse feed order in hand, Elie walked down Main Street toward Wilson's General Store. The roads were busy with the midday rush of people leaving work for lunch. Groups walked in and out of shops, blacks using colored entrances, and whites using the front doors. Puffs of smog shot out of the mufflers of tri-colored buses moving to and from their stops.

Elie observed several police cars at different points on the roads. A few hard-faced officers stood outside their vehicles, hands resting on gun belts, Dobermans at their sides. Other uniforms sat inside their cruisers and watched those passing by. It was no secret several officers on the police force were members of the Ku Klux Klan, and their ability to hide behind the badge made them even more intimidating…and dangerous. Elie considered the upcoming march planned for August. She wasn't sure how the activists would be perceived—marching down the main streets of Freeman—but she hoped to inspire more residents and local officials to petition the state government for integration.

Keeping her focus ahead of her, she continued toward Wilson's. A familiar red truck across the street caught her attention before she reached the store. Shane McDougal lounged in the driver's seat, smoking a cigarette, a small grin on his face. She stopped walking. Was Shane McDougal looking at her? Averting her gaze, she quickened her steps.

Upon entering the shop, she was pleased to see Maisy working at the counter.

Maisy's gaze rested on the paper in her hand. "Lemme guess, feed?"

Elie grinned and nodded. "Two orders. One for my father, and the other for Mr. Montgomery. You'll need to make it double for my father. He's expecting to board a few more horses for the next month or two."

Maisy snatched the slip of paper from her hand, delight crossing her features. "Elie, between your father's and Mr. Montgomery's feed orders, you keep us in business." She moved to the counter and rang the purchases on the register.

Elie chuckled. "Happy to help." She walked around the shop, fingering the various tools and knickknacks hanging on the racks.

"So, are you going to tell me about it?"

"Tell you what?" Elie called over her shoulder, still browsing.

"Don't play games with me, Elnora Brown. I'm talking about you and a certain Mr. Michael Jefferson. What did you two discuss after the meeting the other night?"

Elie flushed. "Well…"

"Out with it!"

Elie laughed. "Mr. Jefferson thanked me for all the assistance I've been givin' him for the march and wanted to know if I'd go for ice cream with him sometime."

Maisy grimaced. "That's it? A thank-you? Ice cream? He didn't ask you to dinner?"

"Maisy!"

"Everyone can see he's over the moon for you, and he asks you for ice cream?"

Elie smiled at Maisy's less than thrilled tone and hid her face from her friend. Truthfully, she didn't know what to think about Michael's attentions. He was quite attractive, and an honest, Christian man who was in the divinity program at Selma University with dreams of being the pastor of his own church someday. He'd a gentle way about himself, always friendly with everyone, even the children of the town. *You and Michael would be a handsome pair.* Her mother's words rang in her ears. She never pushed Elie into anything, but Elie knew encouragement when she heard it.

"Your children will be so cute!"

"What?" Elie snapped back into reality.

"Yours and Michael's. If you could ever get to dinner with the man," she added sarcastically.

"Maisy, please!" Elie could barely catch her breath for laughing.

"Well, did you at least accept his invitation to have ice cream?"

Elie grinned coyly. "Yes."

Maisy clapped her hands. "Ooo, when are you going? Have you decided what you're gonna wear? You should wear someum' yellow. Yellow really makes you stand out."

"Wait a minute!" Elie giggled, holding up her hand for her friend to stop. "He hasn't exactly said when yet."

"*What?*" Maisy threw up her hands in dramatic fashion. "He didn't even confirm a time? What's the man waitin' for?"

"Perhaps, the proper time?" Elie added gently.

"There's no time like the present. And if he doesn't move quickly, the other one will."

Elie was momentarily stunned into silence as Maisy eyed her curiously. "What other one?"

Maisy gave her friend a sly grin. "You know, your long-lost friend, Eric Montgomery."

Heat seared Elie's cheeks.

"Hah!" Maisy pointed a finger at her. "You like him!"

"Shhhh!" Elie put a finger to her lips and rushed over to her friend. "Someone could hear you!"

Maisy laughed hard, holding the sides of her stomach with her hands. "No one," her laughter took over, "is even in the shop!"

"Quiet, will you!" Elie commanded with more anger than she felt. The insinuation she could have feelings for Eric embarrassed her. It was true—she found herself more physically attracted to her best friend than she'd ever considered possible.

Or ever considered, period.

But only physically.

It's too complicated anyway.

"I knew it!"

"You know nothing. I know nothing!" Elie flailed her arms and turned away, leaning her back against the counter and crossing her arms over her chest in frustration.

"I know at the meeting the other night, his eyes were on you like white on rice."

"What?" Elie gave her a dirty look and rubbed the back of her neck to extinguish the flames just beneath the surface of her skin.

"You know what I mean. He could barely take his eyes off you. You should have seen the intensity. I could have waved my hand in front of his face and he wouldn't have blinked."

Elie dipped her head to hide a grin she couldn't control.

The shop door chimed, drawing Elie's eyes. A cold chill swept across her. Shane McDougal stood at the entrance with a somewhat sheepish expression on his face as his gaze shifted from Maisy to Elie.

Maisy hesitantly cleared her throat. "May I help you?"

Shane focused his gaze on Elie for a minute and then answered, "No, just looking."

Skin beginning to crawl, Elie turned away, wiping her clammy hands down the sides of her cotton skirt. She considered leaving, remembering the smile he gave her before she entered the shop. Then she glanced at Maisy, who looked just as uncomfortable. She couldn't leave her friend alone with this character.

"Um, I'm going to see if I have some extra feed in the back." Maisy's voice croaked, and she darted through a door leading to the back office.

Elie walked toward one end of the shop, trying to busy herself with whatever hung on the rack in front of her. She heard Shane's light footsteps and tried not to look in his direction. When the sounds ceased, Elie glanced up to see Shane no more than a foot away…between her and the door. *I should have stayed at the counter.*

"Miss Brown."

Flabbergasted, she lowered her gaze. "Mr. McDougal."

Her attempt to sidestep him was thwarted when he slid in front of her. "How are you?" he asked with a slightly froggy throat.

Elie nodded. "I'm fine, thank you."

"Glad to hear it."

What was going on? Was she being featured in an episode of The Twilight Zone? This man not only hated her people but never spoke a kind word to them. And here he was being civil. *What did I do to deserve this?*

She studied his appearance of a worn red shirt and faded jeans, his dark hair falling slightly over his forehead. He had a thin but lengthy nose and small lips. His green eyes didn't match Eric's for color or brilliance, but all in all, Elie would label him attractive—if she didn't already find him completely detestable.

Shane grinned widely at her appraisal. Elie swallowed the bile shooting up her throat. Dropping her gaze, she attempted to dodge him for the counter. "If you'd excuse me." Shane caught her wrist. Her eyes shot to him in amazement. He licked his lips, a strange confidence in his eyes.

"Elnora, I was wonderin'…" He dropped his head before snapping it up and squaring his shoulders. "Well, I was wonderin' if you had a man."

Elie gave him such a startled look he blinked and stepped back as if affronted. She eyed her wrist, which he still held fast. Shane followed her gaze and loosed his fingers. "Sorry," he said shyly, his face as red as beets.

"I'm, ah, I've been approached by someone I'm interested in." Elie hoped he'd take the hint.

"So you're still available."

So much for hinting. She didn't care for the spark of interest in his eyes or how they warmed the longer they held her own and decided to be firm. "I believe that's my business, sir, and I'd prefer not to discuss it with you." She made a quick escape to the counter and a glance back told her a firm tone might not have been the best approach. Fists balled against his sides, anger smoldered in his eyes.

"Nope, no feed. I'll put your order in and will call when it's ready for pick up," Maisy said after returning from the back.

Shane stomped to the front door and yanked it open but pivoted, fixing his gaze on Elie. His eyes still held the same fury but with a twinge of assurance. He spat on the floor of the shop. A disapproving grunt came from Maisy.

"Whoever he is, he won't last long." With a cocky half-grin, he marched outside, slamming the door behind him.

When she no longer heard his footsteps, Elie sighed in relief. She walked to the front door, pulled a tissue out of her small wristlet, and stooped to clean Shane's spit off the floor.

Maisy hurried from behind the counter. "Don't—I can do that."

"No, it's my fault he forgot his manners, so I'll clean it up." She wiped the last of the saliva off the floor, and Maisy grabbed the tissue from her.

"There's a wastebasket behind the counter. I'll throw this away. What was that all about anyway?"

Elie sighed, pinching the bridge of her nose. *I can't believe I'm going to say this…*"I think he wanted to ask me out."

Maisy burst into laughter. "Shane McDougal? A McDougal showing interest in a black girl? Has he gone mad?"

"Maisy, please!"

"Well, don't you just get all the men."

"I don't *want* all the men."

"He must be crazy."

"Whatever he is, I hope he never talks to me again. Do you think he meant what he said before he left?" Elie bit her bottom lip, fearing harm would come to someone she knew.

"You mean about your man not lastin' long? I'm not sure. You know what a hothead Shane is."

"That's why I'm concerned."

"I wouldn't worry about it. We'll be back in school in a month or so, and he won't be able to control who you date." Maisy wagged her brows and gave her friend a mischievous grin.

Relief flooded through Elie, causing her to smile. She considered Michael again. He'd never give her a moment's scare, not the way Shane McDougal did. Neither would Eric. But Eric denied God any right to his life and Elie couldn't consider a man whose life didn't include the Lord. The thought of Michael being the right man loomed large in her mind.

Elie picked up the receipt for the feed Maisy had placed on the counter.

"How 'bout I come over for dinner tonight? We can further discuss how many men have their eyes on you. I'll be finished at the shop around five and can have my grandfather drop me off at your house."

Elie chuckled. "All right, Maisy, I would love to have you over for dinner, if you're free."

"Why, thank you for the invitation!"

Chapter Ten

MUSING

Eric rubbed the space between his brows. Reviewing audit results was always tedious. Morgan had sent Amanda on some errands this morning, much to Eric's relief. One last review of the audit paperwork and if he was satisfied, he'd submit it to his father.

Morgan Montgomery was an excellent businessman. His files were in order, previous audits were clean, and the bank was well funded. Customers were more than pleased.

Eric found himself falling in love with the banking business. It was different from the corporate world in France—a much smaller pond—but just as enjoyable. He was grateful for the lack of upper management and the endless red tape he'd dealt with in earlier employments. The natural choice to inherit the business, once his father released the reins, was a thought not as unpleasant to Eric as it used to be.

When he reached the last page of the report, Eric breathed easily. Another spotless audit. Everything was aboveboard, no errors were reported, and the business was making money. A smile stole over Eric's face as he leaned back in his chair with his eyes closed, putting his hands behind his head. A job well done. He was still grinning when he heard a knock on his office door. "Come in."

"Sleeping on the job? I didn't realize you wanted to get fired so soon."

Eric grinned wider at the familiar female voice. *Amanda.* He opened one eye, and then two. She stood in the doorway with a small but teasing smile, arms full of files. He hadn't seen her all day and the view—stunning. Dressed in a light green wrap-around dress with bright yellow heels, the front half of her hair was pulled back and the rest hung in large curls floating on her shoulders like golden silk. "You forget I stand to inherit the business. I'm irreplaceable."

Amanda laughed lightly. "You're very sure of yourself, sir. However, you lack longevity and could just as easily be demoted to say, a janitor, and would have to work your way back up to the top."

Eric laughed loudly. Amanda walked into his office and softly closed the door. His laughter ceased as their eyes held. She didn't seem to be poison, but he knew a narcotic when he saw one. Did he want to risk the trouble again?

Any relationship with Amanda could only end badly. He knew nothing about her, and she knew even less about him. He wasn't interested in what she liked or disliked, and Amanda seemed only interested in herself. Eric found the opportunity amusing. He'd never cared one way or the other about whether he needed a woman in his life—they could only temporarily fill a void. No sense in caring much for something he'd never commit to. He'd plug the hole with something sweet for a while, and Amanda was right in front of him—and willing.

Long legs brought her and a demure smile around his desk. She flipped through a couple of files in her arms. "Mr. Montgomery wanted me to give you the paperwork for the

Perkins and Jones' loans, to get your opinion." She placed the files on his desk and waited for his response. He held her gaze. A small blush tinted her cheeks and he almost smirked at the color. She wasn't a woman who'd blush out of embarrassment or timidity. She blushed for his benefit and he appreciated the effort.

All of a sudden, Elie entered his thoughts. He recalled her blush while with him and his father in the small office at the Montgomery estate. He'd confronted her with a challenging gaze, and heat rose from her neck to her cheeks. *That* was the blush of an innocent. Not comparing the two women was an impossibility, but Elie's display was far more attractive; however, she was nowhere in sight, nor was he even sure he wanted to fluster her further.

Eric casually flipped open the Perkins file and glanced at its contents. The address for the business caught his attention. It was in Selma, not Freeman. "I'm going to take a few minutes on these. How about we discuss my plans of tenure over dinner…tonight?"

"Why, sir, if you mean a professional dinner, then I believe I can clear my schedule."

Clear her schedule.

"Because I do believe that fraternizing with management would hurt my career options."

A wave of exhaustion hit him. Tired of their game, he was eager to review the loans in front of him. However, if he was going to try this new muse, he'd venture to make a wholehearted effort, like he'd do with any project. "Dinner tonight, Miss Wilcox, and that's an order."

Amanda grinned and flounced toward the office door. She paused at the doorway and flashed him a seductive smile before exiting the office. Eric leaned back in his chair and sighed. Amanda was stunning, that was a given, but the crater-sized hole in his heart was too big a job for just one beautiful woman to fill. He wasn't about to give up trying.

He'd tolerated numerous nameless beauties in the last several years and a few more wouldn't hurt.

Eric pulled the Perkins file close. *Father does banking outside of Freeman?* The funds for the approved loan were delineated through different channels than their other loans. After a close examination of the financial transactions, he jumped up from his desk and, taking the file, walked quickly from his office, passing a startled Amanda at her desk, and into the hallway leading to his father's office. The door was slightly ajar and Eric let himself in. His father didn't look up from the paperwork that littered his desk. *No wonder he needs Elie to organize.* His father would get lost in his own home if he handled it all himself.

Eric seated himself in a plush leather chair opposite his father and waited quietly for him to share his attention. He didn't have to wait long. Morgan cleared his throat and looked up at his son. Locking his fingers on his desk, he smiled warmly.

Eric smirked. Morgan, always calm and deliberate, had Eric wondering how the man managed to have such a persona. Eric's mind was in a constant state of unrest, which morphed into his present sarcastic and pessimistic nature—a contrast to his father's gentle spirit. Even after his wife passed, Eric never witnessed anger from the man, only a calm peace.

"What can I do for you, son? Wait, nothing is wrong with your position here—"

"No, no, Father. I enjoy working here." His father's expression softened. "I'm not going anywhere anytime soon. I'm here about the Perkins loan."

"Good, good." His father nodded. "What about the Perkins loan?"

"Several questions, actually. Why are we funding this loan for them, where are these funds coming from, and I didn't know you did business in Selma?"

His father's lips twitched in amusement. He looked

toward the door, still open. "Do me a favor and shut the door, will you, son?"

Eric complied, and when he returned to his chair, Morgan explained. "Yes, I do business in Selma. I enable certain people to establish businesses other bankers would overlook—for obvious reasons."

"And what reasons are those?"

"The Perkinses are black," Morgan stated as a matter of fact. "Race relations are as tense in Selma as here in Freeman. Any decent, respectable white businessman showing too much favor to prospective black businessmen would more or less be persecuted, and possibly ostracized from white society. And in the business world, white consumers are a vast percentage of the market. Losing their support would be a death sentence for any business."

Eric sat back in the chair and crossed his arms over his chest, thinking. "So, you provide the funds for blacks to own their own businesses—"

"Or own a home."

Eric waved a hand in acknowledgment and proceeded. "And these funds are from," he paused considering, "the bank?" His brows went up. How did he miss the funneling of money for "special" purposes in his audits? *I haven't been out of work that long to be making mistakes this badly.*

Morgan chuckled softly. "No, no, son. I have what you could call a silent partner. A businessman in Selma assists in funding loans I legitimately process through the bank. You could say it's a type of grant program my partner and I would appreciate remain hidden from the public eye."

Eric breathed a silent sigh of relief. *Still sharp.* However, his father's philanthropy continued to surprise him. Not just a generous man, but also one with an apparent propensity for pseudo-clandestine activities. His father would risk his livelihood to make a difference in someone else's life, even with the strain between the races. Someone he neither knew nor had any relationship with would be worth the trouble. Morgan Montgomery had strong convictions, and he was doing something about them.

Admiration for his father grew exponentially. More than an active member of the anti-segregation movement, he facilitated opportunities and rights for black people. Eric couldn't remember what it felt like to have the compassion and desire to sacrifice for others the way his father did in his life. A layer of scab peeled from his heart. He looked down at his hands and found them trembling. He clamped them together. Too much emotion, too soon.

"Have you met this partner?" Eric asked.

"Um, no. I was given his name and we've been in contact through a third party."

"A third party? *Dad.*"

Morgan held his hands up. "I know, I know, and in any other situation I would agree with what I know you are about to say. However, I've had his references and finances investigated and the money is legitimate."

"Do you at least know his name?"

"Yes, Madson Hoover."

"Hoover, hmmm."

"You recognize the name?"

"No, no." Eric held his father's gaze evenly. "You're sure this is completely legitimate?"

It was Morgan's time to smirk. "Do you doubt your own father? I didn't spend the better part of my life building this business, with the grace of God, to throw away my stewardship responsibilities on careless research." He didn't blink. "Everything is aboveboard. I just need a review of the loan for any discrepancies I might have overlooked and then your stamp of approval. Please."

Eric nodded. "You'll have it."

His father gave him a nod as well. "Thank you."

****

Poor Amanda. Admittedly, the bank's loans held more interest than the chatty blonde before him. Eric hadn't shown Amanda the attention she deserved, and the way she was dressed this evening demanded attention. He glanced over at her as they walked silently in the parking lot outside a quaint family-owned restaurant that served the best spaghetti in town. Warm wind lifted the hem of her blue dress ever so slightly, revealing shapely thighs. She sported an impressive V-neck and he was suddenly sorry he hadn't spent any time examining it during dinner.

Smiling up at him, she looped her arm through his. Eric couldn't remember what she'd said during the course of their meal. It wasn't earth-shattering, or even remotely interesting, or he'd have recalled some details—or at least he thought he would've.

When they reached her car, she breathed a content sigh and faced him, the moonlight hitting her hair and casting her in a subdued golden glow. Her lips turned up and she rested her hands on his arms, rubbing them up and down. Eric involuntarily stepped forward.

"That was a lovely work dinner, sir," she stated softly, a slight note of tease in her voice.

At least she had a good time. He placed his hands on her small hips and eased her closer. She tilted her head to meet his kiss, wrapping her arms around his neck and kissing him with more force than he'd anticipated. Fire and lust shot through his veins, causing an involuntary groan as he held her tightly, matching her enthusiasm. Her heavy musk scent lured him deeper into a licentious haze, her nails digging into his biceps. The sound of footsteps in the distance cleared the fog in his mind. He ended the kiss, but took pleasure at the look of satisfaction in her eyes. Waiting for the usual regret to surface, he relaxed when desire was all he continued to feel.

The rustle of close footsteps drew his attention and he turned in the direction of the noise. He'd just released Amanda when something hard struck him over his upper left eye. Eric could feel his feet lift from the ground, his body falling until he hit the gravel of the pavement.

Amanda screamed.

Eric shot to his feet, rising to full height and seeing Chase McDougal, fists up.

"Chase McDougal, my uncle is the chief of police and he will hear about this!" Amanda yelled vehemently, her hands on her hips. Chase ignored her.

"Well, someone's jealous," Eric said lazily, straightening his jacket, unperturbed by Chase's stance.

"Amanda is my woman," he seethed.

Eric laughed. "I'd say the kiss she just gave me proves otherwise."

Chase let out a snarl and leaped toward Eric, who ducked the left swing and landed a solid uppercut to Chase's chin. Chase staggered backwards until he lost his footing and fell right on his rump. He scuttled backwards a bit, and then surged to his feet. He stole a glance at Amanda, who smiled triumphantly at Eric. Growling like an enraged animal, Chase rushed forward, a bull against the matador. Arms wrapped around Eric, they both landed on the pavement, wrestling for dominance.

Eric felt a blow to his left shoulder and he responded with a fist to the side of Chase's left ribcage. Eric wrapped a leg around one of Chase's and shoved the opposite shoulder up, flipping Chase on his back with Eric on top. A startled Chase gave Eric the second he needed to land another punch to his face. Chase cried out at the impact and his other cheek received the same treatment. Blood trickled from Chase's mouth. Eric disentangled himself and stood over his opponent's body. Chase moaned, half-conscious.

Breathing heavily, Eric wiped the sweat and grit from

above his mouth.

Amanda ran to his side and clasped his arm. She played the dutiful nurse, reaching a hand up to gently caress the side of his face.

"You're hurt. Oh, Eric!"

Eric fumed. He grasped her hand and held it away from him, in no mood for sentiment now. That idiot McDougal had dared to start a fight with him! His jacket was no doubt ruined, his left temple pounded, and he was sure this fight was only the beginning if he kept seeing Amanda. Half of him wanted to rid himself of this mess, but the other half was too egotistical to let go and let a loser like Chase McDougal steal a woman from him. He took Amanda's elbow and steered her back toward her car.

"I think you'd better head home. I've never seen the McDougal brothers apart, and I doubt the other two are far away."

"But —" she began, a twinge of disappointment in her voice.

"No buts. It's late."

They reached her car and she slipped out of his grasp, turned, and planted a solid kiss on his lips. He didn't push her away. "Thank you," she whispered. She opened her car door and slipped in gracefully. Eric closed the door and backed away as she started the car. With one last look of longing, she drove away.

On the walk back to his car, Eric's gaze swiveled to where Chase lay to find he'd disappeared. Eric expelled a long breath, feeling his heartbeat and his adrenaline slow. He yanked his car door open and sank into the driver's seat, wincing at the tightness of his back and the pain above his left eye. Warm liquid slid through the hairs of his eyebrow. *Great.* He was cut.

****

Eric slammed the front door of the house before wrenching his jacket off and throwing it against the wall. He fingered the cut above his brow. A shower. He needed a shower.

"Eric!"

He paused mid-stride. Elie rushed forward, stopping abruptly when she eyed the discarded jacket. Her gaze settled on his face, and she reached up to finger his brow. "You're bleeding!"

Grabbing his hand, she pulled him into the front office, where she sat him down, rather gruffly, on the settee and ran quickly from the room. Eric arched his stiff back, the tight muscles crying out in pain. He groaned, closed his eyes, and lay back, letting out a breath of air.

"Sit up," Elie commanded.

Eric rolled his eyes, complying. She sat beside him, a small white container in her lap. She opened the box, revealing pieces of gauze, cotton balls, medicine tubes, and a dark bottle of liquid. She untwisted the bottle's cap and set the cap aside before tipping the bottle onto a cotton ball. Elie looked up at him, the muscles in her round face tense. She eyed the cut on his forehead. "This might sting a bit," she said hesitantly. Tentatively, she raised the moist gauze to his forehead and just before she touched his skin, he jumped and yelped.

Elie reacted in the same manner, her eyes wide with fear. He grinned at her and for that, she frowned and punched him in the chest.

"Ow!" He gave her a dirty look and rubbed his right pectoral. "Aren't you supposed to be nursing me back to health, Miss Nightingale?"

"If you'd let me!"

"You should really work on your bedside manner." He stared at the cool, damp cotton ball as it touched his cut. He held back a wince.

"What happened?" she asked still dabbing the wound.

"I got into a fight."

"That's obvious. What was the fight about and with whom? You look absolutely terrible."

"Thanks," he said dryly. "I looked almost handsome earlier, trust me."

Elie gave him a look of curiosity. "Are you going to tell me?"

The longer he stared into those inviting eyes, the more he wanted to say, and not just about the scrape he'd had with Chase. Her look displayed no pretense. In truth, he could trust a woman like her. "I got into a fight with Chase McDougal."

"Chase McDougal?" Her brows knitted. "Why? How?"

"He started it. I was in a parking lot and he attacked me."

"But why?"

"It's not that important."

A flash of annoyance mixed with disappointment crossed her eyes but then she was back to Nurse Brown, her gaze unreadable, her actions deliberate. She squeezed a medicine tube, placed a small amount of clear gel on her finger and lifted her hand up to rub the medicine on his cut.

Eric leaned back with a hand up. "Are your fingers clean?"

Elie's lips twisted into a grimace. Using her left hand, she reached to pull the back of his neck closer to her until their faces were mere inches apart. The heat of her body penetrated the air between them. He inhaled her soft lavender scent, his senses heady. Remarkably, her attention remained on his cut.

Eric allowed his gaze to roam over her face, taking in her russet-colored eyes, and then lingering on her full lips, shining from lightly tinted red gloss. He swayed slightly toward her, but she didn't seem to notice. She rubbed a cotton ball around the cut, and then placed it in a small pile of used ones collecting on her lap.

Looking pleased at her work, she met his eyes. "All finished. I recommend bed rest for one night and you should be much better in the morning." Her smile faded. He heard her breath hitch.

He leaned forward.

****

Elie couldn't help noticing how handsome Eric looked up close. Firm chin, lovely round lips, a strong brow, and his eyes were as green as the estate's lawn, freshly cut on a warm summer day. His gaze rested a while on her lips. She swallowed, her throat dry. Would he kiss her? Would she allow him to?

Her heart thumped. Pleasantly. She should make some excuse and leave. Wet signs for the activist march waited for her on the veranda. She could see if they were dry.

Eric reached a hand up and gently brushed the tips of his fingers below her left ear and down the side of her neck to the laced edge of her high-neck bodice. A million nerve endings erupted beneath the trail of heat he left on her skin.

How her body shivered.

"Eric," she breathed, hearing fear in her voice.

"You did an excellent job of fixing me up, Nurse Brown." His husky voice sent ripples of pleasure over her flesh. "Care to receive your payment now?" His gaze never left her lips.

I'm going to faint. Her own eyes betrayed her, leveling on his lips and the thought of them taking her own was almost enough for her to lean in and start the kiss herself. It took all of her willpower to edge back and fiddle around with the medicine box. She exhaled loudly and then met his hooded gaze.

"No payment is necessary. As a friend, I provide this service for free." She frowned at the look of frustration in his eyes, disappointed at his anger over her refusal. She longed to tell him her desire matched his own, but she stopped herself, convinced the fight with Chase was over another woman. It was no secret Chase McDougal carried a torch for a certain bank assistant. Eric had missed dinner tonight to stay at the bank and work.

Work. Right.

Rising from the settee, a hand restrained her. "I'm afraid I must warn you, Miss Brown, I'm not accustomed to refusal."

Elie jerked her hand from his grip.

Eric scowled, putting a hand to his wound. "I'm sorry. I don't know why I spoke to you like that just now. I must be more out of it than I realized." Eric smiled lopsidedly. "Chase did get a couple of good licks in, especially the first one," he grumbled. He leaned back against the settee, his eyes wide with contrition, his bottom lip turning down.

She never could stay mad at him. "All is forgiven, Eric." She turned to go, but his voice halted her.

"What is it about you?"

Confused, she faced him. "I'm sorry?"

"You're different from the rest."

His voice was low, his gaze narrowed on her. Did he mean the other women he'd known?

"What would it take for a man to have you?"

Her jaw dropped. "Eric—"

"I'm just curious, is all. You're beautiful and smart. Why are you unattached?"

Was she lacking? The thought hadn't occurred to her. She graciously received the subtle attentions Michael had given her over the last couple of years, but she had an active life, full of people who depended on her, not to mention the children she taught during the summer months. "The Lord has someone for me. And he will be handsome, smart, and most importantly, will have a heart for Jesus."

Eric dropped his gaze, mouth twisting into a frown. "A high price."

"Too high for some, but not for one."

Chapter Eleven

SCHOOLMARM

Elie flew out of the bathroom and nearly ran face-first into her father's thick chest. Emmett gave her a wry glance as she yelled an apology over her shoulder and rushed to the kitchen. If she didn't hurry, she'd be late for her class. Saturday at the school on Wimbly Lane would be filled with students from lower-income families who couldn't afford to send their children to school during the regular season. Most of the children had to work odd jobs during the week to provide income for their families.

I won't be late. I won't be late. She had lain awake long into the night, reliving her encounter with Eric in the office. At first she was angry with herself for not allowing him to kiss her; at least she would've known what it was like to be kissed. However, wisdom prevailed, to her initial discomfort, and she knew his kiss alone wouldn't have satisfied her.

Her heart was more vulnerable than she'd ever considered and his kiss would've sealed her doom. The fresh realization put fear into her heart. Where Michael Jefferson never gave her a moment's alarm, Eric's waywardness would break her heart.

Enough. She'd have no more distractions today. *The kids will be enough trouble.*

"Don't forget your gradebook. It's on the kitchen table," Elie heard her mother call from the living room.

"Thank you, Momma," Elie responded as she came into the living room. Her mother finished a stitch in her newest knitting project before sending a warm smile to her daughter.

"Since when do you run late?"

Ever since I've been daydreaming about Eric.

"I'll be on time," she affirmed. She twirled around, her head moving from side to side as she scanned the room.

"Whatcha lookin' for, honey?"

"Um..." Elie double-checked the items she held and smiled in relief. "Nothin'. I have everything." She darted for the door. "Bye, Momma."

"Bye, sweetie, and have a good day!"

"Bye, Daddy!" Elie called as she ran out the door.

****

Eric rubbed his eyes and squinted at the streams of sunlight shooting into his room. He'd had a restless night's sleep. The old dream of someone chasing him, of running but never quite losing the presence, plagued him during the night.

Too high for some, but not for one.

He cursed and covered his face with his hands. He'd forced himself to sleep the night before, determined not to think of her. A better time would've been spent ruminating on his lovely nurse than dreaming of a faceless demon.

Frustrated, Eric hopped out of bed, scraping fingers through his thick hair. Elie's words haunted him. Challenged him. He walked over to the window, his bare chest warming from the heat of the sun's rays. Fresh summer air flowed through the open window, and he inhaled deeply, willing the soothing aura to calm his agitated spirit. Off in the distance, horses neighed and Mr. Brown shouted commands.

What's today? Saturday? Elie would be teaching at the schoolhouse. Eric ran to the bathroom for a quick shower. Elie was always a bit overdramatic...and self-righteous. What made her so different from other women? He'd go to the schoolhouse and discover her weakness. And afterwards? With any other woman, he'd take advantage...

****

"Okay, last week we studied multiplication with the number eleven so now we'll look at the number twelve."

Eric silently ascended the short stack of steps to the schoolhouse. He leaned against the doorframe, shoving his tattered hat high on his head, chewing gingerly on the wheat shaft between his teeth.

It'd been years since he'd seen this schoolhouse. A tiny, one-room building owned by the Wimbly Baptist church, it served various uses from storage to a meeting house. Furnished with low wooden tables and rickety chairs, rows of kids sat in the sweltering room, backs rigid and attention focused on their young teacher.

Elie stood at the front of the class, writing equations on the chalkboard, leaving each one without an answer. "Now, we'll start with twelve times one and go all the way up to twelve times twelve." She continued to write. "I hope all of you are prepared to answer these equations." Elie neared the end of the chalkboard.

A small boy in red overalls rotated in his chair. Spying Eric, the whites of his eyes grew large, and his lower jaw slacked. "Miss Brown?"

"Yes, Jeremy, you want to answer the first question?" Elie finished scrawling the last equation.

"Miss Brown, that's a white man!"

"Jeremy, what are you talking about?" Elie turned around and her eyes widened, her lips parting in surprise and her cheeks flushing to a soft pink. "Yes, Jeremy, that is a white man, but we don't address people by their race," she said, steadying her voice.

"Ya here to get some learnin'?"

About thirty sets of eyes stared at the new student.

"Maybe," Eric answered, his eyes never leaving Elie's. She shifted her stance and then fingered a loose curl. Observing her nervousness caused a slow grin to spread across his face.

"Aren't you a little old for learnin'?" Jeremy asked and several of the children snickered.

Eric cocked a brow at the young boy whose eyes studied him in wonder. "Jeremy, do you think your teacher is pretty?"

"Eric," Elie breathed in a warning.

"Yes sir, she's the prettiest lady I know!"

"Well then, you see, you can never be too old to learn from a beautiful lady." His challenging gaze came back to rest on her. The children laughed and "oohed." Elie's gaze darted from Eric to the children and back—her tawny cheeks reddening.

"Children, this is an old friend of mine, Mr. Eric Montgomery. We grew up together, and I spent many days on his father's ranch. Some of you pass the ranch as you walk here to school."

"The one with all the horses?" Jeremy nearly shouted in awe.

"That's the one. Class, say 'Hello, Mr. Montgomery.'"

"Hello, Mr. Montgomery," the children echoed.

"I've never ridden a horse before. Ya think I can ride one of yers?" Jeremy got up on his knees in anticipation of a yes answer.

Eric smiled at the little rascal. "Sure you can. You know, I taught Miss Brown how to ride."

"Ya did?" Jeremy's eyes widened and he looked over his shoulder at his teacher for confirmation.

Elie cleared her throat. "He did give me a few lessons, yes." Elie glanced from Jeremy to Eric. Eric winked. Elie's blush deepened. She marched to the small desk set apart for the teacher and dropped the chalk in a tin can before picking up a sheet of paper and fanning herself. Eric smothered a grin with one hand.

"Class, thank Mr. Montgomery for allowing all of you to go home early today." The children erupted in cheers. "However," she called out over the voices, "you'll have a quiz next week on the entire multiplication table and you better be prepared."

The kids gathered their things, their exuberant voices drowning out the news about the quiz. "Bye, children!" she called as they ran out of the schoolhouse returning her farewells and thanking Eric as they passed.

When the last of the children sprinted out the door, Elie's warm smile cinched and the heated schoolhouse froze. Ignoring his presence, she grabbed an eraser and worked the chalkboard, no doubt rubbing the board hard. No further conversation, just wiping away every last white speck. With schooled patience, Eric indulged his gaze. Admiring her from the rear would satisfy as much as the front. Her baby blue cloth dress with a white collar was fitted right below her neck—a style she obviously preferred over the drooping necks he'd seen on quite a few girls in town, including Amanda. Half of her deep brown curls were pulled back into a tie and allowed to flow over the remaining loose tresses gracing her shoulders. Setting the eraser down, she reached for her skirt, but must have thought better of it and instead, walked to her desk and pulled a tissue from her purse. She wiped her hands.

After returning the eraser to the tin holding the chalk, she looked up, meeting his gaze. "Finally," Eric commented. "One would think you were taking your time with Mr. Chalkboard. I'm almost jealous."

Elie rolled her eyes and walked around the classroom, picking up the few extra things left by the children. One by one, she placed the collected objects in a drawer in the desk and set about the task of straightening a few of the chairs.

His gaze narrowed; she definitely knew how to try a man's patience. He walked up the final step and into the classroom and reached behind him to grab the door. His eyes came back to Elie, who still paid him no nevermind. He slammed the door shut.

Elie gasped and jumped, turning toward the door with a hand over her heart. Ah, there it was—fear. Eric tried not to smile in triumph, not wanting her temper to flare or she'd leave before he had a chance to pick at her armor.

Fear vanished and a dirty look appeared. "Would you stop playing around and help me finish, please?"

Eric smirked and, taking two chairs at a time, angled them like the rest. He helped clear miscellaneous papers off a few of the desks to hand to Elie when they met in the middle of the classroom. Elie reached for the papers without looking at him. She tugged but he didn't release them. Her questioning gaze met his. He still held the other end of the papers and for a moment they didn't move.

Once he had released the papers to her, Elie immediately smacked them on the top of his head, knocking his hat off. She flounced smartly to her desk and placed the papers on top. He retrieved his hat from the floor, and placed it on his head, his lips turning upward. "You're a natural at teaching, you know?"

Elie peered at him through hooded lashes. "How would you know?"

He feigned shock over her sarcasm. "I didn't need to see the entire class to know you had your students hanging on your every word, even if it was about math."

A relaxed smile softened her taut features. "I do love it—especially when I see their little eyes light up when they finally comprehend what I'm saying." She laughed lightly. "Mother's a teacher, but you know that. I hope, one day, to be as good as she is. Sometimes I think I need to work on how I deliver the material."

"I doubt it."

At his compliment, she reddened and busied herself with the papers on her desk. He glanced toward the closed door, and then back to her. "Are you on your way home? Can I accompany you?"

Apparently satisfied the stack of papers was indeed a stack, Elie moved away from the desk, her grin bright. With purse in hand, she bounced lightly toward the door. Eric opened it, ushering her through before he followed. She locked the door and placed the key under a small stone positioned beneath the first step. Eric jogged to where he'd tied Nessie's reins. When he undid the knot, he caught her look of comprehension.

"Oh, you wanted to ride?"

"Isn't it a few miles away?"

"About three miles, yes."

"And you walk?"

Elie shot him a peculiar look. "Yes." She chuckled. "It appears living in Europe has made you lazy," she commented dryly and she started forward on foot.

"Hmm," Eric murmured. He trudged after her and soon matched her steps. A warm wind blew the hem of her frock, brushing the soft fabric against his hand. He stole a quick glance, taking in her cinnamon-toned skin, the soft chestnut curls bouncing around her high-necked blue dress. *So different from Amanda, so conservative.* He recalled the low-cut dress Amanda had worn the night before. It clung to her every lust-inducing curve. Elie's wasn't nearly as revealing, but her ample bosom and small waist, the curvature of her hips—none could be hidden by an inexpensive piece of fabric whose collar seemed to be choking her. The image of his hands ripping the constraining neckline constricted every muscle in his body as blood pounded in his ears.

"How's your head?" she questioned, her eyes taking in the dressing on his forehead.

He touched the small bandage absent-mindedly. "Oh, it's feeling much better, thanks."

Elie's gaze flitted over his face, studying him intently. "Is that a bruise on your jaw?"

"Chase's entire face should be a bruise."

Elie's laughter didn't last long. "Did you really have to fight him?"

The criticism in her voice startled him. "You expect me to 'turn the other cheek'?" he answered sarcastically.

"Well, at least you remember a verse…or part of one."

"Elie, he punched me square in the face, and I landed on my butt. There was no way I wasn't fighting back." Eric whipped the shaft out of his mouth and hurled it as far as he could. The light grain barely floated ten feet in front of him.

Elie bit her lip. They continued to walk in silence until she giggled.

Eric cast her a glance, his eyes narrowed. "W-h-a-t?" his voice exaggerated.

Her brown eyes were bright with glee. "I was just imagining you landing on your butt," she quipped before sprinting ahead.

Eric let out a low growl as her laughter filled the air. He released the horse's reins, and was quick on her heels. It didn't take him long to catch her, wrap his arms around her waist, lift her off her feet, and twirl her around. Her squeal brought a smile to his face—and a lightening of his heart. For an instant he felt free until the burden on his spirit caused him to frown. Her laughter faded, and he set her on her feet.

Horse trotting behind, they were again walking in silence

with Elie gazing at him from the corner of her eye. Eric kept his focus on the road straight ahead of them. Before long, she looped her right arm through his left and leaned slightly on him.

"Tell me about graduate school."

They'd spoken so little about their lives spent apart, and he knew she'd been eagerly awaiting a chance to hear his stories. Eric settled his gaze on her face. Her eyes were expectant, her tanned cheeks marooned by the exertion of energy. A sudden comfort came over him, like nothing he'd experienced before with any other woman. He found it loosened his tongue and for the next hour they slowly strolled along, discussing school, living in Europe, and the changes that had occurred in Alabama since his departure.

"You missed a lot of holidays."

This time, her voice held a sadness that was devoid of criticism. Yet, he couldn't help his defenses; they rose from instinct. Anger swelled in him as the sensation of being attacked heightened. He gritted his teeth in an attempt to calm his nerves.

"We missed you very much…your father, my parents, Miss Hattie," Elie paused, "and me."

Guilt knifing him in the gut, Eric released a yell, flailing his arms in frustration.

Elie stopped in her tracks, but he surged forward, his pace increasing. After a few moments, he stopped and whirled. "How many times do you have to throw it in my face that I left? Huh? How many times, Elie?"

****

She took in a deep breath, but it did little to alleviate the hard line of her jaw or soften her tightly pinched lips. She'd simply wanted him to know how much he'd been missed. Not light a fuse—especially one she didn't know he had. What made him strike out at her? Was he feeling guilty for abandoning them all these years? *Well, he should.*

"I wasn't throwin' it in your face! But you oughtta know how your actions have affected the people who *really* love you." She stormed past him, recalling his fight with Chase over a woman and hoping her insinuation took root.

"You have no idea what I feel."

The slither in his voice propelled Elie around and she walked backwards in order to see his face. "You told me you felt nothing!"

He matched her pace, neither willing to close the divide. "I needed to do what I did for me. Do you understand? For me!" He pointed a finger emphatically at his chest.

It was Elie's turn to throw an arm up and groan in frustration. "And did that help any?" She whirled and bolted.

"Elie!"

She heard him on her heels.

"Elie! Quit running!"

She turned a corner onto the street leading to the land owned by her family and slowed her pace as she neared the driveway. "Why don't you try something different?" she suggested ruefully.

"I am."

His stern reply drew a chuckle from her, but there was no humor in it. "You mean Amanda? You think a woman is going to fill what's been missin'?"

Eric grabbed her arm and spun her around to face him. She gave him a look she hoped was severe, yet flaming green eyes and a steel square jaw told her he wasn't easily intimidated. They stared at each other for a long moment and then Eric flashed a couple of perfectly round dimples, a roguish glint in his gaze. "Perhaps you wish the woman was you?"

Her breath hitched, the statement closer to the truth than she'd ever admit. Letting out an exasperated sigh, Elie turned swiftly on her heels to her house. "Why don't you try something that really helps," she called over her shoulder to Eric, who still followed.

"Oh, Elie, how little you know men. A woman can ease a man's frustrations in so many ways."

Elie whirled around. "You're disgusting," she responded and then faced the house again, hoping he didn't see how she flushed at his argument. Eric's bitter laugh had her snatching the house key from her purse and jamming it into the lock. A verse from the Psalms suddenly entered her thoughts. *But My people did not listen to My voice; and I gave them over to the stubbornness of their heart, to walk in their own devices.*

The verse sobered her. True, Eric was on a path of his choosing, but for all his arrogant pronouncements, he wasn't happy. Elie decided to try a different approach. Drawing in a deep breath, she released it slowly, hoping to calm her nerves so the tone of her voice wouldn't be dictating, but gentle. Facing him, she frowned at Eric's hard eyes, the harsh slant of his mouth. She'd deny him the retort he'd expected.

"Why not give your heart to someone who will not hurt it, but heal it? Someone who truly loves you—Jesus."

Eric's eyes clouded over and her heart sank. This wasn't going well at all. She'd allowed his anger to fuel her own and now her witness was tainted.

"No. I'm not going to do what you or anyone else wants me to do. I'm going to do what I want to do." Deep-seated rebellion laced his voice.

"Haven't you done that for years? Has it worked? I don't think so. You're still angry." Elie fought hard not to grit her teeth. "It's not working, Eric, and I'm tired of fightin' you. I want you back!" A stunned look crossed his chiseled features. His eyes filled with uncertainty and concern. Sensing perhaps she'd made some headway, she edged closer to him, laying a gentle hand on his arm. "I don't want to see you like this. I want to see you happy and loved. I want to see the old Eric."

His lip curved up into a snarl. "That old Eric died a long time ago."

"I don't believe that."

"I guess we're at an impasse then. Our beliefs follow two separate paths and never the twain shall meet."

"You're doing this on purpose," she whispered scornfully.

"God always gave us the choice, right?" His eyes challenged her. "When someone has made their choice, why don't you just leave well enough alone?"

"Because you're not well!" She flung open the door of her house and trudged inside. Eric entered behind her.

"Stop psychoanalyzing me!"

Elie tossed her purse on the sofa, and placed her books and papers on a nearby coffee table.

"It's my choice, Elie."

The grit in his voice grated her nerves and baited her temper. "It's the wrong choice," she muttered underneath her breath. She shot him a glance. The veins of his neck throbbed. *He heard me.*

In a stride, he was beside her, grabbing her arm, pulling her toward him. Upset, she thrust a fist square in the direction of his chest. He intercepted her punch and secured both arms behind her back. When he drew her in, she released an audible sound of shock as her chest slammed into his. Heat rippled through her body as it hummed in response to the firm press of his. They stared at each other for what seemed an eternity and then his gaze dropped pointedly to her lips.

In an instant, everything changed. The look in his eyes—from fury to fervor. Her emotions—from annoyance to ardor. The air between them—from icy to inflamed. She knew if she didn't escape now, she might never have another chance nor want one. Heart beating wildly in her ears, she suppressed a moan as her body slid closer, expectant—to her shock. With a low, earthy growl, his lips crashed into hers.

She writhed, trying to free herself from his grip, but it only made him drag her nearer, molding her into the heat of his hard body. Elie couldn't catch the soft moan her lips let loose as he forced her mouth wide, angling his mouth and deepening the kiss. His grip gently tightened, easing her surrender. Slowly, the fight in her died, replaced by desire—urgent and needy. Resistance ceasing, her lips shaped to his, her body melting in his scorching embrace.

In the distance, a car door slammed and the laughter of a woman filled the air. Eric loosened his hold, and Elie wrenched herself free. Breathing heavily, they both gaped at each other, the utter disbelief in his eyes surely matching her own. The laughter drew closer. *My parents!*

Jacqueline was speaking, and Emmett let out a bellow laugh. Panicking, Elie put her hands to her face and rushed into the bathroom nearby as her parents entered the house.

Coward.

"Why, Eric, we weren't expecting you here. How are you, son?" Jacqueline asked him warmly.

"Mr. and Mrs. Brown, hello," Elie heard him choke.

"Is Elie here? She was at the schoolhouse earlier," Mrs. Brown asked.

I can't hide from them. How would Eric explain how he got into our house? Elie smoothed her clammy hands against the sides of her dress and bolstering her courage, took a deep breath before leaving her hiding place.

"I'm here, Momma." Eric turned toward her, their eyes meeting briefly. She winced at the look of irritation he blasted her. *Okay, so I panicked.* He'd kissed her. What was she supposed to do? Be an incoherent pile of mush in front of her parents? They'd surely guess what had just happened between her and Eric.

"How was school, dear?" Jacqueline kissed the top of her daughter's head.

"Oh, fine, the kids were as rowdy as ever." Elie avoided

her mother's gaze and reached to give her father a hug. After a tight squeeze, he lifted her chin to look into her eyes, and Elie knew he recognized her distress. With pursed lips, he shifted his gaze toward Eric. Elie backed away and went to busy herself with the package her mother had placed on the sofa.

"Would you like to stay for supper, son?" Jacqueline asked Eric.

"Huh?" he answered, a confused look on his face.

She smiled, patting him on the arm. "Supper. You stayin'?" She started toward the kitchen.

He shot Elie a glance for approval, but she frowned. "Um, no thank you, ma'am. I need to head back home. I'm sure my father is expecting me," he mumbled. In a few strides, he was at the door. Elie caught the look between him and her father. Emmett Brown didn't look pleased. Eric's lips tipped downward. "Good evening."

"Be safe, dear," Jacqueline called after him as he exited the house.

Emmett raised questioning brows to Elie. Her father never needed to inquire; she'd always confessed to whatever rule she'd broken. Only this time, her lips remained tightly sealed. What would her parents say if they knew just moments before they entered the house, she was wrapped in the arms of Eric Montgomery? What would they think? She knew they loved Eric as one of their own, but the expression of disapproval on her father's face when Eric passed him caused her heart to quake. In fact, her father's silence terrified her. Did her father suspect something?

Without waiting to find out, she forced her lips into a smile and then hurried into the kitchen to help her mother with dinner.

****

Elie lay in her bed long after the meal, rubbing a hand

over her full stomach. Dinner went just as usual in the Brown household, except Elie had kept her mouth full so she wouldn't have to talk. She'd listened as her mother lively chatted about her week teaching in the local Negro high school and her shopping spree that afternoon. Emmett joked and teased his ladies, and every now and then he'd reach over and give his wife's hand a squeeze. The simple gesture of love between them gave her heart a peaceful sense of warmth. Their love was true and honorable, not at all what she'd experienced earlier with Eric.

Elie sighed, remembering the passion of his kiss. On his day off, he chose her company instead of Amanda's. The thought thrilled her—his kiss thrilled her. But after almost being caught in his embrace and the horribly guilty feeling in the pit of her stomach afterwards, she wondered whether his attention was worth it. Had Eric stopped courting Amanda? Did he intend to court her instead?

The moon's rays filtered through the sheer curtain hanging from the top of the window. When she was little, Eric would often sneak away from home and tap on her window at night, and they'd set off for a midnight adventure, running along a worn path toward the creek, trying to catch frogs as they croaked loudly in the night.

The memory brought a wistful smile to her face. *How time changes people!* She couldn't believe how long it'd been since her last romp in the woods with Eric and how their relationship had all but disappeared. The kiss between them was a dramatic twist in their long history. But where would it lead? Eric was a man with a deeply troubled spirit. Yet, she couldn't deny his kiss had ignited a longing in *her* spirit she feared wouldn't be extinguished.

****

Eric lay in bed, staring out the window and wishing he

could run forever in the night. His father had tried in vain to reach him through conversation at dinner, his mind wholly engrossed in the kiss he'd shared with Elie. He wasn't sure what had possessed him to kiss her. All he remembered was how angry she'd made him, and wanting to silence her lips in the only way he knew how. She'd struggled against him and at the time he'd found her crusade humorous, her movements against him flaring his lust, his own ego expanding at the thought of her inevitable surrender. He closed his eyes, recalling her eventual capitulation, the feel of her lips beneath his own, her body eagerly casting into his.

Eric groaned and rolled over on his stomach, burying his face in his pillow and hoping to stifle the sudden rush of passion churning in his belly. He'd wanted to taste her lips in the library after the fight he had with Chase McDougal, and now that he'd sampled her supple mouth, he couldn't believe how unsatisfied the experience had left him. Shouldn't this feeling be over, this desire, this longing for her plaguing him?

Sitting up, he fluffed the pillow with determination. Whatever was drawing him, he'd find it and sever the tie. Control was something he'd always maintained, but with Elie, command over his feelings and his body was slipping.

He was connected to her in a way he could not comprehend—a bond they'd shared since birth. She'd recognized this bond, and was desperately trying to hold on to it. Elie, however, had never given him an indication this linkage was in any way romantic. This afternoon, he had crossed the line. He'd turned their relationship into something neither of them had fathomed before.

The night's cool breeze wafted over him; the pale moon cast an iridescent glow over the stables and training pen in the distance. He imagined following that lit path, swept away by wind toward a familiar house and girl. His emotions were spiraling out of control and the honest truth was the only person he could think of to save him was Elie.

Chapter Twelve

THE MARCH

The sun had not yet risen, but the men of the Montgomery household had. Today they'd march with other civil rights activists into downtown Freeman. Morgan had been eagerly awaiting this event and attended the prayer meeting the night before at Wimbly Baptist. Eric opted not to accompany his father, and it wasn't because there'd be praying at the church.

Since their kiss, Eric had spent more time at work, determined to put Elie out of his mind. After long hours at the bank, he'd come home to a house with no Elie. She, too, worked away from the estate, in touch with his father through phone calls and notes left when Eric wasn't around. Morgan had mentioned her absence to Eric, but he never questioned Elie about the cause, nor did he confront Eric. What could he say? Regret at not seeing her increased his madness for a woman he couldn't have.

Eric sat opposite his father on the back veranda where Miss Hattie served a light breakfast of bagels and cream cheese with mixed fruit. The smell of fresh homemade biscuits preceded her entrance onto the veranda. Morgan immediately put down his paper when the biscuits were placed on the table and gave his cook a warm smile. "Miss Hattie, you do outdo yourself. How did you know I wanted biscuits?"

She returned the grin and gave his stomach a look. "Sir, I don' know how you manage to keep yo' figure when you eat dem every morning!"

Morgan laughed heartily, picked a buttery-glazed biscuit and took a large bite. Eric helped himself to two. Even though he was a man in his late forties, Morgan was still in remarkable shape. If that was his future, Eric also had no qualms about the number of biscuits he ate either.

Morgan lifted a piece of bagel to his mouth. He still wore his wedding ring. Evelyn Montgomery had been dead for years, but his father continued to display his symbol of commitment to her. "Father, how did you win over Mother?" Miss Hattie gave him a curious look, cleared her throat, and left the veranda.

Morgan's jaw stopped chewing, a questioning look in his gaze.

"How did you get her to, um…" Eric trailed off. He put his hands up to his face and then ran them into his hair. He'd never broached this subject with his father. He could easily win a woman's favor, but love? Letting out a long breath, he sat back in his chair, his eyes on his father.

"Does your gloomy attitude this morning have anything to do with a woman?"

The answer stuck in Eric's throat.

"A certain young woman this estate employs who I can't seem to find?"

Eric sighed and tilted his head back, raking fingers from the nape of his neck through his hair before mauling his face. Either his father was too perceptive or his poker face needed work. "I just want to know how you knew Mother was the woman you needed to marry—and how you convinced her."

Morgan chuckled. "Your choice of words, 'convince...' What made you think she needed convincing?"

Eric gave his teasing father an annoyed look.

Morgan held up his hands in surrender. "Okay, okay, I'm sorry. Whatever you need to know, I'm here."

"Mother? When did you know you needed her?"

Morgan smiled. "My son, the romantic." Eric crossed his arms in light defense and Morgan nodded his acknowledgment of it. "I first met your mother in church, the week her family moved into town. They were late to the service, entering in and taking a seat in the back of the sanctuary." Morgan looked out toward the back acreage, his gaze a thousand miles away. Eric leaned forward in anticipation. "The sun streamed through a window, hitting her golden hair and it shined so brightly, I didn't see anything else in the room. I don't even remember breathing." He chuckled at the memory, setting a wistful smile on his son. "That's when I knew I needed her." He laughed lightly.

"There isn't another word that comes to mind to describe..." Eric trailed off again.

"Describe...?"

Eric's eyes narrowed at having to share his feelings with his father. They'd done many things in life together, but discussing their emotions was never one of them. That was something ladies did. Even when his mother died, Morgan had offered little comfort to him, handling his grief in his own way, and leaving him to deal with it alone. Part of him hated his father for it, but Eric couldn't blame him. It taught him a hard lesson. What kind of man would he be if he couldn't solve his own problems?

What other choice did he have but to talk to his father? Since his last encounter with Elie, he was slipping into an even deeper state of denial and frustration. His budding relationship with Amanda was suffering; he'd buried himself in so much work he, too, had avoided her teasing gestures and hadn't thought about inviting her out for a second date. She'd done her best to distract him, and he'd all but ignored her. Her attempts at seduction had dwindled.

"Dad, I…I need something." Eric fixed his gaze on the back lawn, not wanting to admit the real issue to his longing.

"What do you need?"

"There are times when Elie makes me question if I should have come back, and there are other times just being beside her…seeing who she has become, what she does…I want to be a better man."

"Go on, son."

Eric met his father's gaze. "How do I resolve this?"

Morgan lifted a brow. "What exactly do you need to resolve? Have you two had an argument?"

Yes. A couple of times. But only one of them had ended with them locked in each other's arms. He wrestled with the idea of their re-creating the moment—that would mean actually seeing each other, and a fight would soon follow. He didn't want to quarrel with her. He preferred to do battle in her arms, to assault her mouth.

Eric abruptly pushed his chair back and stood facing the lawn. He wove a hand through his wavy hair and placed the opposite hand on his hip. He could say it. It wouldn't be so difficult to confront it if he could just let it out.

"Eric?" Morgan's voice interrupted his thoughts.

Ignoring the heat in his face, he turned to his father. Morgan leaned forward, his eyes narrowing. Eric let out a breath. "I don't…I…" Eric groaned, lifting his eyes to the ceiling and then crossing his arms over his chest. "I think I'm in love with her."

Morgan arched back slowly, crossing his own arms over his chest, a small smile on his face.

"You find this amusing."

"On the contrary, I'm quite relieved."

"Relieved," Eric responded evenly.

"Eric, my boy," Morgan began, placing his hands behind his head, the smile spreading to his whole face, "do you remember when Elie was born?"

Eric's brows knitted. "Vaguely."

"Well, I knew then what she has known for some time, and what you're just now figuring out."

Eric's lips twitched impatiently. "And what's that?"

"That you're soul mates—in every sense of the word."

The term brought a smirk. "Soul mates."

"The two of you, yes."

He knew he shouldn't have said anything. He expected a solution to his dilemma, not female talk. Soul mates? At least the idea amused him enough to humor his father. "How do you figure?"

"By your connection to her when she was born, and your obvious conflict over her now."

Eric's frustration began to boil. If his father could see it, did everyone else? "How do I end it?"

"You can't," Morgan responded simply.

Blood seeped from his face. Frustration morphed into outright fear. Not even his father's grin could muster enough anger to burn away the feeling of entrapment overtaking him.

"Why fight it? Why not just love her?"

"We're not compatible."

"Based on?"

"Our differences in religious beliefs."

The laughter in Morgan's eyes died, his lips turning downward. "Have you, then, rejected the Lord?"

"Well, Father, He's rejected me."

Morgan's jaw hardened, but Eric refused to recant. His parents had taken time to instill in him a faith from a young age. But what good had it been when his mother lay dying, her lungs drowning inch by inch, day by day? God couldn't—wouldn't—save her, so Eric couldn't love Him.

Morgan sighed and stood, moving to stand in front of his son. He laid a hand on Eric's shoulder. "I've never had to experience what you are now living, I know, but I want you to at least consider what I'm about to say."

"I always consider what you say, Father." Tears stung the back of his eyelids at the sound of his own raspy whisper.

"It's impossible for the Good Lord to reject His children."

"But Mother—"

"Was not rejected, but welcomed into His loving arms." He squeezed Eric's arm. "Now, I know you don't yet see it that way, but your mother trusted God to the end, even though she wouldn't see you grow into the fine man you are or see the children you'll one day have."

Eric's lips twisted and he harrumphed at the remark about his future. His mother might have believed with her last breath, but it was her stolen life Eric couldn't get past.

Morgan chuckled. "You're as stubborn as your mother was. It's funny how I never noticed that part of her demeanor until *after* we were married. I'll have to share some stories with you sometime."

Eric's lips fought a smile.

Morgan grinned mischievously. "It's no surprise to me, but Elie is indeed a woman who could make a man go crazy."

Regardless of the common understanding they shared, a possessive dart struck Eric. *Father's not my rival.* Even if a man of his advanced years seemed young and was in excellent shape.

Miss Hattie cleared her throat and announced the car was ready to take them to the march.

****

Elie distributed the last of the signs to the participants of the day's march. A large crowd of more than fifty people gathered outside a local residence about a half mile outside the main downtown area. She put a hand to her forehead, not wanting the sheen of perspiration to glisten her face. A small woman, with gray hair and thick glasses, approached her with a smile. Elie handed her a sign proclaiming End Segregation before leaning over and giving her gentle hug. Turning away, she nearly bumped into Michael Jefferson.

"Oh! Michael, I'm sorry. I didn't see you."

Michael grinned widely. He stood tall with his hands in the pockets of his navy blue trousers. "Elnora, I've been looking all over for you. Isn't this great?" He gestured around them. "Everyone is here. Those from Selma are arriving now over there." He pointed to a few black cars pulling into the driveway.

Elie trembled in excitement. She'd met some of her friends from Selma the night before when they arrived at their host homes, and now everyone was here. *Well, almost everyone.* She tried not to concentrate on the absence of the Montgomery men by being as busy as possible, but the closer the time came for the march, the more she wondered where they could be.

"Yes, I'm just as grateful as you at the number of people participatin'. I'm still prayin' it will be a success."

Michael smiled and nodded in agreement. "I'm sure everything will run smoothly. Mr. Carter was just on the phone with Asa Randolph. The march on Washington, DC is set for next week, and Dr. King will be in attendance, of course. Mr. Randolph said he'll pass on any news concerning our march here to Dr. King."

Elie's eyes widened. *Dr. Martin Luther King!*

"Are you serious? Dr. King? Are you goin' to announce it? Everyone would be thrilled! It would spark more enthusiasm, although I don't think it's needed." They both glanced around at the group. Laughter, smiles, and joy were all around. Elie and Michael exchanged pleased grins.

Elie's smile froze on her face when a familiar blond head appeared over Michael's shoulder.

Eric.

****

Elie's smile to Michael chilled his blood. Fortunately for him, her gaze had shifted from Michael to himself and lingered. His insides thawed a bit, until her smile brightened at Michael and, taking his arm, they turned to converse with a nearby activist. Eric blew out a breath in frustration.

His father's hand rested on his shoulder. "I'm going to meet with Mr. Blair, the coordinator for the Selma group. We'll be starting soon, and I need to discuss a bit of business with him."

Eric nodded. His father hurried toward a group of men near a line of black cars, and Eric was suddenly confronted by Michael, who greeted him with a friendly grin.

"Mr. Montgomery, I'm glad you and your father could join us today."

Eric cleared his throat. "Mr. Jefferson." They shook hands. "I apologize for our lateness."

Michael held fast to Eric, matching his grip, his eyes holding no joy. "No, no. You are right on time. I have a sign here for you."

INTEGRATE NOW stood out in bold, black letters against a white backdrop. Eric reached for it, mumbling a thank-you.

"Listen, Eric, how 'bout we walk together? Out of all Elnora's friends, I think you're the one I know the least."

Had Elie mentioned him to Michael? Tempering the pleased uptick of his lips, Eric weighed Michael's guarded expression and nodded. With a hard slap to Eric's back, Michael broke his poker face with a grin and moved forward to lead the march.

****

"Miles!" Morgan hailed Mr. Blair standing near a group of college kids from Selma.

"Ah, Morgan." He extended a hand in greeting. "It's good to see you again."

"You too, old friend." Morgan smiled and they excused themselves from the group. "Any more word from your father or the board of trustees?"

"Although my work as the coordinator for Selma's civil rights group has angered my father, he's convinced the bank's board not to fire me."

"The loss of their managing partner would be great."

Miles gave Morgan's shoulder a hearty grip. "I appreciate the support, Morgan. By the way, heard the loans for Perkins and Jones came through. That's good news."

"Yes, we worked hard on those two and were pleased with the results."

"Are you aware of Selma's new bank auditing standards? There are new restraints on the allocation of money and to what amount."

"Mmm, yes, I heard. Freeman banks will be subject to those regulations, as well. Those standards were approved before I could finish the loan process, but the last-minute financial backing from my Selma contact helped."

"This is the anonymous donor you've been working with for the past several years, correct?"

"Yes, it is. I didn't want to impose, considering funds from that donor had been recently used for other loans. I don't like to draw from the same bucket too often."

Miles stopped walking, eyeing Morgan curiously. "How'd you like to meet that 'bucket'?"

Morgan's brows rose at the twinkle in Miles' eyes. Miles had recommended Madson Hoover. He was here at the march? "Absolutely."

Miles smiled. "Follow me."

Before long, Morgan spotted beneath a large white hat a

few wisps of auburn hair sailing over a bright green sundress. She stood directly in their path. His heart did a strange skip, and Mr. Hoover was forgotten.

Then she turned around.

Her pale blue eyes made him catch his breath. She put a hand up to hold the top of her hat as the wind blew her red hair around ivory shoulders. Her lips parted into a wide smile, stopping Morgan's heart. He barely noticed his own mouth had dropped open as Miles introduced her.

"Mrs. Madeline Hoover, this is Morgan Montgomery, of the Montgomery Bank."

Married? Wait, Madeline, not Madson?

"Mr. Montgomery, this is your Selma benefactor."

****

Madeline smiled warmly at Morgan. Since her husband's death a few years ago, she'd been funding loans for the Montgomery Bank. She preferred anonymity, as she did with all her philanthropic endeavors—many of those being civil rights groups. The possibility that Morgan would be attending the day's march hadn't crossed her mind and now she was excited to have met him. Tall, with wavy, peppered dark hair and brilliant chocolate eyes, Madeline's heart fluttered as his eyes drifted, somewhat unashamedly, over her own physique. When he met her gaze, however, his eyes had lost some of the light she'd seen in them earlier. She fought a frown.

"Mrs. Hoover." He brought her hand to his lips. Warmth brushed her skin, a tingle traveling all the way up to her shoulders. Heat burned her cheeks, and she almost chastised herself for acting like a silly schoolgirl.

Almost.

"It's a pleasure to finally meet the person behind so many of my financial dealings."

Madeline dipped her head, slightly embarrassed over her

response to his musically baritone voice. Would she ever stop trembling?

"You don't have any idea how close some of those loans came to falling through without your support."

"Please, Mr. Montgomery, you're too generous. I was more than happy to help."

"I would also like to thank your husband if you could point him out to me." Morgan looked around expectantly.

Madeline's cheeks cooled. "My husband has gone to be with the Lord, Mr. Montgomery. I handle all the affairs of his estate."

"I'm sorry, I didn't realize..." Lines of worry creased Morgan's face.

"I've been a widow for quite some time, Mr. Montgomery, but my heart no longer grieves." She gave him a small smile and, seeing his face brighten, she turned her own away, not wishing to reveal her pleasure over a man she'd just met. Rumor was his wife had been dead for several years, their union having produced one wayward son. She quietly blew out a breath, steadying her nerves and slowing the rate of her heart.

"Would you care to march with me, Mrs. Hoover?"

If he produced those dimples to tempt her, then he wasted the effort—she was already tempted, but she appreciated it all the same. "Madeline, please. And I'd be happy to march with you, Mr. Montgomery."

Two perfect chasms deepened and white teeth gleamed in the sun. "Morgan."

****

After offering a prayer for safety and effectiveness, Michael gave the command to march. The group cheered as they walked down the neighborhood street, making their way toward the center of the city. Eric marched alongside Michael, arms linked in solidarity.

Eric glanced behind him often, searching for Elie, and he found her arm in arm with her skinny friend, Maisy, and another woman he recalled seeing sip milkshakes with her at the ice-cream shop. All three sported giant, purposeful grins and shouted slogans in unison with the group.

His father walked alongside a man Eric assumed was Mr. Blair and…a very attractive redhead. Although he held his sign high and joined in unison with the crowd, at times his father caught the eye of the woman beside him, who flushed deeply with each glance. Eric didn't miss the self-satisfied grin of the elder Montgomery. It nearly brought out a laugh.

"I hear you are in business with your father now?" Michael's question drew Eric's focus.

"Yes, I am."

"You've been away for some time, right?"

"That's right."

"How long do you plan on staying?"

Eric met the man's gaze. Michael raised his chin, his dark eyes stormy, and the smile on his face disingenuous.

"Maybe for good. I'm enjoying my job and the Alabama climate suits me."

Perspiration gathered on Michael's forehead. He shouted something out to the crowd, who responded in kind. "This heat? You prefer all this humidity to, well, any other climate? Now, that I can't believe." He chuckled through thin lips.

Eric watched him peek over his shoulder toward Elie before clearing his throat and shouting, "End segregation now!"

The crowd bellowed.

"Elnora tells me the two of you were very close growing up."

Eric's glanced at him sharply. "You call her Elnora?"

"It's her name, and a lovely one at that. Besides, our level of friendship isn't defined by nicknames."

Eric smirked. "Really? So you two are merely acquaintances then." He caught Michael's gaze and gave him a broad grin. "Those closest to her call her 'Elie.'"

Michael's jaw flexed, his top lip curling a bit.

"End segregation now!" the crowd repeated after Eric.

"We've grown quite close over the last few years. We attend the same church, and we've had a lot of the same classes at Selma University."

He wasn't easily routed.

"She and I are a lot alike. Sometimes we think as one."

Eric thought he would gag. Was Michael being arrogant on purpose? Eric casually surveyed the crowd over his shoulder to catch a glimpse of Elie. Passion for the cause took on life as she beamed proudly. A university student, a teacher, an activist. When had she become this person with these goals, these lofty ideals? Did he even know his friend?

Michael shouted with equal passion.

We attend the same church and have a lot of classes together. Eric recalled how Elie smiled at Michael, the slight curve of her lips and brief flutter of lashes. Although he'd held her in his arms and kissed her, despite his father declaring them bonded from birth—what had he said? Soul mates?—it was Michael who held her interest. Her true match. Eric cleared his throat. "So you're studying to be a preacher?"

Shock registered on Michael's face. "Yes, I am. I feel God is calling me to share His word with those who want to know Him. How'd you guess?"

"It just seems to fit," Eric mumbled.

"Elnora tells me you also grew up in the church."

Eric nodded. Strangely, the spark of defensiveness that flared with Elie didn't ignite—probably because Michael wouldn't look nearly as alluring in the soft pink dress Elie chose to wear to today's event.

"And now you've left the church."

Eric heard the trepidation in Michael's voice but his eyes

were absent of judgment or superiority. He swallowed. "You could say I'm taking some time away." Now why did he downplay his opinion with Michael when he was so passionate with Elie? He wouldn't admit he envied her apparent peace, her joy for life.

"And what conclusion have you reached about God?"

Eric let out a stilted breath. "I'm not sure." He squinted at Michael, scrutinizing him. "How come I can calmly talk to you about this and yet with Elie, I lose my temper?"

Michael fought a frown. "Well, Elnora is quite, um…"

Eric raised a brow, eager to hear his choice of words.

Michael pursed his lips.

"Feisty, passionate, unyielding," Eric offered, grinning widely at the look of astonishment on Michael's face.

"I wouldn't say that at all," he stammered.

Smugness filled Eric and he turned away. "You don't know her *at all*."

****

Somethin's not right.

The grinning faces of admirers and the waves of shop owners weren't the only people on the street. Barking police dogs struggling to break free from their handlers, the angry looks of white men standing nearby on sidewalks, and up ahead, the McDougal brothers created a half-moon around the group. Elie swallowed, but tightened her loop with Jasmine and Maisy and yelled louder, feeling her resolve strengthen.

Police Chief Burt Wilcox stood in the middle of the street, a lone barrier to the marchers. As the group approached Wilcox, he held up a hand for them to stop. "Now we'll have no more of this march. Y'all have made your point. Now turn around." Wilcox waved a hand in front of Michael's face, his other gripping the hilt of his gun.

Michael held out a hand to greet Wilcox. The chief

refused to shake his hand. "Chief Wilcox, I do believe it's our fundamental right to meet and protest the laws and policies of this great nation," he said calmly. He re-linked his arms with Eric and another man at his side.

A red flush deepened Wilcox's features. "That may be, but a group this size should have been registered with the city, and the march scheduled and coordinated with the police department," he ground out.

Voices raised in disapproval. "Chief Wilcox, I'm sorry—"

"Yeah, you're gonna be sorry if you don't turn around right now. And the noise they're makin'! Stop chantin', all of you!" He leveled a rigid finger toward the crowd.

The hairs on Elie's skin stood ramrod straight. Police officers, accompanied by their canines, cautiously surrounded the group. White men gathered in groups of three and tentatively approached the marchers. The McDougal brothers flanked Chief Wilcox. Edward stood with hands in his pockets, Chase panted like the Dobermans on leashes, and Shane…

Shane caught Elie's gaze and held it. His cheeks flushed, but worry flickered in his eyes. Uncomfortable with his concern for her, Elie looked away.

"We don't want to cause any trouble," Michael reasoned.

Eric, who stood tall beside Michael, turned once again, locking eyes with her. To know he sought her out in the crowd reassured her and bolstered her courage. If anything were to happen, he'd protect her. Content to look nowhere else, out of the corner of her eye, she saw a white fist fly. A young black man on the front line fell back, and Chase roared in elation.

Women screamed as a scuffle broke out. Men at the front gathered around the man who'd fallen as Edward and Shane rushed forward. The crowd collapsed inward, women grasping at the backs of the men who were locked in a tussle. Chief Wilcox backed up quickly, motioning for the officers to descend into the fray.

Police released impatient dogs into the crowd. People scattered. Wailing children were eagerly scooped up and women continued to shriek at the sounds of fists hitting flesh. An old man had fallen to the ground, crying out in pain as teeth from a large gray dog latched on his arm and refused to disengage.

Eric moved swiftly toward the back of the group, his eyes never leaving Elie's form, his face a contorted look of determination and strength. In the commotion, her link with Jasmine and Maisy was severed. Knocked back and forth by those beside her, she forced her feet forward, keeping her eyes on the man fighting to get through to her. With all her will, she rushed ahead.

Chase grabbed hold of Eric's shoulder and wheeled him around. Eric landed a swift punch to Chase's jaw that sent him spiraling backwards. Unable to celebrate his triumph, Elie lost her footing and the image of Eric disappeared as the gray street came up to meet her. She struggled to stand but blows of legs and feet kept her pinned to the pavement as pain spiked in her calves, her arms, her sides. She nearly cried out to the Lord in thanks when a hand clasped her arm and pulled her from the stampede. She sucked in a breath.

Shane McDougal.

His wide eyes held both fear and relief. Behind him, Eric yanked on the man's shoulder, wheeling him about. He planted his fist in Shane's stomach and then a left hook slammed into his jaw. Mouth open, she wanted to scream at him to stop. No words came. Regardless of Shane's assistance, he was against her and her people. Eric laid Shane flat on the street and grasped Elie's arms.

"Are you all right?" Eric yelled over the noise. Elie nodded, trembling beneath his grip. "We need to get out of here!" Hand firmly on her waist, he hooked her securely to his side and steered her through the mass of people running in all different directions.

"Chief Wilcox, sir, please, you must call them off! People are in need of medical attention!" Elie heard Michael yell. "Chief Wilcox, can you hear me?" Elie glanced at the chief, his eyes wide as he surveyed the conflict, apparently too stunned to speak.

Wilcox shoved him aside. Michael's look of disbelief and pleas for intervention fell on a deaf and dumb police chief. Gnashing of teeth routed her attention to the sight of a dog gnawing on the arm of a man screaming in pain. Blood oozed from the jaws of the thrashing canine and pooled on the ground. Her stomach churned, bile shooting to her throat. Officers used their billy clubs to beat down anyone in their immediate paths.

"Lord Jesus!" someone cried.

"…massive chaos…chief of police non-responsive," said a reporter.

Eric halted a few feet from an officer whirling his stick through the air. He grasped Elie's arms, an imploring look in his eyes.

"Wilson's General Store!" she yelled, sensing his question.

"Huh?" Eric yelled back, his brows knitting.

She leaned in as close as she could. "Wilson's General Store!" Eric swiftly changed directions. They reached a sidewalk and ran down toward the store owned by the Wilson family. It was locked. Eric turned around but over his shoulder, Elie saw the door open and Morgan grab his son's collar, tugging them both in. He slammed the door, and locked it.

Elie collapsed in Eric's arms. Mr. Wilson brought out a beat-up wooden chair from behind the counter and set it down for Elie. Eric, instead, sat on the chair and pulled her onto his lap. A gentle finger lifted her chin, and she gave him a wearied smile. He put a hand on her head and brought it to rest on his shoulder. A soft kiss in her hair, the tender stroke of his hands eased the panic from her, calming her battered spirit.

"Are you two all right?" Morgan asked, concern filling his voice.

Eric nodded, releasing a sigh of relief. He repositioned Elie on his lap and she gave him a quizzical look, wondering whether her weight was too much for him. Eric responded with a reassuring smile.

A beautiful redhead—the woman Morgan was speaking to just before the march—stepped to Morgan's side. "There has to be something we can do!"

"We can't do nothin'. It's madness out there," an older black woman with graying hair countered.

"Did anyone see your niece, Maisy?" another woman asked Mr. Wilson quietly. Unresponsive, Mr. Wilson leaned on the counter, his head in his hands.

Elie suddenly felt sick to her stomach. She'd marched with both Maisy and Jasmine. *Jasmine!* She put her hand on her forehead, a wave of guilt washing over her. Jasmine had been right beside her, but when she saw Eric in the crowd, she focused on nothing—no one—else.

"What is it?" Eric whispered in her ear.

"I forgot about Jasmine and Maisy," Elie whispered back. "They were right beside me when…" She jumped off his lap and ran toward the glass windows. "Jasmine! Maisy!" She unlocked the shop door, and as Michael ushered in the two disheveled women, she pulled her friends into an embrace while they assured her they were unharmed. She noticed a stream of water out of the corner of her eye and peered out the window again.

Fire hoses were being used on the crowd. Smoke rose from the ground and Elie suspected the police were also using tear gas. Michael was at her side. Turning her head away, Elie closed her eyes in disgust. "This is a disaster," she heard Michael mutter under his breath. She opened her eyes again, placing a hand on his arm. His eyes came to meet hers and he forced a small smile.

****

Eric saw the look between them and his eyes drifted to the hand on Michael's arm. Elie was quite a compassionate, empathetic woman. He'd missed witnessing those qualities develop as she grew up and, for the first time since his return home, he felt a pang of regret. He wasn't allowed to linger on that thought after hearing Mr. Wilson calling for everyone's attention.

"We should leave through the back. We don't want to draw attention to the shop." He motioned for people to follow him.

Morgan, who'd hardly left the redhead's side throughout the entire ordeal, took her hand, lifting her from her seat, and secured her arm beneath his. Eric caught his gaze and nodded. He waited until Elie, Maisy, and Jasmine, arms around each other, walked in front of him, and he and Michael brought up the rear of the group.

The eerie stillness of the back alley contrasted with the distant shouts and sounds of the ruckus on Main Street. Mr. Wilson led the small group through a series of back alleys, heading farther and farther away from the carnage. The rustling of approaching footsteps halted the group. Not a single person breathed. A young man appeared, a horrible look of fright on his face. He bent over, hands on knees, his breath coming in gasps. Mr. Wilson grabbed his arm and continued moving through the alley.

Eventually, the group stepped out onto a calm street and started the long trek toward Wimbly Street. People quietly swapped stories of their chaotic experience, continuously thanking the Lord no one had died.

Eric jammed his hands into his pockets. Everything had gone wrong, people were injured, but their faith hadn't wavered. They still placed their trust in a God who wouldn't guarantee even their lives. How could they be so blind? Their attitudes left him perplexed.

"I'm so glad Michael found you, too," he overheard Elie say to Maisy and Jasmine. "I'm so selfish..."

"Elnora, don't—"

"No, Jasmine, I *am* selfish. I only thought of myself, my own safety...what I wanted." She shot a quick peek over her shoulder at Eric. Their gazes had met for only a second, but he'd read the desire for him there, and it aroused uncertainty in him. He shot a glance at Michael, whose face was contorted in demoralized pain.

Eric's jaw clenched. Did she ever think of their kiss? Did it mystify her as it did him? Or was a certain divinity student occupying her thoughts? Michael was a man who held her beliefs, someone with conviction—he'd make her happy.

"The two of you were beside me..."

"Elie, when everythin' started, I couldn't even remember where I was," Maisy said. "All I could see were those dogs." She shivered.

"Everything happened so quickly," Jasmine added. "I admit I'd forgotten about you, too. People just started pushin' and dogs were barkin'...you couldn't see your way out of that mess."

Elie hugged her friends closer.

"This has been a disaster," Eric heard Michael's raw, haggard whisper. The man put two hands on his dark head and slowly shook it.

Eric gripped Michael's shoulder. "You had no way of knowing this would happen."

Michael's wide eyes were on Eric, anguish swirling in their black depths. "Didn't I? Shouldn't I have known? We aren't the first to march for our rights, Eric. Others have gone before us and have faced a similar outcome."

"But it's worth the sacrifice. Isn't it?"

Michael shook his head again, uncertainty marring his features. "There were women and children marching with us." He jabbed a finger to his chest. "I'm responsible for them."

"They knew the risks. I'm sure they'd do it again."

Michael shut his eyes, and a tear escaped.

Eric frowned. Perhaps he didn't have a right to speak. He'd ducked and dodged responsibility for the last several years. Only since he started working for his father did he find he still possessed some semblance of the concept. "Why don't you blame God?"

Michael's jaw flexed, despair eroding away. The fierce look he gave Eric evoked a flinch. "God didn't set those dogs on us, Eric. Man did. We still have free will. So, I don't blame God, because that ain't where the blame lies."

"Okay." Eric put a hand up in resignation. Michael's voice carried, drawing the stares of people in the crowd. Eric didn't want to fight, and he couldn't exactly argue with what the man said. God might not have saved his mother, but if anyone had died today, he agreed it wouldn't have been because of God.

It would've been because of one hotheaded McDougal.

****

It was well into the afternoon when people sauntered into Wimbly Baptist. The ladies cried and consoled each other while the men gathered around Michael, speaking in hurried and angered tones about what had occurred a few hours before. Michael looked exhausted, but still managed to remain calm and de-escalate the emotions of those around him. He eventually broke away from the group and walked unhurried to the podium, his head hanging.

Michael graciously thanked those who'd participated. He expressed his deep sorrow for what had occurred and accepted all blame for the event's aftermath. Murmurs of disagreement started to ripple, but he held up hands to silence them. Multiple people had been injured and were transported to the hospital in town. He encouraged people to visit those in the hospital and he closed his announcements with a prayer. He prayed for the march to encourage more to join the fight against segregation, and for the quick healing of those in the hospital. After the prayer, people began to filter out of the church.

Elie kept her eyes on Michael and decided now was the time to speak to him. She made her way through the crowd and gently took his arm, pulling him away from the group for a little privacy. "Michael, you *can* take responsibility for the positive outcomes." He opened his mouth to protest but she put a hand up to stop him. "*No.* It takes a real heart full of courage and conviction to even plan somethin' like this. And everything was on the news so, hopefully, the nation will see how this city treats those citizens who disagree with its policies. That will be a blessing for us."

Michael didn't argue with her. His eyes grew languid, and he grasped her hands in his. "Elnora," he said softly. His tone—the urgency now in his voice—and his eyes gave her pause. "Elnora, I know this may not be the appropriate time, but you would honor me if I could court you now, and throughout the coming semester."

Shock parted her lips. Courtship so soon? They hadn't even had ice cream. An unexpected pleasure caused her to blush.

Her mind flashed to Eric's kiss, cooling her cheeks and hitching her breath. What did she feel for him? *What can I feel for him?* He'd made it clear he was a different man, and although he'd returned home, she suspected he was no closer to resolving his issues—nor did he want to.

But Michael and she had a solid foundation: their beliefs. She knew he loved God, and she could trust him. They shared many common interests; he not only inspired her, but was a leader among their acquaintances. Michael was a good man—a man she could love.

I'm making the right choice.

At her nod, Michael's eyes brightened and his lips broadened into a generous smile. Pulling her into a brief, chaste hug, he told her he'd call her tomorrow. He excused himself to gather the Selma group together for their trip home.

She watched Michael leave, her head satisfied with her decision, despite the lack of approval from her heart. Yet, she was practical and thought a deeper relationship with Michael would lead to fulfilling love. She hugged herself with her arms, smiling.

Her eyes found Eric standing off at a distance by himself, watching his father and a lovely woman with red hair. She'd barely spoken to him all week since their kiss. She maneuvered toward him through the lingering crowd. Not speaking was immature, and now that she'd agreed to a courtship with Michael, she was in no danger from Eric.

She quietly approached him as he continued to eye his father. "She's lovely, isn't she?"

Elie heard a strong level of approval in Eric's voice and peered at the woman Morgan was speaking to. She remembered seeing the two of them together throughout the event. Morgan had been quite attentive, his eyes holding an interest Elie hadn't observed before. She sighed wistfully. "They are very handsome standing next to each other."

Eric raised a brow as he glanced at her from the corner of his eye. She smiled at him, and he gave her his full attention.

"Are we on speaking terms now?" she asked a bit hesitantly.

Eric's even gaze made her breath pause. "Elie, today when the world was falling apart, the only person I was thinking about was you."

He stepped closer. The intensity in his green eyes magnified, holding her hostage. She forgot how to breathe. A few fingers slowly drifted down the side of her face, leaving a heated trail that caused an inward quake. How was it that Eric could evoke such a physical response from her and with Michael, she was completely rational?

"Elie, I might have missed more than a few years with you, but I don't want to waste another moment not knowing you, not speaking to you." His hands on her arms eased her to him. "Not being with you," he murmured.

Her heart pounded painfully against her ribs. Jellied knees threatened to give way. His lips were a breath away, jeopardizing her will. Surrender would be so easy, but nothing that came easy was worth more than the price. And she wanted more…more than just a physical attraction. She wanted a meaningful relationship, something Eric was incapable of comprehending.

Yet, he drew her like nothing she'd expected. Even in a crowd, she noticed no one but him. Since his return, fresh feelings about him—feelings other than friendship—had been steadily building within her, threatening control over her heart. How it yearned for the man before her, and not the man she was courting. *Michael!* Something deep within her longed to be with her best friend, but at the moment, her head made more sense than her heart.

She swallowed the thick lump choking her throat. "I can't."

Eric's hands were like granite on her arms.

"I'm sorry, Eric, but I just can't!"

The sharp jaded glass of his eyes speared her. *"Can't?"*

He wasn't the only one not believing her excuse. Elie's ears couldn't stand to hear the irritation in his voice. "Eric, there's been so much time lost, maybe too much time." Her voice trembled, but she was resolved. "I know you and yet I don't. My heart is so confused, but my head is on straight." She paused to gather the strength growing in her. "My beliefs are too important to me to brush them aside for just a kiss—a kiss under the wrong circumstances."

Eric released her arms.

"It's probably best that we not, um—"

"I understand." His voice was even. "Elie, I don't want to fight anymore with you—against you." His hands cupped her face and he held her close. "I'm not going anywhere, Elnora," he said, planting a gentle kiss on her forehead. "Don't take off for school before saying goodbye." He gave her a tender smile and walked toward his father.

She stared after him in amazement. Her rejection hadn't angered him? His assurance that he was planning to stay home both thrilled and unsettled her. They would see more of each other, and with her pledge to Michael, she wasn't convinced that was a good thing.

****

Eric sighed as he plopped down into the front passenger seat of the car, his father already behind the wheel. Morgan's smile met him. "Something troubling you, my son?"

Eric contemplated the color in his father's face. It matched the hair of a certain woman in a green dress. "It appears nothing is troubling you. So the fight after the march was just what, something that happens every day?"

He watched his father fight to keep a straight face. Morgan returned his eyes to the road and pressed on the accelerator.

"The redhead…"

"She happens to be one of the bank's benefactors—"

"And she happens to be quite beautiful."

"How did we start talking about me when we were on you?"

"I never answered the question. Back to you—"

"Oh no, no, no. I saw you talking to Elie earlier and she looked frustrated. You two didn't argue again, did you?"

Vainly, he tried to quell the sick churn of his stomach. "No, we didn't argue," Eric mumbled. "We came to an understanding."

"And what's that?"

"She's interested in Michael because he's…"

Morgan let out a breath. "Something I should have done a long time ago was tell you how I wooed your mother."

Eric snickered. The thought of his father wooing anyone…yet, the redhead seemed a goner. Perhaps his father knew something he didn't. *Not likely.*

Morgan smiled at his son. "Letters. I wrote her many, many letters."

Eric dismissed the hint. "I can't woo her," Eric said flatly.

"Son, you're a Montgomery man. If there is one thing we can do, it's woo women." Morgan glanced at his son. "I suggest you write to her while she's away. Get to know her again—understand her. You may learn a thing or two about what's really important to her, and you can build on that."

Eric kept his face unreadable. He knew what was important to her. God. But Eric wasn't so sure he could build on Him. "You're encouraging me to steal her from a man of God?"

Morgan let out a weighty sigh, full of irritation. "How many times do I have to tell you—"

"I know, I know. I'm a Montgomery."

"That's right. Our horses don't come in second place, and neither do we."

Chapter Thirteen

BETWEEN THE TWO

Needing space from Eric, and time to develop her relationship with Michael, Elie and Michael traveled back to campus for the semester a bit earlier than expected. Michael wanted to get a head start on his capstone project and was scheduled to meet with civil rights leaders in Selma. Despite the unfortunate ending to their march in Freeman, Elie was eager to continue her efforts with the Selma civil rights group and assist in their plans for their own march.

She received a generous offer from Mrs. Madeline Hoover to board with her until school dorms were ready to receive students for the term. She'd been rooming for only a week and Elie already loved the widow. They spent many evenings discussing history and politics and, at times, the Montgomery men. Elie lightly teased Madeline about Morgan, volunteering tidbits about the elder Montgomery to a blushing Madeline.

Elie and Michael met a few times after arriving in Selma, once at Mrs. Hoover's house for dinner, and then several afternoons for light lunches. Michael's qualities revealed themselves in fascinating ways. He was kind in speech, generous in paying for their lunches: a man who cared a great deal for her.

Yet, as the semester progressed, they saw less and less of each other. As a graduating senior, Michael was extremely busy with his senior project, activism, and creating new relational contacts, and Elie dedicated her hours to her practicum and a women's activist group. But Michael called faithfully every night and they spent hours on the phone talking about the day's events. It was nice and comfortable.

Safe.

Nothing wrong with safe.

Nothing exciting about it, either.

"Sometimes love is gradual and less like a romance novel," Madeline had told her one evening.

Elie cocked a challenging eyebrow at her friend. "What about Morgan?" At Madeline's fiery cheeks, she continued. "No, no, you're right. Morgan Montgomery couldn't *possibly* be exciting." Madeline conceded defeat, but Elie's lack of enthusiasm over her victory dispirited her.

Love should be exciting.

One late unexciting Friday afternoon, Elie and Jasmine walked to the post office to pick up a week's worth of mail.

"I can't believe I have a term paper already due," Jasmine complained loudly. "This is our final year. Shouldn't everythin' be easy now?"

Elie laughed. "I think you have it backwards. Because we're seniors, it'll be difficult."

Jasmine huffed her disapproval. "Clearly I picked the wrong subject to study." Jasmine sighed and griped about the junk mail she received yet "oohed" and "aahed" over the Sears catalog. "Now this is the reading I look forward to every night!" She waved her catalog in the air for Elie to see.

Elie ignored her and the rest of the mail in her hand, staring at a white envelope addressed to her in a familiar handwriting.

"What's wrong with you? That's not a bill from the school, is it? Aren't you tired of receiving updated bills after the fact? Why can't they let you know upfront, one time, what the cost is gonna be?" Jasmine snatched it out of her hand, and Elie suddenly came to life with a squeak of alarm. "What are you lookin' at that's more important than a Sears catalog?" Jasmine peered at the writing.

"Give it to me!" Elie tried in vain to snatch the envelope back as her friend twirled away from her.

Jasmine's mouth dropped, her eyes grew big, and a sound of understanding escaped her lips. Elie took her chance and ripped the letter from her friend's hands.

"Have you and Eric been writing each other in secret?" Jasmine whispered thunderously.

Elie released a frustrated breath. "No." She walked ahead, not wanting to draw attention to herself. "This is the first letter I've received from him." Why would Eric choose this time to write her and never when he was away overseas?

"Oh, because it'd be *really* romantic if you two were. Kind of a secret affair." She giggled.

Elie shot her a dirty look. "You know Michael and I are courtin'. I wouldn't be having a 'secret affair' of any kind."

"Have you two kissed?"

Elie continued to walk forward, staring at the envelope. "Yes," she whispered, half listening.

"What!" Jasmine squealed. Elie felt a hand on her arm and then herself whirling. Jasmine gave her a disapproving glare. "Why didn't you tell me you and Michael kissed? How was it? When did it happen? Was it romantic?"

Elie shook her head at the onslaught of questions and gave Jasmine a confused look. "Michael and I haven't kissed."

"But you just said…" Jasmine's mouth dropped again, a knowing look in her eyes.

Elie groaned and rushed away. If she hadn't been so

preoccupied with Eric's letter…he was doing it again. She hadn't seen him for months and still he distracted her.

Jasmine matched her friend's speed. She looked around before whispering, "You and Eric?"

Elie nodded, frowning.

"When?"

"A week before the march. He walked me home, we got into an argument, and he kissed me." Elie forced the enticing taste of his lips from her mind. "But out of frustration, I guess," she added quickly.

"Why didn't you tell me?" Elie detected hurt in Jasmine's voice. "This is crucial!"

"I don't know. It was completely unexpected! It caught us both off guard. And then my parents walked in."

Jasmine jumped, squealing. "Really! Did they catch the two of you?" Her eyes widened in anticipation of scandalous details.

Elie gave Jasmine an annoyed look. "No, they didn't. You're enjoying this, aren't you?"

"Well, I don't have a love life of my own, so I have to live vicariously through you. Two men! Elie, leave some for the rest of us!" She laughed.

Elie's shoulders slumped. "I don't know, Jasmine. When Eric kissed me, it was…I don't even know how to explain it! I nearly burned dinner afterwards and didn't sleep a wink that night."

"Are you attracted to him?"

Holding her friend's inquisitive gaze, Elie nodded.

"Still?" Jasmine's eyes were wide.

Elie's gaze didn't falter. She bit her lip, dipping her head again. "He asked to court me."

"He did?" Jasmine said breathlessly. "When?"

"The same night Michael did!" Elie moaned.

"So you accepted Michael instead?"

"No, Michael asked me first."

"If he hadn't, would you be with Eric?"

Elie chewed her lip, considering. After a moment or two, she shook her head no. "I can't be with him, Jas. Things between us are so different from what they used to be."

"Yeah, he's a full grown, red-blooded male!" Jasmine laughed at Elie's blush. She had no doubt about it, but for reasons she'd already explained to Jasmine at the ice-cream parlor, Eric was off-limits.

"Did you accept Michael to get over Eric?" she asked tentatively.

Elie looked at her, shocked.

"Well, you never did seem interested in Michael romantically, even though we all wanted you to be, then all of a sudden you two are courtin'. Don't be mad at me for saying so, Elie. It's just what I've seen."

Elie couldn't be mad at her friend because she often asked herself the same question. "I'm not sure. But you do talk an awful lot about how great Michael is—somethin' I'm well aware of—so when he asked, I guess I thought it was a good idea at the time."

"Sounds so romantically logical to me," Jasmine said dryly. "You better tell me what the letter says. None of this keeping Jas in the dark anymore."

Elie smiled. "Okay." She hoped Eric hadn't mentioned anything about their kiss, or their conversation after the march.

****

Alone in her room, Elie sat on her bed with Eric's letter in hand. She let out an uneasy breath and opened the envelope.

> *Elie,*
>
> *I know I didn't write while I was away and I decided to try to make up for it. This won't exactly satisfy, but*

hopefully it will prove that I'm trying to make amends, for it was you who said that I didn't realize how my actions have affected the people who love me.

Elie closed her eyes, remembering with sadness the words she threw at him.

Anyway, I don't mean to bring up that topic again, nor that particular conversation but I've thought about it a lot. Of course, that isn't the only thing I've thought of...

Eric penned a smiley face after that sentence, and Elie blushed hot, remembering their kiss.

I simply wanted to know if we could be pen pals while you're away for the semester. I'll start. Work has been good; Father and I have been helping many people get ahead of their difficult situations with the help of generous benefactors. The estate is holding up, although Father seems completely lost without your organizational skills. How he can run a bank and not function at home is beyond my level of understanding.

Elie laughed softly.

How has school been treating you this last year? Hope you aren't suffering under mounds of schoolwork. If you ever need any help, you know you can call me, or come home on the weekends.

The subtle insinuation invoked a cringe. She avoided going home on the weekends, and Eric knew he was the reason.

How is Mr. Jefferson? I know you saw us talking

during the march. He's a good man, Elie. Well, I won't keep you from your studies.

Write me back.

Eric.

PS Happy Birthday.

She sucked in a breath, her gaze pinned to the final two words on the page. *He remembered.* The sentiment warmed her heart and tears unexpectedly flooded her eyes. Tonight she expected a birthday dinner with Michael, and earlier her parents phoned to wish her well, but the one man she hadn't anticipated hearing from, who she'd long ago accepted didn't hold her in his thoughts, had actually remembered.

It touched her that he would admit to Michael being a man of quality. She quickly re-read the letter, noting its lightness. Eric was trying hard to create a sense of normalcy between them. Elie sighed happily. Eyeing her desk across her room, she hopped up from her bed to retrieve pencil and paper, eager to comply with his request. Sitting down, she pulled a clean piece of stationary out of a drawer, put the pencil eraser in her mouth, and mulled over what to write. She smiled as she wrote all about school and the activities of the Selma civil rights group, ending her letter by thanking him for writing and accepting his offer to be his pen pal. Warmth flooded through her as she sealed her reply in an envelope. *Finally…we're friends again.*

****

Another beautiful morning. A few weeks ago, Eric had renewed his budding relationship with Amanda and it was going well. Today they'd ride horses around the Montgomery estate after work. This was all new to him. He'd never spent more than a few days with a woman. If Elie could be happy with Michael, and by the tone of her letters she was, then he could be happy with someone else.

The first employee to arrive, he entered the bank through the back door. Upon reaching the front, he stopped short. Broken glass littered the floor. He followed the trail of shards to one of the missing windows near the door.

A large rock scuffed the marble floor near the broken window.

Eric cursed underneath his breath. The vandal had targeted one of the larger windows. He put his hands on his hips and his eyes strayed to three figures across the street.

The McDougal brothers.

Tendons in his jaw tightened as he watched the three lounging against their truck. Why did trouble always come in threes? He didn't doubt they were the culprits behind the vandalism and he'd settle to fight the one who most likely threw the brick—Chase. However, the fury coursing through his blood tempted him to take on all three.

"You need something? 'Cause the bank's not open yet!"

They grinned. Chase licked his lips, a predator relishing a meal. Eric grunted and stomped to his office to make a call to his father. The soft steps of high heels made him pause.

Amanda walked in, her mouth dropping open at the sight of the damage. "What happened?" she whispered.

He tilted his head in the direction of the McDougal brothers. "Three guesses," he answered grimly, glancing over his shoulders at the McDougals. He kicked a shard toward the wall beneath the broken window.

Amanda eyed the McDougals outside. When he noticed her, Chase straightened, chest puffed out, a self-satisfied grin on his face. Eric glanced at Amanda, who frowned. His lashes narrowed on the woman he was courting. Was there something between them? *Doesn't matter. She's mine.* Turning on his heels, he stomped toward his office.

"What are you going to do?" she asked as he picked up the phone.

Eric snatched the receiver from the holder. "Phone Dad and see if I can get some plywood to cover that opening." He looked away as he heard a voice on the other end of the phone. "Miss Hattie, hi. Is my father still at home? No? Okay, thanks." He hung up the phone. "My dad is on his way in." He came from behind the desk. "Can you stay here and watch the place while I go get some wood? I want to clean this mess up before we open."

Amanda nodded, lines of worry creasing her forehead. "Sure, of course."

He kissed away those lines. "Thanks. I'll be back soon."

****

Elie sighed happily after reading another of Eric's letters. He wrote more frequently now, and she received them expectantly. Their easy rapport returned, and Eric was amenable to conversations about faith, asking many probing questions into the character of God in an attempt to justify his reasons for refusing Him. With more patience than she thought she possessed, she answered all his questions. Recently, he admitted his haste in swearing off God, but he wasn't altogether convinced he hadn't done the right thing. Elie thought of Evelyn Montgomery. She'd lived her life by a high moral code and had passed her morals on to her son. Her impact on him had been strong; Elie feared her own efforts wouldn't be enough.

Setting Eric's letter down on her desk, Elie skittered about the room, preparing for her dinner date with Michael. Her thoughts, however, remained on Eric. It took a conscious effort to consider the man who, for the past few months, courted her like a gentleman. Fancy restaurants, flowers, and chocolate—Michael wooed her like she'd always imagined a man would.

If only she *felt* wooed.

Always the proper gentleman, he returned her to her

dorm at a decent hour, kept his lips to her cheek, his actions always chaste. She appreciated his desire to protect her in their relationship, yet something was lacking. Not able to put her finger on it, but if she could define their relationship in one word, it was *satisfactory*.

At the knock on her door, she fluffed her hair and smoothed maroon lipstick across her lips. On the other side stood a smiling Michael Jefferson. She smiled in return. "Good evening, Mr. Jefferson."

"Good evening, Miss Brown. You look lovely, as usual."

"Thank you." Her eyes drifted over his pressed dark navy blue suit. Michael was always well dressed. She suppressed any unease concerning their relationship. Wouldn't the Lord want her to be with such a wonderfully moral man?

Elie was returned to her dorm room—before curfew—following another tasty dinner at an elegant establishment. Expecting his usual goodbye of his mentioning having a marvelous evening and how he couldn't wait to have another with her, followed by a soft, pulse-deadening kiss on the cheek—and a holding of hands before drifting apart—the intensity in Michael's eyes while standing at her door drew her brows together. *What's wrong with him?* Opening her mouth to voice the question in her head, a gasp released instead when he wrenched her into his arms, planting his kiss squarely on her lips.

The kiss was sweet, warm, his lips hungrily exploring her own. As abruptly as it began, he released her with a sloppy grin that said he took pleasure in his actions. Too shocked to enjoy the kiss, she simply stared at him.

A flash of blond hair, the feel of hard hands holding her to him, Eric's demanding kiss invaded her very thoughts, causing her throat to dry and her palms to sweat. Why hadn't Michael's kiss turned her knees to jelly? Had she been suppressing her passion for him?

Michael's breathy voice sent nervous shivers up her

spine. "I just felt it was time to perhaps experiment in our relationship."

Elie swallowed. "Well then." Completely at a loss for words, she offered a close-lipped smile and backed slowly into her room. "Good night, Mr. Jefferson."

"Good night, Miss Brown."

Elie sagged against the closed door. At a time when most girls would be elated, her recently kissed lips drooped. She didn't want to admit it, but it screamed at her. Although the kiss was pleasant, it didn't send heat through her body the way Eric's had—fear, excitement, and pleasure all coursing through her at once. Her heart thundered beneath her ribs before his lips touched hers, as if it were beating for him.

With Michael…nothing.

Moaning, Elie put a hand over her face. *God, what am I supposed to do? This is the man you have for me. Why aren't my feelings…*

She couldn't trust her feelings. If she did, she'd have agreed to court Eric instead of Michael. Elie whimpered and plopped face down on her bed. She should be thinking how wonderful his kiss was, not about her lack of desire for him. Sighing, she turned her head to the side to breathe. Eric's note lay on the edge of her desk. She reached for it, her eyes skimming the pages again, hearing his voice in her head as she read.

As confusion whirled in her head, her heart ached.

****

It was two days before Thanksgiving, and Elie wasn't even home two minutes before she heard a knock at her parents' door and Eric calling her name. Her heart fluttered with anticipation. She hadn't seen him in months, but his letters had closed the physical gap. She flew to the door and opened it wide.

He stood there in all his golden glory, his wavy hair in shaggy, carefree curls that fell over his forehead in a boyish look. A white shirt accentuated the width of his broad shoulders, while riding pants hung loosely at his waist where his hands rested. A long piece of some sort of grain dangling from his grinning lips, he looked positively country. Elie gave him a coy smile.

He reached for her, and then lifted her off the ground and whirled her outside. "You've been away too long," he said casually, carrying her toward his horse.

"Put me down, barbarian!"

He feigned a wounded look. "Barbarian?"

She enjoyed the feel of his strong arms around her—how they didn't seem to tire from holding her. Her eyes clung to his. "Did you miss me?" she asked quietly, eager to believe she was truly in his thoughts despite the letters he'd written telling her so.

"Immensely," he whispered. He stopped and set her down on her feet. His deep dimples and lopsided grin gave her goose bumps. "I'm glad you wrote me back. I was worried those first few days, waiting for your reply." His eyes shadowed, his tone gloomy. "I thought you wouldn't respond."

She reached up to place a hand to his cheek, and his eyes sparked anew. "Of course I'd respond. You're my best friend. What type of person would I be if I ignored you?"

A devilish grin spread across his face. "Not very Christian-like, that's for sure."

Eric laughed as she rolled her eyes at him.

They rode around on Nellie, enjoying the cool autumn breeze and the changing colors in the trees. After an hour or so, they spent time walking in an open field about a mile from Elie's home. A lull in the conversation had Elie studying her friend. Eyes darkened, jaw in a firm line, Eric spoke before she had a chance to ask why he was upset.

"Elie, this thing between us...I don't like ignoring it."

She bit her lip, uncertain how to respond. Blood thumped loudly in her ears. The unspoken pull between them grew stronger every time they were together. She didn't understand why it was there with him and not with Michael. She was still trying to formulate a response when Eric placed a hand on her arm, and turned her to face him. He took her face in his hands, his eyes captivating her.

"Eric..."

"Elie, I *want* you. And I know you're seeing someone else, but I want..." He stopped, eyes smoldering with the heated need she heard in his voice. "I *need* a chance with you."

His insistence stole her breath. How could she respond? His face leaned into hers, and Elie stilled, not possessing the strength to move if she'd wanted. Her lips parted to beg he put some distance between the two of them but the air died in her throat, as did the desire for him to be anywhere but a kiss away. She closed her eyes, trying in vain to steady her breathing as Eric's warm breath caressed her face.

Kiss me.

She'd chastise herself later for the silent plea, aching for his taste—another chance to feel the fire he'd stirred in her at her parents' home. His lips gently touched the tip of her nose and then settled in the middle of her forehead. Astonished he chose not to rekindle their physical chemistry, Elie's heart relaxed—overflowing with trust and respect for her friend, and relief stole over her. At least one of them remained in control.

"I think the quicker I get you home, the easier it will be for me to behave myself." He chuckled softly.

And here I thought I was the only one...

Cheeks burning from their mutual desire, Elie nodded in silent agreement. Settling behind him on the horse, she laid her face against his broad back and breathed in his masculine scent. Arms firmly around his waist, she closed her eyes. They were still no closer to a decision on what they both recognized as a force beyond their power to keep at bay. Elie silently prayed for wisdom, self-control, and strength to face the coming days.

****

Armed with food for Thanksgiving dinner, Elie exited the grocery store and bumped into Maisy. Both shrieked in glee and embraced each other. They soon fell into step, sharing their stories.

"Picking up a few last-minute things for Thanksgiving?" Maisy asked, peeking into the bag Elie held in her arms.

"Yes, Miss Hattie said Momma didn't bring over enough yams."

"How are you going to stand having Amanda there?"

Elie's head snapped in her direction. "What do you mean?"

Biting her lip, Maisy gave Elie a confused look. "You don't know, do you?"

Anxiety spurted through her. The silence hung between them like a heavy mist, despite the chilly November air. "Know what?" she coaxed.

Maisy sighed. "Eric and Amanda. They're courtin'."

Elie stopped dead in her tracks, the bag in her arms slipping from her grasp. Maisy gasped and reached out to catch the bag while Elie blinked with bafflement. Eric had said he wanted her. *I need a chance with you.*

He lied to me.

Confliction tore at her insides, yet her even voice surprised her. "How long?"

"Um, since September, I think." Maisy eyed her friend. Elie avoided her gaze and instead held her head high, her eyes straight ahead. "Was I right to tell you?"

Elie forced a smile to her lips. She wrapped her arms

around her friend and squeezed tightly. "Of course. Thank you for being a true friend," she whispered into her ear. Then taking the bag of groceries from Maisy's hands, she said her goodbye and marched back to the Montgomery estate.

****

On the back veranda, Elie breathed in the night air and the scent of cinnamon buns being glazed that drifted through the screen door. Thanksgiving dinner had been pleasant, the food delicious, and the conversation lively. Thankfully, no Amanda.

She'd spent most of the meal watching the exchanges between Morgan and Madeline. The day Morgan had phoned the house and invited Madeline to share Thanksgiving dinner with them, Madeline had fussed about what to wear, modeling several outfits before declaring her need to buy a brand-new dress. Elie had giggled and then sighed.

At least one of them had found love.

"So, you're enjoying yourself after all. I haven't caught your eye all evening and was beginning to wonder."

As her heart responded to the rich timbre of Eric's voice, her temper flared. She pressed her lips together, hoping he'd take a hint and leave her in peace.

"Are you gonna talk to me?"

So much for peace. Elie kept her back to him. She didn't have an answer and wouldn't be rushed to a conclusion.

"Can you at least look at me?"

An idea struck her. Elie's lips turned up into a scheming grin. She whirled. "I'm surprised you didn't invite your *girlfriend* over this evening." She did nothing to hinder the sarcasm. "It would've been nice to catch up with the woman my best friend is courtin'."

Eric's eyes narrowed. "Yes, I'm seeing Amanda."

"Well, that's all you had to say."

Crossing his arms over a too-firm chest, he slacked a hip against the doorframe, his dimples hinting at his unperturbed state. "Really?"

"Yes. In fact, it would have been nice to let me know that, right between 'Elie, I want you,' and 'I need a chance with you.'" She glided toward him with her hands clenched to her breasts for dramatic effect.

Eric gave her a fantastic grin. His easy expression unnerved her. She'd hoped to irritate him. The fury she'd spent the night practicing to control shook her. "Well, I guess you're happily involved with Amanda. Of course, I wouldn't have known by your desperate attempts to control yourself," she sneered.

"Why, Miss Brown, I never would have guessed you'd be the jealous type."

Her mouth fell open. "Jealous? Ha! If you knew her connections, then you'd know jealousy was the last thing on my mind." *Second to last, maybe.*

"It isn't Christian to lie." His voice was heavy with steel.

"And your moral compass points true north that you could judge me?" She hadn't meant to sound superior, but the words were out and she couldn't take them back. Her vulnerability made her furious. She had a chance with Michael, a real chance. But Eric's letters, his desire for her, all of it had swayed her to a place filled with longing and now regret. Longing to feel a passion for Michael that matched hers with Eric, and regret Eric had ruined her first.

His eyes narrowed, large hands beneath his arms forming into fists. "You're being quite nasty."

Elie harrumphed. "I'm being nasty?"

"And what do you mean 'her connections'?"

She threw up her arms in exasperation. "*Everyone* knows her uncle is the leader of the KKK! No doubt her politics lean that way as well. How can you march with us and sleep with the enemy!"

Eric stepped onto the veranda, clasping both her arms in steely hands and pulling her toward him. "Keep your voice down. And you have no right to make such claims."

She ignored the rush of heat flaming through her at his touch and struggled against him. "The chief of police is in the KKK, and let go of me!"

"She's never once said she agreed with their cause, and I'm talking about me sleeping with her, which I haven't done!"

Elie sucked in her breath. Did she really say that? Contempt burned in his eyes. Was it for her? Perhaps Amanda? Either way, he was telling the truth. Her muscles grew weak and she ceased her struggle against him. The anger in his eyes gave way to disappointment. He gently set her away from him.

Hard lines between his brows disappeared and the firmness in his jaw softened as his lips sagged into a frown. "Elie, you're seeing Michael, and perhaps that's the way it should be. Because this," he waved a hand between them, "what's between us—this isn't the way it's supposed to be."

She turned away, blinking back hot tears. Her heart cracked at the truth. She was jealous...*and* angry. Jealous Amanda laid claim to a man she couldn't rightfully have, being she was already with one she honestly didn't want.

"Elie..."

She felt his breath on the back of her neck, his fingers gliding over the curls on her shoulders. She brushed by him and into the safety of the house.

****

Eric stood there with his arms limp at his sides, staring into the night. *God, why is this happening to me?* He wove his hands through his hair. Why was he asking God? What had He done for him lately?

Elie's will to refuse him time and time again impressed

him the most. He'd never wanted anything so badly since his mother's passing. He saw the light of God in her eyes and envied it. He considered whether that same light would shine so brightly if she knew personal sorrow—knew her God turned a blind eye to the suffering of people.

A throat cleared behind him. "Mind if I join you?"

Madeline.

He acknowledged her with a nod. She walked over to the ledge and sat, first looking at the stars and then at him. She must have sensed his frustration for she sighed and pointed to a chair. "Sit down for a second, dear," she advised in quite a motherly tone.

Coming from a woman who had no children, her tone amused him. Not raised to be disrespectful, he snatched a nearby chair up, sat it firmly in front of her, and then took the seat, his hands folded in his lap like a schoolboy.

Madeline took one look at his mocking display and laughed heartily. He rubbed at the growing heat on his neck, expecting her to be upset, not entertained.

"You're handsome, trying, and mysterious. It's no wonder she's so conflicted."

He narrowed his eyes. *Elie?*

"Now, I know I'm not your mother, God rest her, and I'm not trying to be, but tell me, what is the problem you're having with such a wonderful girl?"

"Mrs. Hoover, with all due respect…"

"Perfect! I have your respect, and you know that I *am* a woman, so whatever advice I can give would be most helpful. So, start from the beginning."

He stared at her, slack-jawed. Her demeanor surprisingly invoked a sense of trust, so he relaxed his arms to the sides of the chair and told Madeline his troubles. She didn't interrupt with any emasculating comments, or a speech about God and how if he just believed, all his troubles would disappear. Instead, she heartily chewed on a cinnamon bun brought out by Miss Hattie and told him that life was supposed to be wrought with difficulties.

"It's what you do in those difficult situations that counts."

She quickly shared her pain regarding her husband's death, believing he was far happier in Heaven. "I admit," she said with downcast eyes, "my faith wavered at times, during my period of grief. So many dreams…" Sniffing, she squared her shoulders, the look of triumph in her eyes. "My husband was a good steward of his business and finances. His estate has provided for me and has blessed so many others. I doubt we'd have invested in the lives of those less fortunate sooner had he not passed."

Her gaze moved from him to the expanse of the yard beyond the veranda. "I will always love my husband, and I'm grateful for the memories, but God is sovereign and to have had a second chance at…" She blushed prettily, her thoughts clearly on Morgan.

Love.

She came forward and took a hand in hers, uncurling his fingers. "We can't always understand why God allows certain situations in our lives. But our job isn't to understand. Our job is to trust Him, no matter the situation or the consequences."

Madeline intertwined her fingers with his and smiled. "How about this? How about you sincerely ask God what He wants from you now and see if He doesn't answer you." She paused before continuing. "And I'm sure your situation with Elie will all of a sudden work its way out."

Chapter Fourteen

THE RESCUE

Every week since his father's bank had been vandalized, new incidents of destruction were discovered around town. As if their presence were a calling card, the McDougal brothers made an appearance near the scene of each crime. No other white businesses were targeted, and an unfortunate pattern emerged: the business owners had all been loaned money by the Montgomery Bank.

When Eric discussed his conclusions with his father, they couldn't agree on whether or not the acts were part of an elaborate scheme, or coincidence. He assured his father that he had double-checked the records and there could be no doubt those targeted were connected to the bank. The list of businesses and homeowners that hadn't been attacked grew shorter each week.

No arrests were made, and police reports on the damage were not investigated after the initial filings. According to the police department, none of the incidents was connected. The blatant injustice made Eric's blood boil.

He spent all fall reading as much as he could on the subject of integration, and soon found the cause as near and dear to his heart as his father's. For the first time since graduating from college, he knew his life would have meaning. He regretted spending so much time away from home and, one evening before Christmas, he admitted it to his father.

Morgan had smiled and told him his prayer for God to bring some direction into Eric's life was being answered. Eric didn't argue. He still believed God remained aloof, but he enjoyed the intimacy he and his father were developing and the thought often made him reevaluate his relationship with Elie.

Elie had recently returned home for the winter holiday, and Eric thought it best to keep his distance. Her staggered responses to his letters left him more determined to have a relationship with her, but he'd wait for her to initiate.

After Thanksgiving dinner, Eric had severed ties with Amanda. Elie had been right; Chief Wilcox was leading the Klan's Freeman chapter. Even more troubled was how Amanda had tried to downplay her family's involvement. Her lack of conviction in the rights of blacks made his decision to end things with her easier.

And now he could concentrate on regaining Elie's trust. Hearing she'd gone out to the barn, Eric sprinted from the house to the large building. He crept as quietly as he could on the hay, following Elie's whispers to a brown mare she was brushing. The horse neighed Eric's presence, startling Elie, who gave an excuse of waiting for her father, before attempting a quick exit from the barn. Eric stepped in front of her path, blocking her escape.

"There are other ways out of this barn, Mr. Montgomery." Elie crossed her arms.

"If you are suggesting the *loft*," he began slowly, "I suppose I could follow you up there and try to stop you."

At the sight of her thorough coloring, he couldn't help grinning in victory. He guessed his insinuation pleased her, despite the rolling of her eyes as she tried to step around him. He laughed lightly, grabbing her upper arms.

"I'm sorry, I'm sorry. I promise to behave." He stepped back, holding up both hands. "Stay with me?"

Elie eyed him with suspicion but nodded her agreement. Relaxing his arms, he followed her back to the stall where she picked up the brush she'd dropped upon seeing Eric, and resumed attending to the horse. Eric nonchalantly asked about her grades and what classes she'd have for her last semester. Elie responded in kind, and the whole conversation occurred on eggshells.

"I'm sorry, what did you say?"

Eric's eyes narrowed at her. She'd spent the last minute and a half gazing at him as he spoke about the vandalism in the city. He hadn't expected that response from her; perhaps anger, but not the blank expression on her face. "How long have you been tuning me out?"

Elie flushed and hid her eyes. "I'm sorry, Eric, really I am. I guess I'm just a bit preoccupied."

He quickly rehashed the details about the businesses attacked, and how the victims were linked to loans they received from the Montgomery Bank. Elie's eyes widened at the seriousness of the issue.

"How…?"

Eric blasted out a breath, hands on hips. "We don't know."

Elie laid the brush down and leaned against the side of the stall. She crossed her arms over her chest, her face set in determination. "They have to know the bank is workin' with them, or it's just a…a coincidence."

"I'm convinced it's not a coincidence, even though my father argues it's a number's game given the large number of businesses in town the bank has assisted." Eric stood against a side pillar of the stall, opposite Elie. "I don't know how, but they know we've approved loans for those businesses."

"Someone had to have told them."

Eric's bottom lip puckered out, and he blew at a lock of hair that had fallen over his forehead. "Only a handful of us at the bank know the real identities of the people who've received those loans."

"What about Amanda?"

If Elie had suggested Amanda a couple of months ago, he'd have dismissed her notion as one rooted in jealousy, but he considered the blonde in silence. She had handled files, if only to deliver them to him or Mark Greene, but Eric had a hard time believing she'd actively seek to injure anyone. It was no secret she despised the McDougals. Eric slowly shook his head. "I don't think so. She isn't involved in the loan process. I'll admit, she doesn't harbor the same sympathy that we do toward integration, but I can't see her purposefully undermining the bank and its customers."

Elie frowned but didn't pursue the matter further. She moved to the front of the stall and stood just a hair away from him. He inhaled her lavender scent, an appropriate choice with the soft purple coat she wore. Mahogany waves fell around her shoulders, creating a lustrous brunette halo. He ignored the sudden surge of blood throughout his body, the heat warming him to the point of mild perspiration.

"What do you and your father plan to do?"

Eric forced his thoughts—and eyes—away from her lips and the aching need her mouth aroused in him, and back on their conversation. "There's little we can do. We've met secretly with each of those who haven't been attacked and they've all established a security watch. In fact, they're so terrified they'll be hit next, there are people who go out at night and walk around just to watch the businesses."

Hay crunched beneath Elie's feet as she paced in front of him. Her pretty bottom lip was pinned beneath her top teeth, her dark eyes hardened with determination. She was doing what he'd already accomplished, running through all the possibilities.

"No one has actually *seen* the McDougals do anything," he offered. "It's frustrating."

Elie's brows knitted as she absorbed all the information. "What about the benefactors? Are they at risk?"

"I'm not sure. The bank has already been hit, but as far as I know, none of the financial contributors have had any incidents. I believe Father has already contacted them and explained the situation."

"And you're sure it's the McDougals?"

Eric held her gaze. "Absolutely," he stated firmly. He cracked his knuckles. If only he could be present at one of the businesses *before* the McDougals showed up, then he'd have the proof he needed and could go to the police. *The police.* What if they were involved?

"Perhaps some documents found their way into the trash, or someone who works at the bank said something to somebody?" Elie grasped at ideas.

"We've all been careful. If anyone leaked any information, they'd be putting themselves at risk as well."

Elie shrugged her shoulders. He was at a loss as well. The only course of action available was to catch the McDougals in the act, and there wasn't any way of knowing where and who they'd strike at next. He rubbed at the headache forming between his eyes. "Are you staying for dinner tonight?"

Elie stopped pacing, her eyes rounding at the invitation.

"You haven't been over since you've returned from college," he whispered.

She averted her eyes, wrapping her arms tightly around her waist. "I can't. I have to finish preparing the last of the decorations for the children's Christmas pageant." She moved toward the open barn doors. "Wimbly is putting on a play of Jesus' birth using only the children's church." She turned around when she reached the doors. "You should come see the play. The children are so cute."

"Thank you, I will."

Elie stumbled.

A chuckle escaped his lips as she righted herself with a lift of her chin. "Elie, before you leave, I want to talk to you about something." He left the stall, meeting her at the barn doors. He cleared his throat. "It's about Amanda and me." How would she react to the news? He didn't expect her to leave Michael, but one look from her and he'd know whether he had a chance to win her.

"I have to go." She rushed out, without a look back.

****

Elie sighed in exhaustion as she finished sprinkling glitter on the remaining snowflakes. The volunteers had left the old schoolhouse hours ago. The moon was high in the inky sky and she had to get home. As she locked the schoolhouse doors and bounded down the steps, she wished her father hadn't dropped her off earlier; it would have made more sense to drive herself. Nevertheless, it was only a few miles to home and it wouldn't take her long to walk, if she hurried.

Elie stared for some time at the dark sky above her head as she swung her arms by her side. Home not far off, she slowed her pace, soaking in as much of the cool night air as she possibly could. She whistled a made-up tune until she noticed a dark figure moving a short way down the road. Elie's steps became smaller and smaller as she squinted her eyes at the figure. *Who is that?*

A loud belch stopped her in her tracks, the hairs on her neck rigid.

"Ellllnoooraaaaa!"

Elie sucked her breath. A face crossed a path of moonlight shining through the trees. *Shane McDougal!* He strode toward her, his brothers trailing behind, casually raising something, bottles possibly, to their lips.

Elie retraced her steps, keeping her eyes on her predators.

"Where ya goin', sweetheart?"

Chase.

"It's late, gentlemen, and I need to get home." She quickened her steps backwards.

The boys lengthened their strides. "We just got here." Edward's voice hinted of a grin. "And home is a long, long way away."

Elie swallowed, the cool air drying her throat. "You're all drunk and—"

"And you think you're too good for us, Miss High-and-Mighty Brown?" Chase snarled. "You've always acted like you were too good for anyone."

Was that true? For a split second, Elie considered the possibility she'd given off an air of superiority. *Have I been acting high-and-mighty?*

Chase burped loudly, thumping his chest.

Not a chance.

A soft, almost delicate voice was carried on the breeze, chilling her to the bone. "I still like you, Elnora…In fact, why don't you let me show you?" Shane sprinted toward her.

Elie screamed. She whirled and ran in the opposite direction, forcing her legs to move faster than they'd ever taken her. No matter how much she pushed, the footsteps of the McDougals grew louder and louder in her ears. Howls, laughter, and the crunching of pebbles beneath rapidly moving feet muffled the sound of her labored breathing.

God, please!

Tendrils of her hair stuck to the back of her neck as she perspired beneath her coat. The muscles in her legs burned. Darkness was in front of her, the Wimbly church still off in the distance. If she could just make it…

A low growl emanated from Shane, and she turned her

head to see his hands stretched out for her. She cried out at his touch and they tumbled until her back struck a hard object, drawing a grunt at the pain shooting up her spine.

Hands were everywhere. Her arms, her hair, her waist. They yanked her from the ground and forced her back against a tree. Hot breath, heavy with the scent of liquor, filled her lungs and she gasped, desperate for fresh air. Senses peaked, the pressure from their hands hit her like a wave of claustrophobia. Laughter deafened her ears. A rough tongue lashed the side of her face, saliva searing her skin.

They mocked and jeered at her while their hands ripped off her coat, tugged at her dress, and stroked her cheek. "It's going to be okay, Elnora. Don't worry," Shane whispered in her ear, his tongue flicking along her lobe. Hot tears threatened to spill from her eyelids. "I want you."

With a sudden surge of defiance, Elie grabbed the nearest shoulder to her and with her knee, plunged it as hard as she could into Shane's stomach. He doubled over, clutching his abdomen, and sunk to his knees with a groan. Momentarily stunned, Elie surged away from Edward and Chase. Cursing, they stumbled after her.

Knife-like pain shot through her right arm as it was pulled from behind in a rapid jerking motion. Elie yelped at the pain. Her body turned against her will and collided into Chase. Two hands were around her neck, squeezing.

"You don't touch my brother!"

He dragged her to the tree, his hands still wrapped around her throat, the pressure collapsing her airway. She clawed at his hands, her lungs on fire. *Please God, send someone!*

His hands dropped and the force of air into her constricted lungs caused Elie to cough uncontrollably. She sagged against the tree, her strength waning. A sharp sting to her face diverted her attention from the ache in her lungs. She put a hand to the impacted skin, and blinked away the black spots in her vision, zeroing in on Edward's pointed finger. His voice was deadly calm.

"That's for kneein' my brother."

She squinted her eyes in the darkness, her tears blurring the men moving in front of her. Her wrists were bound with the rough hemp of a rope. Tears streamed freely down her face, the hope of rescue fading. The rope scraped against bark, raining pieces down onto her face, and her arms snapped over her head. Body stretched, her heels were lifted from the ground until only the tip of her shoes rubbed the earth's surface.

Elie knew what would happen next. She thought of Leonard and the fate she'd soon share with him. But first…

Fingers singed the flesh of her thighs, tracing the curve underneath the folds of her skirt. Elie whimpered, locking her ankles and squeezing her thighs together. Her mother was right about walking the lane alone. If only she could drift off to sleep and not feel what was about to take place. Her eyes closed.

Eric.

****

Elie, I'm going to make you listen to me.

She'd run out on him at the barn, but their conversation was far from over. He'd meet her at Wimbly, or he'd go to her house. Eric raced Nellie down the dirt lane leading to Wimbly Baptist, his heart beating a mile a minute. What if she refused to break her relationship with Michael? He licked his lips, remembering their kiss. *One kiss…that's all I need, Elie.* Then she'd be his.

A scream pierced the night air, turning his bones to ice.

Elie!

He reined his horse upon seeing a red truck parked ahead on the side of the road. His eyes narrowed, and his fingers clenched the reins. He glanced around the area, seeing nothing but empty beer bottles littering the ground. A slap cracked the silence. Several hundred yards ahead, figures moved in the shadows of the tree line. Eric reached underneath his right thigh, pulling a rifle from the sheath attached to his saddle. Heels nudging Nellie's belly, he set the animal into a steady walk.

The loud voices of the McDougals masked his approach.

"Chase, would you stop? Punchin' her in the stomach won't make this pleasant for her," Shane argued.

Laughter. "You 'spect this to be pleasant for her? It ain't 'bout what she wants, but what you want," Edward offered.

"I want her to like it…" Shane trailed off as his hands ran down the sides of her face to the curve of her collarbone.

Eric cocked his rifle.

All three turned at the sound.

Eric sat high on his horse, his rifle at the side of his face, his gaze focused with deadly intensity on Shane. Seeing the line of sight on him, Shane stumbled away from the tree. Eric's rifle followed. Shane halted, his eyes on the weapon.

"Aw, you gonna spoil the fun!" Chase slurred.

"If you two don't release her right now, you'll have one less brother." The warning came in a low, dangerous tone.

"Eric." Elie whispered his name faintly, the tears in her voice unmasked. His skin grew hot as his blood boiled at the sound of her pain. Breath coming rapidly in and out of his nose, Eric labored to master his fury. He raised the rifle by an inch and fired a round over Shane's head.

Shane's eyes were shut tight—his brothers stood like stone statues.

"Now!" Eric growled his command. Edward fumbled with the rope, pulling it from around the tree branch as Chase clumsily tugged at Elie's wrists to free her.

"Can you walk over here?" Eric asked her. Her hesitant first step had her bending over, arms around her abdomen, but she pressed forward. Eric freed one hand from the weapon and reached for her arm. She cried out in pain as he lifted her onto the back of the horse, and with his gun still pointed at Shane, his finger tapped the trigger, itching to ram it back. She was hurt far beyond the slap he'd heard earlier.

"Don't tell Pa," Shane whispered with a trembling bottom lip, his eyes leaving the barrel to watch Elie mount the horse.

Eric nicked his heels into the belly of his horse and backed it slowly from the group. His rifle scanned the three profiles, lingering for a few seconds on Chase. He then maneuvered the horse around, and it broke into a full gallop toward the Montgomery estate.

When they were at a safe distance, Eric pulled on the reins. Nellie obeyed the command, slowing to a standstill. Elie's form rested heavily against his back, a death hold around his waist. Eric glanced around and listened intently. Owls hooted in the distance, and leaves rustled in the gentle breeze. He closed his eyes and inhaled the cool night air. *Thank you, God.*

"Elie," he whispered.

Silence.

"Elie, are you all right?"

She answered by tightening her hold on his waist. He stifled a chuckle and began to loosen her arms from around him. Elie's head came up with a sob.

"No, no, no, no, no." He twisted around and latched hold of her waist, pulling her around and onto his lap. He wrapped his arms around her, and Elie cried softly into his shoulder. "You're safe," he whispered into her ear, stroking damp locks of hair around the crown of her head. The mare made a restless move beneath them, and Eric masterfully steadied the horse. He then lifted Elie's head from his shoulder and, with a finger beneath her chin, tilted it to the moonlight to see her face.

A tough mound began forming on the right side of her face. The slap. Gently, he traced the warm skin, angered she'd been abused. He recalled how she had clutched her stomach. Gently, he pressed a hand to her abdomen. She winced but gave him a weak smile. "That's not convincing." Eyes faltering, she offered no response. "Are you all right?" he whispered again.

Elie nodded, but tears continued to flow. He placed his lips to the space between her brows, and lingered there. Hands on the sides of her face, he softly kissed her cheeks, unbothered by the salty tears he tasted. He met her eyes for a moment before grazing her lips with his own, wanting to ease, if only for a moment, the strong desire in his blood to consume her mouth. But he didn't want to scare her. She'd experienced enough terror for one night. Elie sank into his chest, placing her head once again on his shoulder and heaving a sigh, quieting her sobs.

"I think I should get you home." He maneuvered the horse into a comfortable trot toward the Brown farm.

****

A few hours had passed since Eric had rescued and returned her home. She stared at the ceiling above her bed, clutching the covers to her chest, her breathing shallow. She couldn't sleep. Over and over, she thanked the Lord for sending Eric, and for keeping her from further wounds. She choked back a sob. If Eric hadn't arrived, she'd still be hanging. How long would it have taken her parents to find her? Would Edward, Chase, and Shane have paid for their crimes? *How Momma would have wailed if she'd seen me there…*And her father? How would the death of his only child change the gentle, loving caretaker of horses?

Elie blinked back tears for the fourth or fifth time since her rescue. God had been with her tonight, but even now, in the safety of her own home, she felt alone. A soft tap at the window made her breath hitch. It had been years since she'd heard that familiar rap.

Stifling a moan from the soreness of her stomach as she sat up, she slipped out from under the covers of her bed, and tiptoed to the window. Drawing the curtains to one side, she unlatched the window. A soft breeze swept into her room, billowing her calf-length nightgown—and locks belonging to a dark blond head. She stepped back as Eric slid through the opening. He quietly shut the window, turned around and reached for her, and they met in a crushing embrace.

Elie buried her head in his chest, breathing in the night air mingled with musk and concentrating on his strong, steady heartbeat. She let out a long sigh, dispelling the sobs bubbling in her chest, and she almost yelped in surprise as he lifted her from the floor.

Eric carried her to the bed, gently setting her on the sheets. He reached for the covers to tuck her in, but she moved to one side. His movements paused, his eyes reading the invitation in hers. He discarded his boots and settled onto the covers. Arm wrapped around her, Elie snuggled into his side, laying her head on his chest as he brushed back the few strands of hair that had fallen across her cheek. His fingers lingered along the length of her jaw line, tingling her skin and sending massaging warmth down through her fraught nerves.

"I prayed. I prayed to God that someone would find me." She spoke against his chest. "What were you doing out there?"

"Looking for you."

"Looking for me?"

"I…I wanted to finish our conversation—the one we were having at the barn? Right before you walked out."

She chuckled at the sound of his teasing smile. "I ran because…because…"

"It's okay, I know why." He squeezed her tightly, encircling her with his other arm. "I just thank God I was on the road when—I'm just really thankful."

Tears coursed down her cheeks. God had answered her

prayer for a rescuer. And Eric thanking God? "You're praying now? Does this mean—"

"You're getting me wet."

Elie laughed, and sniffed loudly.

"Shh." He put a hand over her mouth. "Do you remember what happened the last time your father caught me in here?" She nipped his hand with her teeth, and he released her. Giggling, she settled back against him.

Of course she remembered. She was thirteen, and Eric was sixteen. She'd never seen her father so angry. A switch hung in the kitchen and Emmett had grabbed it and threatened to thrash Eric if he'd touched her. Elie snickered at the memory. Eric had just come to tell her Nellie had been born. Why would her father think he'd had his hands on her?

"I'm glad you can laugh about it now. I thought Emmett was going to murder me."

Despite his light tone, she frowned. Since that moment in her bedroom, Eric had kissed her. Although it'd been months since, she often replayed the memory in her mind—often yearned for his touch. The night of Nellie's birth, when her father had caught Eric in her room, Emmett had forbidden her to ever be alone in her bedroom with her friend. *You can never be too careful, girl. He's a man now. And you, a black girl...you can never be too careful.*

In a couple of weeks, her father had cooled down and trusted Eric again, especially after she'd convinced him that she and Eric were not sweethearts. Elie shuddered, her father's warning too close to reality. After her encounter with the McDougal brothers, she now understood her father's fears.

Sweethearts.

They weren't lovers then, but now...

Eric leaned over and planted a soft kiss on her forehead. "You should sleep," he whispered.

She clung to him out of both panic and longing. "Please don't leave me."

"I'm not going anywhere."

"You promise?"

His hold tightened. "I promise. I'll never leave again."

****

Jacqueline slipped out of the bed and into her soft slippers. She tiptoed to the dresser, careful not to make too much noise. The top middle wooden drawer creaked as she opened it. Finding a pack of matches, she lit a small candle.

The events of the evening had robbed her of sleep. She spent much of her waking moments in prayer, thanking the Lord for her daughter's rescue and safe return. Afraid she'd been snatched away, with light footsteps, Jacqueline walked to the door of Elie's room and eased it open. Seeing her daughter in Eric's arms, she inhaled sharply.

Eyes strained against the darkness, her gaze took in Eric on top of the covers, holding Elie in a position of comfort. Across the room, Eric's boots were on the floor near an armchair; no other clothes had been discarded.

Jacqueline found her breath again and her mind flashed back to the last time Eric was in her daughter's room. Emmett had been furious with the boy, suspecting the worst had happened. Elie hadn't spoken to her or Emmett for two whole days, angry Emmett had threatened to wallop some sense into the boy.

Guess he still ain't got no sense.

They'd forbidden him to sneak inside Elie's room. Yet, Jacqueline couldn't muster any ire against the boy tonight—not after he'd saved the life of her only child. Earlier, Elie had clutched his arm, her eyes pleading with him to stay, but at the insistence of her parents, he disentangled and excused himself. After he'd departed, Elie became mute, only nodding and shaking her head to the questions she and Emmett asked.

She didn't doubt her daughter and Eric had a connection.

He'd been present at her birth, and they'd spent almost every day of their lives together until he moved away to attend college. Elie was so elated when he returned, but discovering how different he'd become had stolen her daughter's joy. She'd compensated by spending even more hours working on errands for Morgan and volunteering more time with the children's church. Jacqueline's lips trembled, as did the candle in her shaky hand. If it hadn't been for Eric, her daughter wouldn't have stayed so late at church.

No, Lord, he saved her life. Please help me not to be bitter.

Jacqueline closed the door quietly and walked back to the bedroom she shared with Emmett. When she entered, he was sitting up, trying to shake off semi-consciousness. "Where have you been this late at night, woman?" he teased gently.

Smiling, she blew out the candle and sat it on the dresser before joining him under the covers. "I was watching our daughter sleeping."

"Is she okay?" He yawned while drawing her into his arms.

"You'd have to ask Eric. He's the one holding her."

Emmett grunted in confusion.

"You remember when we used to find them in her room in the middle of the night? Well, he's come back," she ended quietly, not sure how her husband would respond to the new development. Emmett was silent. "He's holding her like you are holding me now," she whispered, relishing in the comfort of her strong man. How could she fault Elie for doing the same?

Emmett breathed steadily, yet his heart thumped faster and faster.

"You're angry."

"I told that boy—"

He shifted, but she put a restraining hand on his arm, halting his movement from the bed. "At least, they're just sleepin'."

"Just sleepin'!"

She flinched at the thunder in his voice. "Shh, please, Emmett. You saw the look on her face when he left. She was terrified. She hasn't said a word since he's been gone. She needs him to be with her right now."

Even in the dark, she could see his stormy expression. Anger rolled off him in violent waves. "I don't approve of that boy in my daughter's bed, underneath *my* roof," he growled.

"I know, I know. But can't we just let it lie, at least for tonight—"

"I think we've let him do enough lying around tonight." He tossed the covers and leapt out of bed.

"Emmett!" She jumped after him, rushing ahead to block the doorway. "Emmett, wait."

"Move out my way, woman."

"Emmett, please! Think of our daughter!"

His eyes glittered like black ice. "I *am* thinkin' of our daughter."

She sighed and ran her hands down her face. "He's fully dressed. He's just holdin' her."

"Jacqueline, I can't have him doing anything with our daughter, dressed or not."

"Emmett, you sound so serious." Jacqueline bit her lip and wrung a piece of her nightgown in her hands.

"You know our daughter's in love with Morgan's boy."

Jacqueline swallowed the lump of resignation in her throat. Emmett was right. Elie had been in love with Eric since she could say his name. "He's not with the Lord now," she whispered.

"That ain't the real issue. Our daughter's as stubborn as some of Morgan's stallions." He sank on the bed with a defeatist look, crossing his arms over his chest and releasing a heavy breath. Jacqueline sat beside him, laying her head on his broad shoulder. His gruff voice held a twinge of sadness. "We have to make her see he ain't right for her. Maybe if we continue to encourage her and Michael. He's courtin' her now."

Jacqueline shook her head. "I can't force her on a man she don't love."

"Well, she can't be with Eric, even if he did love Jesus. This town is being ripped apart at the seams with whites and blacks fightin' all the time." He ran a hand down the side of his face, and expelled a weary sigh. His voice softened to a forlorn murmur. "Them being together would never work. It's best she be with her own kind."

Jacqueline sniffed, nodding her approval. She rubbed at the moisture in her eyes. Her baby would be heartbroken, but it was for the best. They'd get no justice for her after tonight. How could they go against the mayor's sons? Their daughter would be humiliated, but even more so if she married a white man. She and Eric would face such prejudice...Jacqueline hid her face in her husband's shoulder. She wouldn't be able to stand seeing her daughter in such pain. At least she and Emmett could protect her this one time.

Chapter Fifteen

FALLING

Eric's eyes squinted as the sunlight streamed through the thin white curtains in Elie's bedroom. He hadn't meant to stay all night—only until she was sound asleep—but he was so comfortable he'd drifted off soon after she did. Judging by the light, he guessed the sun had just risen. He glanced down at the sleeping beauty in his arms and smiled. Her face looked perfectly relaxed, her breathing deep and steady.

He strained his ears for sounds outside her bedroom door.

The switch.

Emmett Brown had almost killed him the last time he was here. Accusing him of doing things the McDougal brothers attempted the night before. Eric stretched his tightened jaw. He would never harm Elie. He loved…

If he catches me again, he'll murder me.

Eric cleared his throat. Removing Elie's arm from around his waist, he eased from underneath her weight.

Elie stirred. "What?" she asked in a dreamy haze.

"Shhh," he whispered, hoping she'd return to sleep.

Elie blinked rapidly, awaking from slumber. "Where are you going?" she said, raising her voice.

He waved his hands in a downward motion. "Shhh, Elie. It's morning, and I have to leave before your parents find me." A sudden ache weighed on his chest. Waking up next to her *felt* right, and now he couldn't stay where he belonged.

"My parents love you. They'd welcome you here," she argued weakly, yawning.

Eric reached for his boots and, sitting on the edge of her bed, he worked to put them on. Welcome him? Doubtful. He grinned. "They would, would they? They'd love finding me in your bed?" he teased.

Elie waved a hand at him. "It's not what it looks like." She yawned again before snuggling deeper into the covers, her head burrowing into a pillow. Chuckling, he sat near her head and bent to kiss her forehead.

"That excuse didn't work last time, if you remember."

"I don't want you to go…" she trailed off, her lids closing.

"I don't want to leave," he said, his voice softer than hers. He kissed her forehead again and stood. As Elie drifted back to sleep, Eric quietly retreated toward the window.

****

Elie decided to go against her parents' suggestion and work for a few hours at the Montgomery estate. Work allowed her to focus and she needed something to preoccupy her thoughts other than trees…and rope…and rough hands. Her father insisted on driving her to the estate and she thought it wise not to argue. She was sure she'd be safer in the daytime; the McDougal brothers wouldn't think to reattempt the act in broad daylight. However, at the urging of her parents, Elie agreed to her father driving her to work.

Yawning, Elie rolled down the car window, hoping a

little cool air on her face would wake her. The air whipped through her hair as she and her father traveled down the road adjacent to the Montgomery acreage. The vision of Eric's embrace caused her to smile. In his arms, she was safe and secure.

"Are you tired? It is a bit early. Perhaps we should have waited a couple of hours."

"No, Dad. You have a job, too."

"Mr. Montgomery would understand if I was a few hours late," he said gruffly.

Elie gave him a sideways glance. Her father had been unusually quiet this morning. At first she assumed it was because of the incident last night, but it was more than that. His abrupt mannerisms, his gruff tone when he did speak, his silence at the breakfast table—he'd barely looked her in the eye. He seemed…angry.

"Did you sleep well?"

"Hmm." Elie nodded, recalling how comfortable she'd felt falling asleep in Eric's arms. She angled her head more toward the breeze in an effort to cool her heating cheeks.

"Elnora, the Christmas pageant is tonight. Couldn't your work wait until next week?"

Elie bit her lip, considering. It could, but she'd promised Morgan she'd be able to assist him more than usual during the Christmas holidays.

"Elie, we need to talk about you and Eric."

The abrupt change in subject by the blunt statement completely startled her. It implied there was some level of intimacy beyond the friendship her parents had observed. Or was she just assuming that's what her father had meant? She cut a glance to the man behind the wheel. *Did they perceive more?* She was afraid to ask. Fiddling with the strap on her hobo, she feigned ignorance on the premise of the question. "Um, me and Eric?"

"Yes, Elie," he replied in a weighty voice. "Your mother

and I are concerned that your relationship with him might be crossin' some boundaries."

She sat mute, hoping her silence would end the conversation. *They can't know he was there last night.*

"Does he still deny his faith?"

Elie once again looked out the window wondering when, if ever, they'd reach the house. Did her father take the long way around?

"Elie?"

She shrugged.

"If the two of you are thinkin' of startin' some kind of romance, don't."

Elie faced her father, mouth opened in surprise. How did he know they were dancing around a romantic relationship?

Her father's lips twisted lopsidedly. "How'd we know? We're your parents, Elie. We've watched the two of you from birth. Did you think it was such a secret?"

"Um, well, when did you 'spect?" she stammered.

"The day your mother and I returned home and found the two of you in the livin' room, unable to look at each other or cough up a sentence." He chuckled and then cleared his throat, struggling to replace his smile with a frown. "After he left, you nearly burnt dinner."

She smarted under that recollection. "I didn't *nearly* burn it."

"You're right, ya' burnt it. Look, honey, he don't love Jesus, baby. And…"

Elie held her breath. Why else did her parents disapprove? Eric was reconsidering his faith—he'd said as much in his letters. In the meantime, he'd mended his relationship with his father, and he'd started working at the family bank. Didn't that count for something?

"And what, Daddy?"

Emmett kept his eyes on the road, his fingers tapping on the wheel. Was he nervous? He cleared his throat again but didn't answer.

"Daddy?"

"Your momma and I think you should be with your own kind."

The air from outside went through her, icing her veins. Her own kind? They didn't approve of Eric because he was white? As the words sunk in, their meaning took on a dreadful reality. Even if he did love Jesus, her parents couldn't see past their own prejudice to accept him as more than just a family friend. Hot tears burned the back of her eyes. Elie turned away before the first one slipped down her cheek.

"Now, baby, we love that boy, we do. But honey, you two would have a bad time at it." He reached over and squeezed her shoulder. "We, your momma and I, don't want you to have a life more difficult than what you got now."

How could life be more difficult? She'd already lost him once…the thought of not ever having him *now*…"You forbiddin' me to see him?"

"No, of course not. Just…"

She nodded, understanding. Her cheeks wet, she leaned toward the open window, allowing the breeze to dry the tears. Perhaps she should have waited a day or two before returning to work. How could she face Eric now, knowing this?

You should be with your own kind.

The longer she dwelled on those words, the stronger defiance stirred in the deepest part of her soul. She wanted her friend. Craved his presence and his touch. Hungered for his mouth.

Her father squeezed her arm again and then patted it gently. She knew her parents only wanted her happiness, but a life without Eric would be too devastating.

****

Eric walked into his father's downstairs office and

stopped short, seeing Elie in front of the desk. She placed a stack of papers in her hand on top of the desk and gave him a weak smile.

He closed the door before leaning his back against it and crossing his arms over his chest. "You should be at home," he said disapprovingly.

"Resting?" Elie's lips twisted into a grim expression.

He narrowed his eyes at her sarcasm. Hers didn't falter and they stared at each other, weighing the strength of each other's wills.

Eric sighed, realizing the futility of arguing with her. "Elie, I just want you safe. You don't have to do anything if you're not ready." He paused, glancing at his shoes, while carefully considering his next words. "Last night was, um, pretty traumatic, especially for you." He lifted his head and noticed her downcast eyes. "No one expects you to continue as if nothing happened," he whispered.

Elie breathed deeply, her chest rising and falling slowly. She locked her trembling hands behind her. "I needed to do something to keep my mind off of—" Her voice broke and she put her hands to her face.

Eric was in front of her in a heartbeat, pulling her hands from her face to see her eyes. Tears streamed down her cheeks. "You're trembling. I wish you'd stayed home."

Elie's lips tweaked upward. "I'm fine," she whispered, her eyes summoning courage that shocked him. If her smile reached her eyes, he'd never guess the performance was for his benefit. Eric wiped away a stubborn tear lingering on her pale cheek. Her eyes warmed, before slowly traveling southward. The parting of her glossy lips caused the muscles in his gut to tighten. Releasing her hands, he took her elbows and gently pulled her toward him.

"Eric?" she whispered softly, asking.

His fingers skimmed to her waist as hers traveled up his torso. *Gentle, gentle. Don't force her.* Her frightened scream still reverberated in his ears. How had the McDougals emotionally scarred her? Sure she let him hold her, but…Her eyes were heady, her gaze still on his lips. He wrapped her securely in his arms. Nose to nose, he brushed his lips across her top one. She sighed softly and tilted her head back, inviting his kiss.

The kiss was far different from the one they'd shared in her parents' house. Not demanding but softly, respectfully, he explored every part of her gloriously round mouth, and she whimpered when he parted her lips, the taste of her drawing him in. Slow, deep. Elie's hands moved up his shoulders and around his neck. With one hand on the small of her back, he lightly slid the other up the center of her back to cup the base of her neck. The space between their bodies closed to almost nothing as they melted into each other's embrace. Blood pounding in his brain, he groaned, squeezing her tightly, his kiss intensifying and drawing her soft moan.

He could feel her desire as her lips matched his own for passion and desperation. But he had to release her. She wasn't like any of the other women who'd satisfied him for a brief time. He loved her—respected her beliefs. Grunting his disappointment, he gently pulled away. Foreheads touching, they breathed heavily the air between their lips. And for long moments, neither of them moved.

Elie kept her eyes closed and her hands slid down until they gripped his biceps. He cupped the sides of her face, drawing her once again into his arms. "Father is going to see if something can be done about last night," he whispered, lightly resting his chin on the top of her head.

"We all know the chief of police won't go against the mayor's sons."

"They almost—" He paused, gritting his teeth, as his anger rose. "They can't get away with what happened."

Elie squeezed him as they held each other. "Eric, I don't want to harbor any anger or bitterness. I'm sure you've mustered enough for the both of us." She tilted her head back and he saw her grin, but her smile held no humor. "Let the Lord—"

He pulled back but didn't let go. "Elie," he began, his anger being replaced by annoyance.

"Stop it," she whispered gently. "While you were gone, I prayed every night for your return and here you are. There was nothin' I could do to bring you back, so why should I worry about whatever is coming to the McDougal brothers? They're gonna get what's comin' to 'em."

He stared at Elie evenly, her words taking root. Had God really brought him back to Alabama? Did Elie's prayers have that strong of an impact on his life? He recalled how desperately he'd prayed for his mother's healing and, when she died, he was convinced his prayers had gone unheard. Now Elie's eyes implored the truth he'd long ago dismissed, a truth she lived every day.

"Do you know how stubborn you are? God sent you to rescue me. He kept me safe, and still you resist Him."

He was unable to admit she was right. *At least not to her face.* But he'd come to the same conclusion the night before.

"I'm not worried, though." She let out a reedy breath, mouth broadening into a grin. "I thought your return would be the miracle to end all miracles until last night. Seeing you ride up on Nellie—" Her voice broke. He reached for her, but she held up her hands. "I'm okay." A lone tear slipped down her cheek, ending near her smiling lips. "I know your faith will return."

"And you think *I'm* stubborn?"

"Persistent. That's completely different."

"Whatever." He moved her arms aside, locking his hands at the small of her back and nudging her closer. His lips briefly took hers before she stiffened and angled back.

"Eric…" she protested weakly.

"I know you love me," he whispered pointedly. He ignored the pleading in her eyes. His hands caught her waist and dragged her to him. "One day I'm going to hear you say it."

****

How can I? Elie's heart rammed against her ribs, desperate to be free of its cage. Fear gripped her spirit. How long could she go on denying her heart? But she had no choice. Elie wrenched free from his hold and took more than a few steps back. "I'm still with Michael." As soon as the words left her lips, guilt consumed her. She hadn't ended their courtship. When had she discovered her heart had belonged to Eric? She couldn't remember, and now she was being unfair to Michael.

Eric sauntered forward, his smile devastating. "There's an easy solution to that. I've already said goodbye to Amanda."

Perhaps you shouldn't have. Even if she ended her relationship with Michael, a divide still existed between her and Eric. Faith, for one, and the other…How could she convince her parents to look past his skin color? Surely, they wouldn't be the first couple to experience hardships brought on by their races. Every day she lived in hardship. When life became rough for him, Eric ran away. Would he do so again?

His eyes—sharp jade—full of determination and desire, moved steadily forward, ensconcing in her the answer to all her fears. "You love me."

Legs heavy as wooden beams, she plodded backwards until she bumped into the edge of the desk. Her desire manifested into a shiver and she struggled to remain steady.

His eyes sparked and a sly grin formed. "I saw that. You love me, and I love you."

His size left no room for escape.

He loves me! The words reverberated in her ears, shouting down all efforts to resist. Together they could accomplish anything. He wouldn't leave her now. He'd promised her last night. She took a step forward and with that invitation, his arms went around her, crushing her against him.

His mouth ravaged her—her cheeks, her lobes, her jaw. Soft, but persistent, his lips parted her own to explore untouched depths. She moaned, her arms coming around his back, her hands gripping his shoulders, holding on for dear life.

"Miss Elie!"

Elie tore herself free, and gasped. In the doorway stood Miss Hattie, her eyes wide with alarm, her mouth tight with disapproval. She harrumphed and stalked away.

Humiliation flooded her. "Miss Hattie!" She surged forward but a hand on her arm restrained her.

Eric's mouth curved up in an amusing grin. "Elie, don't worry about her."

Irritation rose at his unbothered expression, causing her further embarrassment. "Eric, this isn't funny!"

"You have to admit, it's a little funny."

She struggled against his hand, locked tight around her wrist.

"Why are you fighting me? Look." He put a finger underneath her chin, and raised it to look into her eyes. "It's okay. If you want, I'll talk to her."

She whimpered, impatient to be free. "You don't understand. She'll tell my parents!"

Eric frowned. "Okay, I admit, your dad has given me 'the eye' lately, but I'm sure once we've had a chance to talk—"

"No, they won't accept you! You're white, Eric."

She hadn't meant to put it so bluntly, but it was out. Eric's hand dropped and he took a step back. The shock on his face, as if she'd just slapped him, tore at her heart. If only she could explain…but there wasn't time. Miss Hattie could have gotten to her father by now…

"I have to go, Eric."

"Elie!" He called after her but she stepped into the hall, colliding with Morgan.

"Whoa, Elie. Forgive me." He steadied her. "My dear." He wrapped her in a fatherly embrace before cupping her face between his hands and giving her a soft smile. "You don't have to be here, Elie."

She sent him an unsteady smile, exhaustion from last night's events and the silent threat from Miss Hattie beginning to take its toll. "I know, but I need to keep busy."

Morgan squeezed her shoulders and nodded in agreement. "I understand. Have you spoken to the police yet?"

She eyed the floor. "I doubt speakin' to the police would do any good." She raised her chin, hoping her smile would cheer him. "Next time you offer to drive me home, I promise to accept it." Her light tease was met by Morgan's frown. He bent to place a kiss on her forehead and he gave her another hug before releasing her. She glanced over her shoulder at Eric. He stood in the office, hands in pockets, his face unreadable.

****

Eric watched Elie disappear into the hall. *You're white.* He hadn't thought that mattered to her. Her kiss had given him all the assurance he needed, but clearly he'd misread her intentions. Out of all the things she fought for, why not him? *They won't accept you.* What excuse did her parents have? They'd known him since birth. Had they been lying to him this whole time?

Morgan entered the office, his face downcast. "She won't go home, will she?"

"No. She wants everything to be business as usual." He plopped down on the couch, frustrated. He'd just done some of his best kissing on that woman, and she'd run out. He crossed his arms over his chest.

"A strong young woman, that one," Morgan murmured.

Not strong enough. Ego bruised, he'd just have to break

down her will—with more kissing.

"Do you really believe something can be done by speaking to Asa McDougal? His sons seem to be cut from the same cloth." He flicked a piece of lint that had found a home on his pants as he asked his father the question, needing to get his mind off the growing seeds of rejection Elie had recently planted.

Morgan snorted. "Indeed those rotten apples didn't fall far from the poisonous tree. Whether or not Asa does anything, he needs to be spoken to. His position as mayor doesn't give his sons the right to terrorize the citizens of this town."

Elie's parents rejected the idea of reporting Edward, Chase, and Shane to the authorities. *The mayor owns the police,* Emmett said. Eric understood their hesitancy. No one had been charged for the violence against the marchers in August. Those severely injured by beatings and dog bites were still on the long road to recovery. Emmett and Jacqueline wanted justice, but believed the battle was already lost. Eric was glad his father still had the will. "Will you speak to him today?"

Morgan's jaw was set. "Yes, I will. In fact, I'll see you later at the bank. I'm going straight to Asa's office." Eric nodded as his father left. He remained in his spot, still fuming over Elie's words. *I can't help my skin color!*

God made all colors, Eric. He loves them all, his mother once answered him when he asked why Miss Hattie looked different from her. What had Jacqueline and Emmett told their daughter? They'd marched side-by-side, but he wasn't good enough to court their daughter.

So, God can accept me, but they can't. Eric smirked. What a cruel twist of fate.

****

Morgan removed his hat as he walked into the

government building in the heart of the city. He turned to his right, noticing the office directory on a nearby wall. Asa McDougal's mayoral office was located on the fourth floor. Morgan headed toward the stairwell and the climb to the fourth level.

As he climbed the staircase, Morgan was somber. Outside Eric's welcome home dinner, Morgan had little interaction with Asa. He remembered when they were growing up how much of a bully Asa was and believed with the addition of political power, little changed.

Morgan wondered how Asa would respond to the accusations Morgan would confront him with. The attempted rape of Elie and the beating she received were grave offenses. Asa couldn't be in the dark about his sons' wild and criminal behavior. They were frequently seen in the public, during daylight hours, beating a black person for walking near them, or an old man for drinking from the wrong fountain. It was as if they were the enforcement squad of the corrupted police force.

If there was anything Asa desired the most, it was high society distinction. Asa was always surrounded with an entourage that would rival any celebrity in Hollywood. He constantly vocalized his opinion through television interviews, newspaper editorials, and once, Morgan heard him on a local radio station. Already in hot water with the negative publicity regarding the civil rights march in August, any further press, especially on his personal life, would no doubt ruin him.

And if I'm not ready for the backlash...

Morgan stood outside the mayor's office and inhaled and exhaled slowly. He closed his eyes and said a brief prayer for God's guidance. Upon opening the door, he was greeted with a friendly smile from the mayor's secretary, Ms. Graham.

"Oh, Mr. Montgomery! I didn't know you would be coming in today. Um, did you make an appointment?" She fumbled through her calendar.

Morgan gave her a small smile. "No ma'am, I did not. This is kind of spur of the moment. It shouldn't take too long." He looked toward the mayor's closed door, straining his ears to hear if Asa was in a meeting with anyone. "Do you think the mayor could squeeze in a few minutes to see me?"

"Oh, I'm sure he could, but he does have a meeting with the fire inspector in about a half an hour. You know, over the last incident?" Her voice dropped to a whisper.

Morgan nodded in recollection. A nearby watch repair store had caught ablaze early one morning. Everything inside was lost.

The storeowner?

A black man, who was a patron of the Montgomery Bank.

Ms. Graham beckoned Morgan to follow her as she walked to the mayor's door. She knocked lightly and called out to Asa. When given the affirmative to enter, she opened the door and announced Morgan.

"Ah, my friend, Mr. Montgomery!" Asa, sitting behind his desk, stood up, extending his hand.

Friend?

"Mayor McDougal." Morgan shook his hand.

Asa waved a hand around and laughed, obviously pleased with the title in front of his name. "Please, none of that title stuff. I'm Asa to you." His lips put forth a swarthy smile. Morgan nodded his head in respect to the change, but fought a smirk over Asa's attempt at distaste over his own title. He took Asa's hand. "Please, have a seat," Asa said, motioning to the plush leather chair situated in front of his own deep mahogany desk. "Oh, and Ms. Graham, please hold all my calls."

Ms. Graham had lingered near the doorway. "Remember you have a meeting with Inspector Geddy in a half an hour."

"Thank you, thank you," he responded dismissively as she closed the door.

Asa landed in his chair with a heavy thud and leaned

back, locking his hands behind his head. Morgan eyed Asa's bulk, which to some, could be intimidating. He remembered how Asa ate several plates at the dinner party.

Morgan cleared his throat, hoping to dispel the air of superiority Asa emulated. "Asa, I wanted to bring a couple of things to your personal attention in hopes that your," Morgan paused a half second, deliberating on his word choice, "leadership would calm fears and set behavioral precedent." Morgan tried not to choke on the words, knowing they meant little when describing Asa.

"Of course, of course, Morgan. As the mayor, I see it as my duty to provide solid supervision. I've always held," he too paused, looking up at the ceiling, clasping his hands in front of him and then looked at Morgan with authority, "that I should have a personal hand in any matter—"

"Forgive me, Asa," Morgan interrupted, "but I wanted to make sure you received all the details before you leave for your next appointment."

Asa's eyes narrowed slightly at the interruption but his features began to relax at the mention of details Morgan thought needed is immediate attention. Asa cleared his own throat. "Of course, continue."

"As you know there have been a string of businesses that have been attacked. I read the editorial you provided the local paper, and it is well known that your three sons are the first ones at each scene when discovered." Morgan braced for any response from Asa.

Asa was silent, his eyes darkening.

"It doesn't look good and I'm afraid they may soon be implicated in these attacks."

"Implicated." Asa's voice was as granite as he echoed Morgan.

"It's no secret their feelings toward the minority population, and they've been witnessed starting fights with people on the street." Morgan lowered his voice in an attempt to sound sympathetic to the McDougals, although it was sympathy for the McDougals he completely lacked. "And I have information about an attack on a young woman just last night…"

Morgan didn't finish as a growl emanated from Asa's lips before he jumped to his feet, his eyes blaring.

"You dare accuse my sons of these petty criminal acts, and…and *rape!*" he yelled, saliva flying from his mouth, sweat forming heavily on his forehead.

Morgan didn't expect Asa to have a stroke over the news but the veins in Asa's neck grew larger by the second as Morgan's accusations sunk deeper and deeper. Asa's eyes burned red with fury and his fists clenched in anger.

Determined to show Asa he was not intimidated by his erratic behavior, Morgan stood slowly. "You cannot deny your sons are out of control. They're attacking the people who expect their mayor to protect them, and helpless women on the side of the road at night!"

Asa's breath came in heavy, ragged gasps, as he shook with rage.

Morgan tried to de-escalate what he suspected was Asa's rapidly approaching brain aneurism. "You're their father." He leaned on the desk, urgency in his voice. "You can control them. That's your responsibility." His fist hit the desk in earnest.

"Bah." Asa waved a hand in the air and walked around the desk to eliminate the distance between Morgan and himself. "They're grown men," he growled. "Responsible, law-abiding citizens who don't need to be managed." Nose to nose, Morgan was engulfed in overbearing cologne and lingering peppermint on Asa's breath. The whites of Asa's eyes seemed to eclipse the color of his irises. His finger jabbed Morgan in the chest. "My son's did *not,* I repeat not, rape some darkie female. And if you say anything about this to anyone, you will reap the consequences, Mr. Montgomery—don't think that you won't." He leaned away, licking his lips, satisfied with his own threat. "Your bank is well-known in town, and services the highest clientele. I'd hate to have to see you close your doors due to bankruptcy. You know, being a bank and all."

Morgan sized up Asa, weighing the seriousness of the threat. He didn't believe for a second that his bank would at all falter. It wasn't just the black population that was unsettled by the rash actions of Asa's sons, but the white community had its own doubts about full-scale dissension in the city, divided along the lines of the shades of skin. Morgan was confident that despite Asa's threat, the community would not follow through.

Asa began to walk toward the door.

"Asa…" Morgan whispered entreatingly.

Asa turned sharply on his heels, his eyes once again ablaze. "Don't address me so informally, *Mr.* Montgomery. It's *Mayor* McDougal," he seethed. "Now if you will excuse me, I have a very important meeting with the city fire chief to review the evidence of the latest attack on a black business by *unknown* assailants."

His emphasis of "unknown" wasn't lost on Morgan. Either Asa was in denial over his son's actions, or he was refusing to admit their guilt. Either way, it was Asa's position that his sons had nothing to do with the attacks.

Morgan's lips made a tight line as he watched Asa open the door to his office and with restrained fury wait for Morgan to exit. Morgan sighed and reached for his hat. He walked toward Asa, their eyes never breaking contact. When Morgan turned to exit, he spotted Ms. Graham sitting at her desk, the shocked look on her face leaving Morgan in no doubt she'd overheard their argument. Morgan tipped his head toward her. "Ms. Graham," he said and walked out.

Morgan fought against anger stewing in him. Asa's response wasn't a surprise, but that knowledge didn't help stay the effect. Morgan burst through the doors of the administration building, and blew out a breath as the air hit his face. The slightly cool breeze began to calm his nerves as he analyzed the conversation he'd just had with Asa. He half envisioned Asa being coolly collected when confronted with the allegations. However, Asa had been so furious; Morgan wasn't prepared for anything but a civil conversation. He now realized he grossly underestimated Asa's retort.

Christmas was everywhere the eye looked. Lights were strung around businesses and light poles, small decorative trees were displayed in windows, and red and green seemed to be all around in various forms. Jolly, fat men dressed as Santa would hand out candy to children passing by and a few trios had been performing well-known Christmas songs for nearly a week. Even though tonight was the night of the children's pageant at Wimbly Baptist, Morgan was not in the Christmas spirit.

Morgan reached into his pocket and pulled his car keys out. As he approached his car, he paused as a disturbing thought came to mind. Would Asa retaliate? Asa was more than a little upset about the possibility of negative backlash if his sons were ever implicated in any of the recent criminal attacks, but Morgan decided to give Asa the benefit of the doubt. Asa wouldn't jeopardize his position as mayor by choosing to exact violence against a particular group, or family, for a personal quest. As Morgan drove to the bank, a sickening feeling in his stomach began to grow that he couldn't seem to quell. If Asa's behavior was any indication of what was to come, then things were going to get a lot worse.

Chapter Sixteen

BAPTIST BURNING

Elie was grateful for Michael's assistance at the pageant. She'd no idea how taxing the attack on her last night—or Eric's kiss today—would be on her. She barely had a moment alone with Michael and she wanted it that way, needing time to think what to say to end their relationship. After hours of decorating, she still hadn't formulated a coherent explanation. The thought of his disappointment weighed heavily on her mind and impeded her contemplation.

She did her best to ignore the intense headache that had developed since she'd arrived at the church and had seen Michael, and instead focused on straightening the kids' costumes and gathering others into an area where she wouldn't have to chase after them. After tying the laces to one of the children's shoes, she straightened up too quickly, and the room began to spin. Losing her balance, she fell backwards, into the arms of Michael, who swooped her up before she hit the floor.

She moaned as Michael gently sat her down on the back

steps of the church. "Wha...what happened?" She touched her head, still feeling it swimming.

"You fainted." He set a hand on her back to steady her. "Are you feeling any better?"

"Mmm." She tilted her head back, the air cooling the moisture on her forehead.

"Perhaps you are overdoing things, Elnora. You worked earlier today and you have to direct the pageant? Maybe you should let one of the mothers handle tonight's event."

*And the McDougals last night...*He didn't know about their attack and she had no intention of telling him. She answered with a defiant shake of her head.

He rubbed her back, his voice soothing. "Many of them attended the rehearsals and I'm sure one of them wouldn't mind."

She had to end it now. "Michael..." The worried look in his eyes caused her throat to tighten, choking the words.

"What happened?"

The sound of Eric's voice had her sitting up straighter, her vision clearing, and her mind suddenly less foggy. Michael glanced behind him and she caught his look of disapproval. He grasped her hand and slid closer to her on the step.

Eric bounded down the steps and stood before them. His critical gaze took in Elie and he squatted to her eye level. He took a hold of her wrists, pulling her hands from Michael and enclosing them in his own. Michael's gaze burned into the side of her face but she couldn't bring herself to pull away from Eric.

"Michael, what happened to her?" Impatience laced Eric's voice. "Are you all right?" Eric asked her.

"She fainted," Michael spat.

Elie dipped her head, embarrassed by the attention. She felt Eric's finger beneath her chin, lifting until their eyes met. "You fainted? Do I need to tell you I told you so?" he teased lightly and the back of his fingers stroked her cheek.

Sniffing, Michael shot to his feet, anger flashing across his features. He knocked Eric's hand away.

Panic seized her. "Michael!"

Unhurried, Eric stood to full height, his green eyes burning with annoyance, the muscles in his face rigid.

She attempted to stand, and both men reached for an arm to aid her to her feet.

"I'm all right, Eric. If you wouldn't mind," she cast a glance at Michael, "I need to speak to Michael." She swallowed and then sent a pointed look at Eric. "Alone."

Eric eyed Michael with suspicion and then refocused on her. "Are you sure?"

She nodded. "Please. I'll see you inside." She smiled, hoping to dispel any concern and prove she was stronger than she felt. Without acknowledging Michael, Eric gave her arm a gentle squeeze and jogged up the steps and into the church.

Nerves wracked, she blew out a thick breath, her heart thumping in worried anticipation to what she was about to say. She hadn't rehearsed any speech and hoped the words would come to her. Behind Michael, the sun slowly dipped into the oncoming night. Michael's expression dropped with it. She opened her mouth—

"You're in love with him. Aren't you?"

Elie sucked in a breath. *He guessed? But how?* Michael's bottom lip trembled, his dark eyes glittering with fury and hurt. Guilt ripped through her, leaving her mute. She could only nod.

"Since when?"

She dropped her lashes, the torment in his voice stripping her courage to look him in the eye.

"I think you owe me an explanation." Rancor sharpened his voice.

She nodded again. "I don't really know. Maybe I've always loved him."

With a shudder of humiliation, he turned away.

"Michael." She reached for his arm but he jerked away.

His head snapped back to her. "What do you know of him? He doesn't even believe in God."

Elie winced. It was true, Eric had lost his way, but she was sure he'd find it again. When, she didn't know, but she'd wait for him. She had to. "He has changed, you're right. But he's had some pain a few years back and he's workin' through it—"

"You're making excuses for him, Elnora." He shook his head, his look of disappointment shredding her heart. He seized her hands. "You're a precious gem. Why would you throw yourself away on a man who doesn't love God, and a white one at that?"

Her cheeks warmed with embarrassment, but she stiffened at the insult to Eric's race. "Michael, you don't mean that. We've worked hand in hand with other white men and women for integration—"

He flung her hands away. "Those men weren't stealin' my woman."

Elie bit her lip, averting her eyes. She couldn't blame his feelings of betrayal; she'd been dishonest with him and herself. *I should have never agreed to this courtship.* The disdain in his eyes cut her. She'd ruined their friendship. "I'm sorry, Michael. I should have said something sooner. I..." She swallowed, her gaze full of the pain of rejection lingering in his obsidian eyes, the anger-flared nostrils, and hard jaw. As he turned away, she grasped his arm, hoping he'd believe her words. "I tried with you, Michael. Really I did," she insisted desperately. "Please forgive me. You're so kind, and wonderful. Everything a woman could want..."

Her hand fell away at his sneer. "Don't pretend you gave any effort. If you wanted me, then you'd be with me, seein' as how I'm so wonderful."

Tongue dry from the air she sucked into her open mouth, she couldn't summon her voice. Never had she witnessed this side of him. Guilt compounded. She'd turned him into something nasty and he was unrecognizable as her friend.

Narrowed eyes pinned her to her spot as he stepped closer until he was only a breath away. "Have you given yourself to him?"

Mortified at the accusation, she wrapped her arms around her middle and backed away. "No," she breathed hotly.

His features relaxed into cool indifference and he edged back. "I believe in integration, but I don't believe in mixin' the races. Just thinkin' of you with him..." His top lip curved up in disgust.

"You're not the only one. My parents don't approve either."

"And they're right." He pointed a finger at her. "You've always been a good girl, Elnora. You should listen to them."

She nodded, but disagreed. She didn't see the problem with "mixin' the races" as Michael had labeled it, but she was in love with a white man and perhaps she was biased. His expression was one of mute wretchedness, and her spirits sank. "Please forgive me?"

He looked away, a tic trembling in his jaw. "I want to forgive you. But I'm not sure I can, now."

Elie swallowed a sob. *This is my fault.* If she hadn't been so focused on avoiding her feelings for Eric—judging Michael to be the perfect suitor and Eric lacking—*I wouldn't have hurt my friend.* She reached out to him. "Michael, I'm so sorry."

Maisy burst through the door. "Are you all right? I heard you fainted on stage!" Maisy took hold of Elie and pulled her into a hug.

"I'm fine, I'm fine," she said breathlessly. Michael's gaze darted from her to the ground and then back to her. Fists jammed in his pockets, he took the stairs up to the door, two at a time. Elie gripped Maisy, hiding her face in her shoulder.

"Oh, okay. I thought you said you were fine." Maisy

hugged her back, stroking her hair.

Elie sniffed, blinking away tears. "I'm sorry. Guess I'm a bit shaken up."

Worry lines creased between Maisy's brows. "Are you sure you're okay?"

Elie nodded, smiling. "Yes."

"Well then, if everythin' is all right…the children are ready for you. I believe we're about to start."

Maisy and Elie climbed the stairs and entered the small sanctuary. Proud parents waved and called out to their fidgety children in home-sewn period costumes, while churchgoers milled about, searching for places to sit in the crowded sanctuary.

Michael stood at the opposite end of the stage. He and Elie exchanged a pained look before he cast a hardened glare at Eric, who ignored him, his attention on Elie with a look of concern in his eyes, a leg bouncing in anxiety. She flashed him a quick smile and focused on assembling the children for the pageant.

****

What did he say to her? What had she said to him? Calm and a bit timid at the march, Eric hadn't guessed Michael to be the jealous type. When Michael had practically shoved him away from her, he wanted nothing more than to punch him in the gut.

Eric felt his father's eyes on him. "What happened?" he whispered as the kids took the stage.

"Elie overdid things and fainted."

Morgan sighed deeply, the space between his brows deepening. "How is she?"

"I think she needs to rest, but she claims to be fine."

Eric forced himself to concentrate on the children in front of him and soon found it hard not to look away. The story of

Jesus' birth was played out in all the simplicity of its youthful actors and the childlike rendition struck a heartstring. God sent His only Son to die for all of humanity. He glanced at his father. He was sure his father would give his life for him, and he'd do the same. In the end, it would be an easy sacrifice, but for God? Eric's soul stirred in a way he hadn't felt in a long time.

A rock shattered through a window close to the stage. A loud roar from outside accompanied the startled gasps of a few of the attendees. Men jumped up from their seats, sprinting toward the doors, and a few women made their way to the windows. Women backed away from the glass, their screams filling the air. A few of the children on stage began to cry and Elie and Maisy rushed forward, gathering them to crowd the center of the stage, away from any windows. Eric stood, catching sight of a faint reddish glow beyond a pane of glass. The double doors at the back of the church opened to a blinding, thunderous blaze.

The church was surrounded. Hooded figures dressed in white, carrying torches, were roaring at the top of their lungs. A large wooden cross burned on the front lawn, its flames flickering high into the night.

The howls of the hoods ceased.

As a few of the men quieted the women in the church, the pastor stepped forward onto the outside steps. "Y'all aren't welcome here tonight. We ask y'all leave in peace."

Not a single man moved.

"There are women and children in here. God does not desire any trespasses against them."

In unison, the white hoods advanced one step.

Women gasped. Men grumbled in frustration and anger. Smoke from the crosses drifted through the front door of the church and those in the back pew began to cough.

Morgan made his way through the crowd toward the entrance but Eric stayed behind, near the pew. He turned and met Elie's frightened gaze. She was speaking softly to the children, her eyes clinging to his. The children huddled around her and Maisy, some sniffing, some crying, and others with their heads buried in Elie and Maisy's laps.

All sound left Eric's ears as every fiber of his being focused on Elie. It was quite possible they would die tonight. What if he'd never returned? What if Elie, her family, and his father died here, burned alive in a church, all while he wasted his life in France? Would their thoughts have been on him, and how he'd denied them a chance to meet one last time? The regret would have killed him. A sickening feeling formed in the pit of his stomach at the thought of it all ending. *God, where are you?*

Eric joined his father and the other men who'd congregated outside on the doorsteps. If there was going to be a fight, then he'd be in the thick of it. *Where's Chase McDougal?* His fists clenched, itching for flesh. You'd better be out here.

"We're prepared to fight," the pastor stated firmly. "As the Lord is our witness, we will be victorious!"

On Christ the solid rock I stand, all other ground is sinking sand...

Behind them came the powerful singing voices of the women and the children, permeating the walls of the church, bursting into the night air. The sounds of their voices carried, pushing against evil and a few Klan members backed away, glancing at one another almost as if in confusion. A small number of hoods gathered together, speaking in hushed tones. The men on the steps began to pray fervently for grace and a divine rescue. The voices of the Klan members rose as they spoke among themselves. Eric thought it strange they could hear themselves over the singing.

When darkness seems to hide His face, I rest on His unchanging grace!

Several times, a few hoods turned in their direction and then back to one another. Eric strained in vain to hear the voices, trying to identify familiar ones. Finally, one hood waved his torch in the air, motioning the others to fall back. Many disappeared slowly into the darkened woods that surrounded most of the church. A few remained behind in front of the building. The pastor and men of the congregation stood their ground. The hoods were now outnumbered by men ready to defend their families, their church, and their God.

From the distance, a nondescript black vehicle approached the church, braking not far from the remaining Klan members. Torches thrown near the burning cross, the hoods dove into the car. The men on the steps watched the last of the taillights fading quickly into the inky shadows.

Churchgoers cheered, shouting praises to God. Soon, the sounds of the organ flooded the tiny church and members provided vocals to the hymn.

After dousing the flaming cross with water from the church well, men rushed to reposition their cars to face into the trees surrounding the church, their headlights lighting up the foliage. Guns were secured, and a plan to escort those without vehicle transportation home was agreed upon. Everyone gathered inside for a final prayer.

For the first time in a long time, Eric bowed his head in prayer. Why had the hoods retreated? They could've easily rushed the church and set it on fire. And who would convict them? Police Chief Wilcox had to have been among them, and probably authorized their actions. Eric couldn't explain their survival. Was God on their side tonight?

Morgan and Eric stayed to offer security and were two of the last to leave the church. Michael had since left, and Eric took the opportunity to speak to Elie alone. "Thank you for inviting me tonight," he said, pulling her aside to a private corner. "You didn't tell me the Klan would be the second act."

Elie smirked, raising a shaky hand and dragging her fingers through her loose hair. "Eric, things could have ended so badly. And the children!"

"Shhh." He pulled her into her his arms. "They're safe. You're safe. God protected us tonight." Arms around his waist, she tilted back to meet his eyes. He let her inquisitive gaze search his and watched as a spark of understanding simmered in the chocolate depths.

"Elnora!"

At the sound of her father's voice, Elie wrenched free. Hardened lines accompanied a rigid jaw framed by a grimace usually reserved for the wildest and untamed of their horses. Elie murmured goodnight and brushed passed them and out the side church door before her father could stop her. Eric rolled his lips in to keep from smiling. *Running away again. She really is scared of her father.*

This time, though, he wouldn't stand dumbfounded before Emmett. Elie was free, and he was going to have her. Eric approached the man who thought he stood between him and his daughter. "Sir—"

"I know you and my daughter have somethin' goin' on." His voice was low and hard. "But I'm gonna ask you to reconsider your choice."

Stunned, Eric's mouth dried and words escaped him. He hadn't expected dismissal before asking for his permission to court his daughter.

"There are plenty of nice *white* girls in town that you could have your pick."

I've already done that. I want Elie. Blasting out a breath in annoyance, he tried again. "Mr. Brown—"

"Now, Elnora's young. She's still in school and livin' under my roof, so she has to obey *my* rules. Our families bein' real close and all, I'd hope you'd respect my wishes as her father."

Eric shook his head in bafflement. It was true. Her parents wouldn't accept him. After all these years, Emmett saw him as no more than the white son of his employer.

Chapter Seventeen

RIOT

The Browns were obliged to join the Montgomery men for Christmas dinner and gift exchange at their estate. While Morgan and Emmett discussed the climate of the black residents in the town, debating the effect a citywide petition would have on the mayor, Elie and Eric sat on the back veranda, drinking hot chocolate and enjoying the cool December breeze.

Eric tried multiple times to convince her that they should challenge her parents regarding their courtship. Morgan would be on their side, and with the approval of one parent, her parents would have to agree to their courtship. When she remained unconvinced, he proposed they court in secret. She denied, refused, dodged, and finally threatened to leave the house if he didn't keep quiet on the subject.

Eric repeated his conversation with her father. "They'll never let us be together. Not when all they can see is my race." He reached for her hands, holding them tightly in his own. "This is why we should court in secret," he urged.

Elie gripped his hands, her eyes downcast. "I can't go against my parents' wishes, Eric."

"Elie, you're a grown woman."

She shook her head. "I can't hurt them like that." She snatched her hands back and hid them beneath the folds of her skirt.

With a fatigued sigh, he leaned back in his chair. "What can I do to convince them?"

"Nothin.'"

How could the Lord allow her to fall in love with a man her parents rejected? Why couldn't she have loved Michael, a man her parents loved, and who loved her? She hadn't spoken to Michael since the Christmas pageant. Jasmine hesitantly mentioned seeing him in town, and only when Elie pressed her did she say how bitterly Michael had spoken of her. Regret haunted Elie and she prayed for a renewal of their friendship, but she'd broken his heart, and it would mend in its own time.

Elie moaned audibly, throwing her head back into the chair. With her head still back, she rolled it until her eyes met Eric's. He grinned knowingly at her.

"You sound like I feel."

"I'm going back to school tomorrow." She changed the subject, hoping her darkening mood would lighten.

"School doesn't start until a week after the New Year."

Elie nodded, not offering more.

"I'm waiting."

"It's the final semester and I have some work to do on my senior project."

Eric snorted. "Elie, you're always ahead in your work. If I know you"—his pointed gaze held her hostage—"and I know you, you're running away. Again."

"Eric, really, I—"

"It was your decision, remember? I had no say in the matter." His voice was clipped. "But just because we can't have a relationship doesn't mean you can't breathe the same air I do."

She smoothed her dress and stood slowly. Tears threatened to spill onto her cheeks. She blinked as rapidly as she could but to no avail. Their gazes locked. "You don't know how difficult this is for me. I'm not so strong and resistant as you may think," she choked out. She labored to breathe and closed her eyes, tears falling. Releasing a raspy sigh, her blurry eyes found him. "You're right, Eric. You've always been right." Her rupturing heart quaked, causing her to tremble. "I love you," she whispered.

Eric rose from his seat, reaching for her, but she rushed back into the house, the screen door slamming behind her.

****

"Rumor or not, we can't dismiss the possibility." Michael bent over his knee, his tone low to Elie and Jasmine, who sat on the steps of the university library.

"But who is spreadin' these rumors? How do we know the Klan is plannin' a rally here?" Elie demanded, hoping a church in Selma wouldn't witness a repeat of the Klan's performance at Wimbly Baptist. The memory of hanging from a tree caused a tremor to course through Elie. According to one of Eric's letters, his father had spoken to Mayor McDougal about his sons' offenses against her. He scoffed at his sons' involvement and they remained free to wreak havoc on unsuspecting women in Selma.

"We don't have to know everything. Reports from all over Freeman and Selma of crosses burnin' on people's front lawns is all the evidence we need to know what they're doin' is only gonna get worse."

Elie bit her lip. What Michael didn't know, and what would spur him into action, was, according to Mrs. Hoover, the homes of those harassed were recipients of money from the Montgomery Bank. Eric and Morgan were no closer to discovering who was leaking information about customers.

"Birmingham is always burning, Freeman is on the brink, and now Selma? It's too much to think about. I just want to graduate," Jasmine grumbled in exasperation.

Marches and lobbies to end segregation were more frequent, in response to the Klan assaults. Local black residents adhered to a community-imposed curfew placing residents in their homes by nightfall. Many were willing to sacrifice personal freedoms for their lives. Fewer lynchings had been reported since the curfew.

"We've a few more months, then we'll receive our diplomas." Michael stood to full height, his chest puffed out in pride.

Ever since her return to school, she and Michael had been thrown together with their work in local civil rights leagues and fellowshipping with mutual friends. For days, he hadn't acknowledged her with anything more than a nod, but within the last week, he seemed to be his old self, with just a slight bit of edge. Elie decided it was best not to attempt another apology. She was sorry for her behavior, but forgiveness depended on Michael. All she could do was pray for their friendship.

In a recent letter, Eric offered to pray as well.

****

Eric drove slowly around the campus, not sure where the dormitories were, but keeping his eyes open for signs. He and Elie continued to correspond via letters, but his impatience won out. Desperate, he sought permission from her father to drive down to the school and bring her home for the weekend. Surprisingly, Emmett had agreed to his request. Perhaps his suggestion would induce Emmett and Jacqueline to reconsider allowing him to court their daughter. Or perhaps she had planned to stay at school this weekend, and her parents wanted her home for a visit. Either way, he'd see her and maybe convince her to broach the subject of courtship with her parents.

Before leaving home, he called Madeline Hoover's residence; however, Elie wasn't at her home. He'd stopped by Mrs. Hoover's earlier and she said Elie was meeting a few of her friends at the university library. She'd given him a knowing look, but not a judgmental one. At least someone approved of the idea of him and Elie.

Passing by a group of women near the post office, he asked for directions to the library. Some of the women giggled and blushed when he questioned whether they knew Elie. They gave him directions to the building, and also her dormitory if she wasn't at the first location. At a stop sign, Eric saw a flash of white in the rearview mirror. He adjusted the mirror. In the distance, several more white sheets ducked behind a structure.

He couldn't deny who they were.

After a sharp intake of breath, he accelerated. A sheet dodged in front of his car, forcing him to brake hard.

They would dare do this in broad daylight?

Ducking his head to find the position of the sun through his windshield, he squinted at the fading light. Fire would soon follow. A woman shrieked and he slammed the acceleration pedal into the floor of the vehicle.

His car whizzed by others, their drivers honking their horns, and people ran in every direction. The sounds of a police siren accompanied the distant screams and shouting. *I've got to get to the library.* One more corner and his destination came into view. Michael, Jasmine, and Elie stood on the grand steps, looking around in confusion as people dashed by them.

The car jerked to a stop, drawing the attention of the group. Eric jumped out of the car. Elie's eyes saucered, and she immediately descended toward him.

"What are you doing here?"

"Elie, we don't have time—"

"I think you'd better explain," she said, interrupting him firmly.

A man dressed in slacks and a buttoned-down shirt dashed up the steps, his face ashen despite his dark coloring. "Michael!" He gripped Michael by the arms, his breathing heavy. "Michael, members of the Klan are on campus!"

Michael's jaw dropped. "What?"

"Some people in sheets threw a few rocks into the windows of the west dormitory and set another part of it on fire. Can't you hear the sirens? The police are searching for them right now!" He struggled to regain his breath.

"It's true," Eric quickly confirmed. "I saw them myself near the post office." He took Elie's elbow. "I think we should get out of here, at least until we know it's safe."

The sirens drew nearer. A fire engine raced past them, their eyes following the vehicle until it rounded the corner and then they gazed upward. Smoke filled the red-orange sky.

"Was anyone hurt?" Michael asked.

The man shrugged. "Someone saw a couple of Klan members near the dormitories. One had a bottle with a lit fuse made of cloth. He threw it into a window at the dorm."

Another fire truck whizzed by, followed closely by an ambulance.

"Oh, no!" Jasmine covered her mouth with her hands, fear etched into her features.

"I'll go speak to campus security," Michael stated absent-mindedly, his eyes still on the smoke. "I'm student body president. I have to get as much information as I can."

Jasmine touched his arm, drawing his attention away from the smoke. "I'll go with you," she offered.

Michael stared at her for a few seconds before giving her a warm smile. "Thank you. My car is parked this way." He pointed down the road away from the confusion. They descended the stairs, stopping when they neared Elie. His eyes questioned whether or not she'd be safe.

"I'll take her to Mrs. Hoover's," Eric responded to the unspoken question. Michael nodded once, and then he and Jasmine hurried to his car. Elie allowed Eric to steer her to his car. He opened the front passenger door and helped her inside. After sliding behind the wheel, he revved the engine and drove off.

****

The sun plummeted as they made their way off campus. From her window, she saw crowds of people gathered. Women crying, others praying, and men clustered in groups, angrily gesturing. Elie could only imagine they were discussing what had happened, and hopefully not what they were going to do about it.

She cast a glimpse at Eric, taking in his firm jaw, his gaze focused on the road in front of him. She lightly touched his arm, and he turned toward her, a look of concern on his face.

"You all right?"

Elie nodded, her eyes searching his handsome face. Why had he come now, of all times? Her heart fluttered with excitement at the possibility of him coming for her, even if it was against her better judgment to see him. She swallowed a sigh. A trying night was ahead of her. She didn't doubt he wanted to discuss courtship, and she hadn't softened her parents to the idea because she didn't know how. The exhilaration of their last kiss flooded her thoughts and she closed her eyes, wanting to shut out the horrors of the world and know only the wonders of this man's love.

They drove into a familiar residential area, not far from Mrs. Hoover's estate. "Why did you come here?"

"Why do you think?"

Elie silently sat staring at the street in front of her, heart pounding hard in her chest, taking her breath away.

Eric angled his head toward her. "I came for you."

She met his eyes and a heated tremor rumbled through her at the sight of the intense love she read in his eyes.

Someone crossed the front of the car and Elie screamed, her hands going to her mouth. The car came to a screeching halt. Two hands slammed on to the hood of the car. Headlights illuminated the white of the sheet covering the person staring back at them. Eric leaned forward, squinting as he stared intently at the person he nearly ran down.

"Eric?"

"Those eyes…"

They shimmered wickedly at them before disappearing into the descending night.

A dart of fear struck her. Many black families lived in this community. Where one member of the Klan stalked, like roaches, more would follow. Elie closed her eyes, putting a few fingers on her temple, images of destruction piercing her head. *How long will this oppression last?* The car jerked forward, and her eyes flew open, scanning the neighborhood for more sheets.

"The sooner we get to Madeline's, the better I'll feel about your safety," he said grimly.

Elie's anger burned as hot as the flaming cross at Wimbly Baptist against the men who'd caused her and her family—her community—so much pain. "Eric, what are they doing here? What if they attack someone in their home?"

"Maybe they followed me…"

Her head snapped in his direction. Had she heard him correctly? He'd spoken so softly. "What do you mean *followed?*"

He closed his eyes briefly, breathing out a frustrated sigh. "I don't know, Elnora. They just seem to be everywhere now. If they know the names of all the black loan recipients, then they'd know who financed those loans. Which would lead them to…"

He trailed off again, his eyes widening. Elie swallowed, her throat dry. To someone they knew? Perhaps that person had already been attacked. She gripped his arm, squeezing. "Eric, who?"

As they continued to make their way through the community, a dark cloud rising upward in the distance drew her attention from Eric and his silence. Even in the night sky it shone gray, lit at the bottom by a strange orange hue.

"What is that?" Elie strained her eyes to make out the cloud as darkness enveloped them.

"Fire!"

Eric took a detour toward the smoke and was forced to stop the car. The neighborhood was in chaos. People were in the streets, women were wailing, children crying, men running past each other trying to make it to the houses on fire.

"My baby! My baby!" a woman cried out, the anguish in her sobs tearing through Eric's car. She sank onto the lawn of a house engulfed in flames. There was no chance of getting close to the house; the heat from the blaze was too great. Fire crackled as it burnt the home, side panels falling to the earth with a thud.

The nightmarish inferno continued to burn around a child. Part of the gutter separated from the roof and crashed to the ground, causing the people in the yard to jump back and the hysterical woman to wail even louder.

"Oh, Eric. That poor child—"

A gunshot rang out.

"Get down!" Eric covered Elie with his body.

More loud screams, and footsteps hitting the pavement. When Eric and Elie raised their heads to peer over the dashboard, a man flattened to the concrete. People scattered in all directions. Where had the shot come from? Children were swooped up into the arms of adults trying to get them to safety.

He lay there, still.

"Jonas! Jonas!"

A few men bent over him offering aid, and an elderly woman rushed forward but upon seeing who it was on the ground, raised her handkerchief to her mouth. She shook her head and then shrieked, "Nooo! Jonas!" Women came on either side to steady her as she shuddered violently.

Elie's breath caught in her lungs as waves of shock knocked into her. Her eyes began to swell with tears. *This can't be real!* Another shot fired and she jumped, this time letting out her own gasp of fear. Another fell to the ground.

Shotguns rang through the air. Men were fighting back, shooting into a tree line not far behind the burning house. In the distance, a man's cry could be heard, and Elie's heart leapt victoriously. She squeezed her eyes shut to his screams, twisting her head away. *I shouldn't feel glee, but I can't help it!*

"Are you okay?" Eric pulled her into his arms. She breathed in his spicy scent, it and the strength of his arms calming her frazzled spirit. "I'm gonna get us out of here. Stray bullets could hit us."

Loud sirens from behind signaled the coming of rescuers. Eric shifted the car into gear, moving out of the way of oncoming emergency vehicles. He continued down the road, right through the middle of the war zone. People helped their neighbors flee their burning homes, a gunshot victim's arm was being wrapped, and scores of people moaned in the streets.

Elie rested her head against the window and wrapped her arms around her stomach, while breathing a prayer for comfort, safety, and healing for those suffering. She uttered a special appeal for the woman whose child was lost in the fire.

A few minutes later, they turned in to the long driveway belonging to Mrs. Hoover. Her house was recessed a bit away from the main road, and almost hidden by a row of weeping willow trees. Tall marble pillars from the ground to the roof lined the front of the two-story house. Even in the night setting, the house glowed pristinely white, reminding Elie of an ancient Roman temple she saw once in a history book.

Eric slowed the car as it curved around the bend, stopping at the massive oak front doors. Elie staggered out of the vehicle. A cool breeze brushed across her skin, refreshing her tired spirit, and the rustling of the willows in the near distance abating her fears. They were miles from the screams—miles from danger. The doors opened and Peter, the lead housekeeper, greeted her, wrapping her in a secure embrace.

"Were you two at the university?" Peter asked as he ushered them into the house. "See what's happenin' there? Me and the missus been watchin' it on the tube." He didn't give them time to answer as he continued repeating reports of Klan sightings in the surrounding neighborhoods.

Madeline rushed through the French doors that enclosed the den, and immediately hugged Elie. "Oh, we thought you might have been hurt. Thank God you're safe." Madeline gave Eric a motherly hug and a swift kiss on his cheek. Taking both of their hands, she led them into the den. "Stella!" Moments later, a second housekeeper, a young woman with chocolate skin and tightly coiled hair, appeared in the doorway. "Please bring tea."

"Yes, ma'am. Dinner will be ready in a few minutes."

Teacup in hand, Elie relaxed against the cushions, allowing the hot liquid to calm her as the warmth massaged her throat. Its sweetness stirred a hunger in her belly for food. Eric sipped his tea, his focus on the news coverage of the fire at Selma University. He appeared to be grimacing, his jaw clenched. Elie touched his arm and they made eye contact. His playful wink settled a bit of her anxiety.

After spending an hour at the dinner table reliving the earlier events of the evening for Madeline, Eric and Elie settled back in the den with desserts in hand. The news coverage of the attacks continued, and Elie shook the fog from her head.

Listening to report after report of fire, destruction, and death was mind-numbing. Stella entered the room and announced a phone call from Morgan to Madeline. Madeline left to answer the phone.

Eric put a hand to his forehead, a sheepish grin on his face. "I was supposed to bring you home this evening. Your parents were going to join us for dinner, and my father is probably wondering where we are."

"My parents!" Elie's hands went to the sides of her face, shocked she'd forgotten about her mother and father. "I should have called. With everythin' that's happened…I better go ask Madeline if she could pass a word on to your father." She shot to her feet, thanked Stella as she passed, and left the room.

After spending a few minutes on the phone with her mother, she handed the receiver to Madeline, who continued her conversation with Morgan. Elie returned to the den, but stopped in the doorway.

Eric sat with his knees on his elbows, a large book in his hands. Elie tiptoed to the back of the couch, and peered over his shoulder. *He's reading the Bible!* Her heart stirred with thanksgiving, and she sent a silent prayer of praise heavenward.

They hadn't argued over his lack of faith in quite some time. He had come to the Christmas pageant, although she was sure his motive was to see her. Her mother had mentioned, according to Miss Hattie, he'd started attending Sunday morning services with his father. Elie bit her lip. None of what she witnessed was a ringing endorsement of Eric's change of heart, but she still hoped.

Madeline entered the room. "Your father is on the phone for you, Eric."

Eric sent her a pleasant grin. "Thank you." Closing the Bible, he stood, and with a swift kiss to Elie's forehead, he exited the room.

Madeline joined Elie on the couch. A sigh filled with happiness distracted Elie from the Bible in her hand. "You're blushin', Mrs. Hoover, and I wonder what the cause could be." She gave her a mischievous grin. Madeline's skin seemed even paler as the backdrop to the strawberry color in her cheeks. "Why, your face matches your hair."

The two shared a laugh. "His father, of course." Her eyes went to the door where Eric had exited. "I'm so pleased Eric doesn't see me as a threat. Morgan told me Eric's heart has never quite healed from his mother's death, and I don't want him to feel as if I'm trying to replace her," she murmured.

Elie took hold of her hand. "I know Eric very well, and I can see his heart is already warmin' to you. He'd love it if you were his step-mother," Elie offered, biting her lip to hold in a laugh. A snort escaped. Madeline feigned a disapproving frown and playfully slapped Elie's arm.

"Don't you start—there's been no talk of that."

Elie giggled, her heart light for the first time since leaving campus.

Fanning her cheeks, Madeline stood. "I'm going to take a long bubble bath. If you need anything, call for Stella. She's too afraid of traveling home tonight so she'll be spending it with us."

"Have a good night." Madeline disappeared and Elie turned to see Eric standing at the other door, his smoldering stare causing her nerves to tingle. She swallowed.

He joined her on the couch. "I apologized to your father for not returning with you this evening."

Elie edged closer, her hand resting lightly on his arm. "It wasn't your fault. How could you have known what was going to happen?" Eric cupped her cheek, his green eyes flickering specks of gold brought out by the crackling fire in the hearth. His gaze, first on her eyes, moved decidedly to her lips. Elie wet them, her heart thumping in her chest.

"I know. I just want him to trust me with you." He met

her eyes again. "I don't want anything to happen to you." His brows angled up, his lips in an ironic twist. "Your father would kill me if something *did* happen to you on my watch."

Elie smiled, but happiness eluded her. Would her parents ever accept the one thing he couldn't change? She watched her fingertips trail down his arm. Goosebumps appeared and she lightly fingered their impressions. "I'm givin' you goose bumps."

"You said you loved me and you didn't give me a chance to respond," he said hoarsely. His other hand moved to her opposite cheek.

Elie's gaze locked with eyes flaming with desire, igniting a blaze in her heart. The air between them hummed in anticipation of what she'd been dreaming of since she had left him alone on the veranda at Christmas.

Something drew her gaze over his shoulder, and she saw the open Bible resting on the sofa's armrest. Clearing her throat, she slipped out of his hold and moved to retrieve the Bible. "Um, what were you readin' when I was on the phone?" She caught his half-grin of understanding. He didn't press the issue. Instead, he motioned for her to come back and sit on the couch. As she settled beside him, he took the book from her hand, focusing his stare at the words on the page.

"Psalm twenty-five. *Do not remember the sins of my youth or my transgressions...Turn to me and be gracious to me, for I am afflicted. The troubles of my heart are enlarged; bring me out of my distress.*" He glanced at her with a look of nervousness. "Father told me he's quoted these words often when he's been distressed."

Elie snuggled close, resting her head on his shoulder. She studied the words of the psalm. "Have they helped you?"

"Nothing I've tried on my own has made any beneficial impact on my life. Not hours and hours of work, not endless travel, not laziness." Dangerous dimples tunneled into a strong square jaw, his smile rueful. "Not women."

Tears spilled onto her cheeks, and she quickly wiped them away.

"That night in the church, during the pageant? Those people could've given up their faith, blamed God, but they didn't." She heard him choke on his emotion. "They had the courage to stay true. What do I know of bravery? I've been a coward. I ran."

Elie took his face in her hands. "But you're not runnin' anymore."

He shook his head. Eyes red, but being a man of strength, he refused to let the teardrops fall. She couldn't help but smile at his efforts. His heart was important, not his tears. The sincerity in his eyes erased all her doubts.

Eric let out a slow breath, a pensive look on his face as he focused on something on the rug nearby. "Elie, I'm still wrestling with myself—still unsure if I can fully trust God, but I know this…I love you."

She trembled, the blood from her thudding heart sending delicious warmth throughout her body. He reached for her hands and threaded their fingers. Heart fluttering, she gasped at the sensation and the heat he brought. But did he truly mean the words? Elie was speechless, but not disappointed. She could hardly contain her joy.

"I know I have no right to ask this of you."

Elie stiffened. What would he ask? About the courtship? Only time and prayer could change her parents' hearts… maybe.

"Will you wait for me? Just a little longer," he hastened to add, hope flickering in his eyes.

Wait for me. To thrilled to speak, she nodded.

Eric laughed away the tension. "Despite my efforts to stay away, to not feel."

She dipped her head bashfully, remembering her vain attempts to put distance between them. Somehow they were always thrown together and each time their feelings for each other threatened to overtake them.

Tears pooled, yet she grinned widely. "I can't pretend that I don't feel, that I can *not* love you. Because I do, and because I believe this can be right, I'll wait—" The words were barely out of her mouth, and his lips were on hers, soft and gentle. The kiss was brief, and Eric slid back, creating a respectable space.

"I'm taking you home tomorrow."

She didn't argue.

"I should probably convince Madeline to join us." He looked toward the French doors, where they had last seen her. "I'm sure my father would appreciate the surprise." He grinned knowingly.

Elie laughed.

Hand in hand, Eric walked Elie to her room and, in the most gentlemanly manner, he said goodnight, yet his eyes revealed a desire to linger until morning.

Elie stifled a nervous laugh, her neck and cheeks hot. Grinning at the pronounced look of resignation on his face, she said goodnight and slowly closed the door.

****

Despite his urgings, Madeline refused Eric's pleas to leave her home and join him and Elie back in Freeman. She wanted to be in Selma to assist the local churches and the university. Early news reported two black men confirmed dead, several wounded, one house destroyed by fire, and several crosses burned on the lawns of residents in parts of Selma's residential districts.

A small boy had also died in a house fire.

After he settled Elie in the car, Eric stood near the driver's door and gazed intently at Madeline as she asked Peter to make inquiries in town about the people who needed aid so she could make a contribution.

Eric rubbed at the pain in his temple. *If they knew who received the loans, then why not the lenders?* Madeline wasn't his mother, yet he couldn't stand the thought of her on the receiving end of such violence, especially if his father planned to marry her. The image of Elie, tied to a tree, at the mercy of her three attackers haunted him too many times; he considered what would have happened had he not intervened. The look of defeat on her face was etched into his mind and were it not for knowing she was alive, and by his side, he'd have gone mad at the memory.

Madeline's face was crinkled with concern. Eric tilted his head to the side as he continued to stare. Catching his stare, she offered him a faint, sad smile. She came around the front of the car to face him. Another plea for her to leave would fall on deaf ears so he remained silent. She had a stubborn streak as wide as Elie's. His lips ticked upward. He and his father were suckers for obstinate women. Madeline stood on her tiptoes and gently kissed his cheek, and then rested her own cheek against his. He gripped her shoulders, holding her to him.

"Goodbye, son," she murmured in his ear. "Hurry now, and remember to take the back road. It may be longer, but at least you'll avoid most of the city."

Eric released her reluctantly, and he slid into the vehicle.

"Tell your father I'm all right, and I'll send news of anything I know."

"Goodbye, Mrs. Hoover," Elie called out.

"Goodbye, dear. Tell your parents hello for me."

Elie smiled. "I will. And thank you for the hospitality."

Madeline quickly rounded the front of the car to stand at the entryway. "Anytime, you know that. Call me when you arrive."

"We will." Elie waved goodbye as the car moved away.

Madeline raised her hand in farewell.

****

Madeline collapsed on the couch in her den, exhausted. She'd spent the day traveling around the city, talking to the neighbors of victims, offering support and supplies to local churches, and visiting the injured at the local hospital. Morgan's agitation over the attacks moved her to empathize with his pain. He was deeply concerned for the residents of Selma being on the receiving end of the McDougal hatred, and she compiled a list of names and residences she intended to pass to him. Madeline sighed, her head falling back against the couch, the back of her hand shielding her eyes from the light of the end table lamp.

The rich aroma of beef roast floated from the kitchen, and her stomach rumbled in reply. She smiled at the thought of relaxing on a full stomach. After the heartache she'd witnessed today, a recess for her drained spirit was just what she needed.

"Mrs. Hoover!"

Madeline jumped, startled. "Peter?" She ran toward the front door, where she'd parked her car, and where Peter had gotten in to drive it to the back garage. She opened the door with a rush, and her heart clenched in fear.

Darkness had descended upon Selma moments after she'd returned home. City leadership had imposed a strict curfew at sunset. But at the edge of her lawn stood a row of white hoods with flaming torches in their hands.

Oh no!

Putting a hand to her throat, she searched for her voice. The white line parted, and two others carrying a large piece of wood came forward. They propped up the wood, and another hood with a torch moved to stand beside the cross. He lowered the torch, and in an instant the flame grew into a blaze. The cross lit, Madeline's ears were filled with the shouts of the trespassers.

They know...

"Stella!" Madeline called the housekeeper's name as Peter drove around the corner and stopped abruptly in front of her, spraying gravel and dust into the air. She turned and nearly ran into the housekeeper, who had a worried look on her face and a gravy spoon in her hand.

"Mrs. Hoover!" Peter yelled from the car.

My purse! No time to grab anything else, Madeline ran back into the house, the yells from the Klan members closing in as she snatched her purse off the foyer table. Clutching the outside pocket in her dress and still feeling the paper with the list of names of those victimized in last night's attacks, she rushed back to the car.

The hooded warriors advanced.

Stella was already settled in the back seat, but she squirmed restlessly and yelped out in fear, her eyes transfixed on the flames closing in.

With no time to secure the house, Madeline flew out the front door, and dove into the vehicle. Instantly, Peter was off. Gravel flew several feet high as he skidded around on the driveway, the accelerator pressed to the extreme. Madeline pulled her legs in and shut the door, despite the opposing physical forces working against her own strength. She screamed as hands from the hoods descended upon the car, pounding against her window, trying to block the passage of the vehicle. One figure jumped on top of the hood of the car and swayed from side to side as Peter drove toward the main road. Stella cried hysterically and Madeline shut her eyes, unable to witness what would happen next.

"Hold on!" Peter said through gritted teeth.

Madeline's eyes flew open and she clutched her seat. Peter jerked the car's steering wheel from left to right and the car responded, veering on and off the pathway. The person on the hood cried out as he flew off the car, tumbling onto the lawn.

Madeline gasped in relief and then bounced, her hands

going to the roof of the car, as it flew off the gravel driveway and onto the smooth pavement. Needing one last glimpse of home, she rotated in her seat. Hoods entered her front door while others stood along the end of the driveway. *Thank you, Lord; we made it out alive!* Back pressed firmly against her seat, her breathing came in ragged gasps, her order faint. "Head to Morgan Montgomery's."

Chapter Eighteen

HEALING

Madeline relayed the horrifying events of what had happened earlier that evening to a captivated audience. Her, Peter, and Stella's encounter with the Klan at the Hoover estate convinced both Eric and his father that anyone involved in the financing of blacks and their families would eventually be victims of Klan retaliation.

Eric glanced at his father several times throughout Madeline's account. Standing near a bookcase, skin reddening by the minute, his face glowered with rage, his fists white. Eric tried subduing his own emotions, seeing his father had enough righteous anger for the both of them, but he understood the fury undoubtedly coursing through his father's veins. Shane McDougal was in his sights the night Elie hung by her tiny wrists, and ever since, he'd asked himself too many times why he didn't just shoot.

Madeline often dabbed tears from her eyes while retelling the stories of the victims she'd visited earlier in the day. "How did we come to this?" she murmured, staring off into some unknown distance.

Stella cried softly in a corner of the room. Elie moved to her side, wrapping her arms around the young woman's trembling body and whispering softly in her ear.

Turning away from Madeline, Morgan slammed a fist on the bookshelf. Eric shifted his gaze to Elie again. Emmett was nearby, watching him with keen interest. Not intimidated, Eric held the man's gaze. Would Elie's parents ever allow her to be safe with him?

Mark Greene entered the room with a clearing of his throat. "Excuse me. Forgive me, Morgan, for coming over unannounced."

Morgan immediately went to his friend with his hand extended. "Not at all, Mark. Please, come in." He gestured toward an empty chair near the door.

Mark's gaze took in the room. "I was wondering if any of you saw the late news on television?"

All of them exchanged curious glances and a few shook their heads.

"We've been a little preoccupied with other matters at present," Morgan explained.

"Well, um…perhaps you'd better see for yourself."

Morgan paused, his eyes narrowing on Mark. He rushed from the room toward the den, with the others close at his heels. Morgan hurried over to the television and, turning the dial, he clicked to a familiar news program.

Madeline gasped, her hands covering her mouth as she saw the flames.

The Hoover estate was on fire.

Morgan was at her side the second she turned away and held her to him as she buried her face in his chest.

> *"It is unclear if Mrs. Hoover or anyone else was in the house at the time of the fire. Witnesses claim seeing Ku Klux Klan members driving away from the general area and authorities believe they may have been involved. The*

Klan was also seen earlier on the campus of the University of Selma, the site of an arson attack, and the organization is being blamed for the deaths of several residents as well as the cross burnings that occurred yesterday evening."

Facing the television screen, Madeline watched as the fire faded into another news story concerning local sanitation. Her eyes came to Morgan's. He tightened his hold around her and she managed a weak smile. "Even if I've lost everything, I have my life. I *know* God is not finished with me."

"Then perhaps," he murmured, placing a finger beneath her chin, and drawing her closer, "the Lord has plans for you to move soon."

And as if their audience had melted away in the fires at her home, Madeline closed her eyes and parted her lips, receiving his kiss.

****

The early glow of sunrise poured onto the veranda, brightening Eric's mood as the chance at a good night's sleep was lost hours before. His predicament with Elie took a front-row seat in the myriad problems he faced. Only two things cheered him this glorious late Alabama winter morning if ever he saw one: the strong brew of the hot coffee he was sipping, and God.

The scent of buttery biscuits assaulted his nostrils, stirring his stomach into a ravenous hunger. His father joined him on the veranda, coffee mug in hand, mouth full of biscuit.

"Dad, everywhere I look, I see Him," Eric whispered, his voice cracking.

Setting his cup down on a table, Morgan laid a hand on his son's shoulder.

"In a sunrise, in a sunset…even in the heat and fire of the Klan torches." Eric chuckled and glanced at his father out of the corner of his eye. "Mrs. Hoover's house burns down, and last night she sits on the couch with a smile on her face."

"Ah, yes, well, I'm not sure God can take credit for *that*."

They laughed heartily, and then Eric turned serious once again. "I must seem pretty selfish and pathetic to you…and to God."

His father's hands were firm on his shoulders. "There's nothing wrong with feeling pain and grief over the loss of a loved one. But this life is bigger than Evelyn passing away, than our grief, and even those who've struggled and given their lives in the fight against segregation. We might not know why things are the way they are, or why people leave us before we're ready for them to, but we know this: God is always there, eager for our trust." Morgan laid a hand on his son's cheek.

Eyes wet with tears, Eric nodded his head in agreement.

Morgan's lips wavered in a melancholy smile as his hands gripped Eric's arms, pulling him into a fierce hug. When he released him, he blinked away the moisture filling his own eyes. "You'll have to forgive me, son. I neglected you after your mother died. I should have given you more support and instead, I chose to work through my grief—our grief—alone."

Eric shook his head. "No, Dad. I used to blame you, but I don't anymore. I think I understand now." His eyes caught a glimpse of Elie entering through the kitchen's back door. "Had I lost someone I loved, I might have shut everyone out as well. In fact, I know I would because I already did that once."

"I pray that it will be a long time until you have to face the prospect of losing another loved one."

Eric groaned in frustration, and he stomped to the nearest chair and shoved it with his boot. He raked both hands through his hair and then latched them to the wood of the ledge. "Emmett and Jacqueline don't approve of me because I'm white." His father's silence left Eric wondering whether the man had heard him. Looking over his shoulder, he saw his father grimace, the worry lines between his brows deepening.

"I wasn't aware they felt this way about us."

"That I'm not good enough for their daughter?"

"No." The sadness in Morgan's eyes tore at Eric's heart. "That she isn't good enough for you."

Eric blinked in shock. *Not good enough for me?*

"Emmett should know better—should know he's more than an employee of mine. He's my best friend," Morgan muttered in disappointment as he joined Eric at the railing. "No doubt the two of you will face some extreme prejudice wherever you live if you choose not to live here. But if you did stay in Freeman, our families are well-known and I'm sure, in time, your union would know some peace."

"If we're ever united," Eric grumbled.

"I could talk to them, if you want."

Shaking his head, Eric raised his hand to halt Morgan's level of involvement. "No, thanks. The real issue is my heart. They don't know how I've changed."

"Oh, I think they have an idea."

Eric raised his brows at his father's insinuation. He glanced over to the kitchen door. Did Elie know her parents had changed their minds?

****

"Miss Hattie, I understand your position. My parents take the same one."

Hands on broad hips, Miss Hattie raised a haughty chin.

Not to be outdone, Elie lifted her own. "But you won't convince me to give him up. I *love* him!"

Miss Hattie's dark skin glistened with perspiration, either from the heat of the kitchen, or the exertion she expended disapproving of Elie's choice. Her wide nostrils flared, her inky eyes coolly dismissing her. "You're a foolish child." Back to Elie, she returned to knead spices into the steak meat.

Elie blinked back tears of frustration and anger. Before she could stop the words, they flew from her mouth with vehemence. "You have no right to interfere, Miss Hattie."

She whirled. "No right? You ain't got no right to him! I've never approved you workin' here, and I told your parents so—actin' as if you was equal to them. But Emmett and Jackie could never say 'no' to you. They never let you see the world for what it is. Now you've gone and gotten a high-and-mighty attitude, thinkin' you deserve yourself a white man. 'Bout time your parents set you straight."

Elie's head jerked back as if she were slapped. Her jaw dropped. She *did* deserve to be treated as an equal. She *did* deserve to love whomever she wanted to love, be it a black or white man. And she had her taste of the world at last year's march—the brutality of prejudice, the hatred brewed out of a difference of opinion. "That isn't fair." Her voice shook. "I wasn't born a slave, and I *refuse* that mentality."

Miss Hattie sucked in a breath and her skin took on a lighter pallor.

A lone tear slid down the older woman's cheek. For the first time in all her life, Elie watched indomitable Miss Hattie cry in pain. The sight stung Elie's conscience and she broke down. "Oh, Miss Hattie," she sobbed, "I'm sorry." She sniffed and wiped the tears from her own cheeks.

Miss Hattie hobbled over, her thick arms suffocating Elie in a fierce hug. "You is young, child. I won't be bearin' no grudge against you." Her tone was low but hard. She dropped her arms and struck Elie with a look of righteous defiance. "I ain't no slave—I just know my place." She nodded her head in a matter-of-fact way before moving to prepare the meat for the Montgomery's dinner.

Elie drew in a ragged breath. She hadn't the strength to even move and comfort the woman. First Michael and now Miss Hattie. *I've hurt her.* It would take time to heal the wound.

"Miss Hattie, are those brownies I smell?" Eric came

through the kitchen doors but stopped short seeing Elie. His eyes filled with concern as his gaze volleyed from the back of Miss Hattie, who didn't bother to acknowledge him, to Elie.

Neither of them moved.

Miss Hattie cleared her throat, but still kept her back to the pair. "As I was tellin' Miss Elie here, those brownies are for lunch. So, I best not be catchin' you in here tryin' to sneak one."

Elie jumped at the sound of meat being pounded.

She looked to Eric for help. If she didn't leave the kitchen now, in a minute she would be on the floor, a quivering mess, groveling at Miss Hattie's feet. That action would be too undignified, even toward the old woman. Eric gave the cook a quick look and then came forward. He took Elie's hand and pulled her out of the kitchen.

"What's the matter? Did you two fight?" he asked, leaning in close to her ear.

"Miss Hattie told me how she felt 'bout us. And I…I was so mean to her." She gripped Eric's arm, and he wrapped it around her waist, allowing her to hide her face in his chest. His hand stroked her hair, his lips brushing her temple.

Elie allowed herself to be led by him into the front room. He closed the door behind them. She walked to the window, the warmth from the sunlight creating a cocoon of comfort around her.

"Miss Hattie loves you like a daughter. I'm sure whatever you said, she'll forgive."

Elie nodded, believing that to be true. Her eyes strayed to where he stood. The light streaming in from the lace curtains created a soft halo around his blond hair. Lips parted and brows knitted, she noticed he kept near the door, searching her face.

He let out a nervous chuckle and then his eyes sparked with renewed courage. "Hello, Elie."

She suddenly felt *very* warm. "Hello, Eric," she responded

softly.

In two strides, he closed the gap between them and took her hands into his own. "It's over, Elie."

"It's...over?" A dart of fear pierced her at the thought she could lose more than his friendship but also his love. What had happened between last night and this morning?

"All the anger, the stubbornness, the refusal to admit I was wrong." His buoyant mood shone bright in his eyes. "I've renewed my commitment to Him, Elie."

Elie's eyes widened with surprise, yet she couldn't help the doubtful crease of her brows.

Eric let out a laugh. "Ask my father if you don't believe me."

Joy and freedom was in his laugh. She shook her head and smiled. "I don't need to ask him." Taking his face in her palms, she said, "I can see it in your eyes, and hear it in your voice." Warmth from his hands traveled up her arms and surrounded her ballooning heart, ready to burst with joy. She crossed her forearms to hold his hands, squeezing them.

A twinge of doubt cut short the soaring flight of her heart. Her parents would be thrilled at the news, but their minds remained steadfast: Elie didn't belong with a white man. She continued to smile in spite of her growing disappointment. Somehow she and Eric would be together.

He leaned over to kiss her forehead, allowing his lips to briefly linger.

"I have to go. I need to pull my father away from his lady and discuss what we are going to do about this loaning business. People can't keep getting hurt because of us. See you at lunch?"

Elie nodded, not trusting herself to speak. Her desire for him was growing exponentially, and she wanted to shout how much she loved him. How would she ever be able to stand loving him from afar?

He reached for her hands and drew her against him. A

single thumb stroked the curve of her jaw. "I know. I want to run to your parents and get their consent." His lips brushed against hers gently, his touch reassuring her. "We'll let God work it out."

As he released her and turned to go, she gazed again out the window, trying to focus her energy on the day's tasks and not the pain of their separation. A multitude of errands had to be done. *Organize. I've got to organize—*

She gasped as hands pulled and pressed her body until it was enveloped in scorching heat. Breathing eluded her as she received the most thorough kiss of her life. Holding her head in his hands, Eric gave her an off-center grin. "That's to hold me over while we wait for your parents' permission." One final press of his lips to hers, he winked and was out the door.

Great. Now how am I supposed to concentrate on my work!

Chapter Nineteen

TESTING

At Peter's announcement that he had a visitor, a woman who'd asked specifically for him, Eric opened the front door and halted, one foot on the porch, and one inside the house. Standing near the edge of the steps Amanda faced him, a distraught look filled with fear and—dread?—in her face. She rocked from side to side, wringing her hands. At times she glanced over her shoulder, and all before he had a chance to greet her.

"Amanda?"

She offered him a small, shaky smile. "Hello, Mr. Montgomery."

Eric's eyebrows furrowed at the formal greeting. "Are you all right? What's wrong? Please, come inside." He reached out to take her arm and gestured toward the door but looking at his hand, she shook her head and backed away, nearly tumbling down the steps until she grasped at the closest column to steady herself.

Again, she shot an anxious look over her shoulder. Eric

followed her gaze. "Are you expecting someone?"

"I, um..." She raked an unsteady hand through her disheveled hair. "No, I don't think so," she mumbled.

Eric put his hands in his pants pockets and waited.

"Mr. Montgomery, I have a confession I need to make."

The hair on his neck stood up. Whatever Amanda had to say, it was serious enough for her to continue to address him formally...and fidget.

"It was me."

"What?"

"It was me," she said a decibel louder. Amanda bit her lip. "The black people who've been attacked by the Klan? Those who have loans with your bank? I took their names and addresses."

Eric was fully alert. "And gave them to who?" He tried to calm his rising blood pressure as images of fires, burning crosses, and the defeated looks of residents and shop owners flashed before his mind.

Amanda swallowed, her voice barely audible. "Chase McDougal."

Even though Eric had guessed Chase was behind the attacks since the assault on the bank, hearing the name out loud was still a blow to his stomach. A full minute passed before he spoke. "And those in Selma?"

Amanda nodded, tears spilling over.

"Mrs. Hoover's estate?" he breathed.

Amanda's eyes closed. "Yes," she choked out.

Eric blasted a sound of aggravation, turning around, hands grinding into his hips.

"Chase told me they'd something special planned for her."

Eric pivoted toward her.

"Is, um...is she okay?" she asked meekly.

Eric looked at her evenly.

Shrinking back at his glare, Amanda put shaky hands to

her cheeks and gave a small cry.

"She's fine. She was able to get away before they set fire to the house."

Amanda nodded. She wiped the tears from her face and again cast her gaze out toward the street.

"Amanda, do you have *any* idea what you've done?"

The tears flowed. "I know. I'm sorry—please. They threatened my family!"

At the moment, he didn't care whether she'd acted alone. "And how many families are without homes, wives without husbands, families without livelihoods!"

Amanda trembled. "Chase, he...he made me do it. I didn't have a choice!"

"Amanda, people have *died.* Do you understand that?" His voice was stern, her tears not eliciting an ounce of sympathy. "You should have said something."

"Is everything all right out here?" Morgan walked onto the porch, followed by Mark Greene.

Eric took a few steps away from the house. He didn't want to relay the news to his father. It was Amanda's responsibility. He heard her clear her throat and with a tremor in her voice, she repeated her confession.

The expression on Morgan's face was grave. Mark gaped.

A loud engine approached, drawing the gazes of all four to the edge of the front lawn. A red truck came rapidly toward the estate's entryway. It missed the gravel driveway and ran front-end into one of the trees hugging the edge of the lawn.

The men sprinted toward the truck, but halfway there they slowed. Chase tumbled out of the driver's seat and made his way around the back end.

"You shouldn't be moving, son," Mark said.

A trail of blood snaked from Chase's hairline to his neck. He whipped the revolver up and pointed it at Mark. "You don't say nuttin'!"

Eric's muscles tensed. The sounds of footsteps behind

him caused his heart to stop. Over his shoulder, Amanda came running with Elie and Madeline on her heels. If the gun went off…

Morgan held a hand out for Mark to move back, and he complied. Chase stumbled, but managed to keep the gun aimed at them.

"So you are here!" Chase acknowledged Amanda. "I didn't think you'd tell 'em." He chuckled and nearly tipped over. "Guess I was wrong," he sneered.

"Chase, please."

"Yeah, beg, honey. You know how I love it when you beg." He laughed, and then coughed violently. Eric glanced sideways at Amanda, who hid her eyes from him.

"Chase, you need to see a doctor." Morgan stepped forward.

He raised the gun to aim at Morgan's chest. "Don't!"

Eric slid an arm in front of his father's waist to drag him back, but Morgan pushed it behind him. His father's voice remained calm and steady. "Chase, you're injured—it might be very serious. Allow us to at least call a doctor, and a tow truck for your car. Whatever the cost, I'll be happy to pay for it."

"Do you think I need handouts from you? The great Morgan Montgomery. My daddy is the *mayor*!"

They stood silent.

"Did she tell you?"

Amanda moved to stand beside Morgan. "I did. They know everythin', Chase. Please, don't make things any worse."

Chase laughed and pointed the weapon at her. "Worse? How can it get any worse?"

"Now, hold on, son," Morgan intervened.

"You li'l slut. Don't you know I did this for you? For us? For the white race!"

Amanda swallowed, her eyes on the gun.

"Who is Eric Montgomery?" he taunted. "Just some

banker's son who came runnin' home to Daddy when he couldn't cut it in Europe. Actin' all high-and-mighty." He sauntered forward. "He ain't the manner of man to please you." Eyes leering, he chuckled. "And I know it, don't I?"

Eric held his tongue. If Chase had made that erroneous insinuation months ago, he'd beat Chase to a pulp for it—and the previous insult. A drunk and highly unstable Chase wasn't worth the effort. If provoked further, he'd fire the gun and someone Eric loved would be hurt in the process.

Amanda flamed. "Chase, you're upset. Please calm down. Let Mr. Montgomery take you to the hospital."

"You had no right." He scratched his head with the gun. Blood smeared across his forehead. "No right!" With a shaky hand, he raised the gun again. He closed one eye, zeroing in on Amanda. "No right."

A blast of smoke from the gun clouded the air.

****

Eric breathed hard, jogging alongside the gurney as the doctors wheeled Morgan toward the surgery room. Nurses loudly voiced Morgan's vitals as doctors responded with instructions for surgery. His father remained still, having lost consciousness soon after the bullet struck him in the chest.

Morgan moaned and his eyelids fluttered. He tried to lift an arm, his hand reaching into space. Eric grasped it. "You're going to be okay, Dad."

"Eric..." Morgan called out weakly.

"Please, sir, you can't go any further." A nurse put a restraining hand on Eric's arm.

"But—"

"I'm sorry, sir; you *must* wait out here." The nurse disappeared with his father through the swinging doors marked Authorized Personnel Only.

With a heavy heart, Eric trudged to the family lounge

where Elie, her parents, Mark, Amanda, and Madeline were already waiting. Elie rushed forward and took his arm, guiding him to a seat where he sat, head in his hands. Why was this happening now? Was this a test? Did God want him to prove his faith by having him watch his father die? Eric groaned. Nothing made any sense.

It all came back to him in a daze. Chase had aimed for Amanda, but his hand shook so badly he missed, and hit his father instead. On impact, Morgan inhaled deeply and looked down as a red spot grew on the left side of his chest. He turned, giving Eric one last look before sinking to the ground.

Madeline shrieked Morgan's name as Eric rushed to his father's side and placed his hand over the wound. In an instant, Madeline fell to the ground beside Morgan and with tears streaming down her face, she steadily spoke words of love and encouragement. Elie ran to the house, calling for Peter to help bring the family car around. Chase trembled violently, the gun slipping from his fingers. Taking the opportunity, Mark secured the weapon as Chase dropped to the ground. His eyes seemed trained on the blood, the whites surrounding his pupils expanding as he repeated over and over, "What did I do?" He glanced around him, blinking rapidly as if disoriented and for the first time recognizing where he was.

All the anger Eric had for Chase had dissipated in that one moment. Nothing was more important to Eric now than his father. As they waited for news from the doctors on Morgan's condition, police questioned all those present during the shooting except Eric, opting to wait until the chaos surrounding Morgan's care had died down. Mark demanded to know what had become of Chase. The police assured him Chase had been taken into custody.

The minutes on the clock ticked by at an excruciatingly slow pace. Morgan had been in surgery for over an hour. No nurses came to report on his progress, yet Eric held out hope.

Thirty minutes later, the door to the patient waiting area opened, and a doctor in scrubs walked through. "The Montgomery family?"

Fingers entwined with Elie's, Eric surged to his feet. "I'm his son," he let out in breathless anticipation.

The doctor rubbed the bridge between his eyes. "Your father is alive."

A collective sigh of relief came from the group.

"The surgery was rather difficult. The bullet bounced around a few ribs on his left side, taking out a chunk of his lung and nicking an artery. I found it lodged just behind the skin of his back."

No one breathed.

"The next few hours will be critical. He's lost a lot of blood and is on a ventilator. If he shows any improvement in the next day or two, then I believe he'll recover. However, I won't lie to you. His wound was extensive and there is the chance he won't..."

Fear snaked its cold fingers around Eric's heart and squeezed. Elie's palm pressed firmly against his, and he drew strength from her nearness. He swallowed, finding his voice. "Can I see him?"

The doctor nodded. "No more than two people at a time, please."

Elie loosened her fingers, but Eric didn't release her hand. "Perhaps Mrs. Hoover—"

"I can wait, dear." Eric eyed the woman he was sure would be his future step-mother—if his father lived. Her gaze was pinned to the couple's clutched fingers. She raised smiling eyes. "Go ahead." Eric was grateful she sensed his need to have Elie by his side.

They paused at the doorway of the recovery room. Morgan lay unconscious beneath white sheets, tubes protruding from his nose and arms. A ventilator droned softly in the corner, parts of the machine moving up and down, providing air to Morgan's damaged lung.

Eric was at his father's side, taking hold of his limp hand while Elie walked around the other side of the bed to grasp Morgan's other hand. She stroked his damp hair, and fingered his arm. "He's cold," she whispered, her voice trembling.

Eric leaned forward, placing a gentle kiss on his father's forehead. "I'm here, Dad, and I'm trusting God that you will heal. You don't need to worry about me." A chuckle followed his whisper. "But, if you see the light, don't go to it."

After everyone had an opportunity to visit with Morgan, they gathered in the patient waiting area where Eric led them in a prayer. Upon ending the prayer, he opened his eyes and found Emmett staring at him again, his brows furrowed. Jacqueline offered him a kind smile, her cheeks wet with tears.

Eric was by his father's side throughout the next week. There were moments he stared at his father's still form and seeds of doubt about his recovery festered in his mind. Many times he came close to giving in to doubt, wondering whether he'd made a mistake about giving his heart and trust to God. *Is this what happens when you turn to God?* Over and over, his mind would ask the question. He relied on the only other man he could trust would provide him the counseling he needed to remain committed to his faith.

Emmett visited the hospital frequently, either early in the morning or late at night, whenever Eric's heart was in crisis. Both scoured the Bible together, reciting words of hope and praying for a strengthening of their faith in God's power, and healing for Morgan.

Chapter Twenty

VENGEANCE IS MINE

The next weekend, Elie returned home, eager to see Morgan. After a week in the hospital, he opened his eyes, and his recovery moved at a rapid pace. He was sitting up and speaking, although still confined to a hospital bed. She and Madeline sat in chairs near his bed. Morgan spoke a few words of gratitude for the visit, but soon drifted off to sleep.

Elie took in Madeline's overall appearance and hid a grimace. A youthful woman in her late thirties, she seemed to have aged ten years. Usually an immaculately dressed woman of fortune, she now wore a simple high-necked cotton dress, and let her flaming hair hang in loose disheveled curls. Elie could see many sleepless nights in her eyes.

Madeline smiled sweetly when Elie asked whether there was anything she could do for her, but Madeline said she was on her way back to the Montgomery estate to sleep a few hours. She offered Elie a ride but the younger woman politely refused, having plans to visit Eric, who had decided to put in a few extra weekend hours at the bank.

Elie hurried her steps to the Montgomery Bank. It was a cool Saturday, the clouds blocking the warm sun. Wind blew through her thick wavy hair, causing a shiver. She snuggled her hands deep in her jacket pockets and wished she'd worn thicker socks.

As she passed a newspaper stand, a headline caught her eye. Chase McDougal was front-page news. Eric had written her, saying the Federal Bureau of Investigation had taken control of the investigation of Morgan's shooting within hours of him being shot. Not wanting justice to slip through their fingers, Mark had contacted the FBI, and the rumor was Governor Wallace had directed the bureau to control the investigation, hoping to keep the focus only on the shooting, and not the activities of the Klan. Chase's arrest did little to soften tensions in the city. Even though Klan activities had ceased, black-owned businesses still closed before sunset, armed men stood outside churches to protect services during the day and at night, and no one walked the rural outskirts alone.

"Ray, don't do this! Two wrongs don't make no right!"

"I knows what I'm doin.' They come and they take away. It's about time someone took some'um from dem."

Elie's eyebrows came together as she walked upon the disturbing scene. Ahead of her, a middle-aged black man and a barber stood in front of a barbershop. She slowed her pace. The man she assumed was named Ray looked agitated, clutching his dark jacket, torn and ragged at the ends, around his deep brown trousers held up with black suspenders over a soiled white shirt. Days' old stubble lined his chin and crept up the sides of his cheeks. Before she even reached the pair, her nose wrinkled; Ray hadn't showered in days.

"Please, Ray," the barber pleaded.

"I can't. I gotta do what I come to do. I can't turn back now."

"Ray!"

"Bernie…if my wife wakes up…tell her I love her?"

The barber extended a hand out to Ray but he backed away from it. He rubbed the back of his uncombed head, still looking at the hand of his friend. The barber let his arm drop, seeing Ray hurry across the street. Shoulders slumping, the barber's eyes followed the man who was on some personal mission that couldn't be deterred.

Elie was relieved when the bank came into view. Stepping inside, she smoothed her windswept hair and gave her numb cheeks a few quick pats. Eric emerged from his office just as she was unbuttoning her navy blue pea coat.

He smiled and motioned her forward. "You mind waiting in my office? I need to hand something to Mark."

In less than a minute he returned, closing his office door. She'd taken off her coat and moved to meet his embrace.

"I saw your father today. He was in good spirits, but quite exhausted."

Eric's arms settled around her waist. "Did you see Madeline?"

"I did. She should be back at your house now. If it's possible, she looked more worn out than your father."

Eric chuckled. "She's been by his side night and day. I've asked her to take a little more time for herself, but she won't hear of it. She loves him."

"She does."

Their gazes locked. Her cheeks incinerated. When his gaze didn't relent, she changed the subject.

"Chase was indicted yesterday."

Eric led them to a pair of chairs in front of his desk. They sat down. "I know. The district attorney's office wants this case to go to court as soon as possible. Despite pressure from the mayor's office, Chase will go to trial for attempted murder."

Elie nodded, biting her bottom lip. "Do you think there'll be a conviction?"

Eric shrugged his shoulders. "I don't know. I was at your parents' house for dinner the other day, and they gave me a history lesson on offenses against blacks by the Klan. Whenever a death was involved, petty minor violations were the only charges."

Elie's brows drew together. Four months ago, four young girls had died in the bombing of the 16th Street Baptist Church in Birmingham. No one had been charged with a crime.

With a loving smile, Eric reached over and clasped her hand in his. "I think we have a good case against Chase. The bullet removed from my father's back will match Chase's gun, which is in FBI custody, and Amanda swore she'd testify against Chase, regardless of the outcome to her reputation."

"Amanda—testify? Are you sure you can trust her?"

Eric's lips dipped down in an off-kilter smile. "She's resigned from the bank and just the other day, she gave a written confession to the FBI. I think she's feeling guilty."

Elie noted the confidence in Eric's voice, and the reservation in his eyes. Chase's imminent prosecution didn't guarantee a conviction. The likelihood a Klan member would be seated on the jury was high and he'd block a guilty verdict.

"Wait, did you say you had dinner with my parents? You never mentioned that before."

A satisfied grin spread across his features. "I did. Emmett invited me over a few days ago."

Elie could hardly contain her excitement. Sitting on the edge of her seat, she squeezed his hand. "Well, you're one for secrets. How did this come about?"

The corners of Eric's mouth spread even further. "It appears I've made quite an impression on your parents."

Elie frowned, despite his smile. "We know that already. Did they tell you again that we can't be together?" Not wanting him to see the tears stinging the backs of her eyelids, Elie stood and tried to turn away, but Eric's hand held fast.

"Would you come here?" He pulled her into his lap. "No,

that's not what they said." He wiped a tear from her cheek, tracing the limits of her lips with his finger. "They gave me permission," he said, voice husky, his warm breath skimming across her cheeks. His mouth took hers in a deliciously sweet kiss.

"Really?" she gasped, after he finally relinquished her lips.

Eric chuckled between the kisses he planted along her jaw, ending with a nip just beneath her earlobe. "Really. Your father said he'd noticed something different, even before I'd asked to go to Selma and bring you home that weekend."

New tears emerged and this time they didn't sting.

"Elie," he murmured against her neck, "my kisses shouldn't be causing you to weep. Stop crying." Eric pulled a handkerchief out of his pocket and dried her tears. She giggled at his efforts, which he put a stop to with a kiss that left her breathless.

****

It was day one of the trial into the attempted murder of Amanda Wilcox and the shooting of Morgan Montgomery. Mark Greene testified to the arrival of Chase at the Montgomery estate, the crash into the tree, and the drunken ravings he made toward the group. Mark recalled Chase waving a gun before pointing it at Amanda. The defense attempted to focus the cross-examination on Chase's inebriation and how he had no control of his faculties. Mark, however, remained committed to his testimony, stating Chase had refused all efforts at a peaceful resolution.

Another traitor, Asa thought glumly as he sat hunched behind Chase's chair on the defense side of the courtroom, watching Mark slander his son.

Klan supporters packed the room, but the judge proclaimed zero tolerance for outbursts, and that a fair trial was the goal of the justice system. A few disgruntled mutterings were heard throughout Mark's testimony, but the judge kept a sharp eye on the gallery.

After Mark testified, the defense requested, and was granted, a brief recess. The legal teams and observers streamed into the outside hall for a respite. Two guards on either side escorted Chase McDougal out through a side door and were on their way to a temporary holding room when his lawyer called out to them and gestured to bring Chase over. Asa, the attorneys, along with Edward and Shane, stood away from the onlookers who talked among themselves about the trial. The guards exchanged reluctant looks until a stern word from the lead attorney, Jack Conner, decided the matter. Another attorney berated the guards for their impudence. One guard apologized multiple times, explaining the room was for Chase's safety during the recess.

Asa laughed harshly. "Who's going to harm my son? Do you know these men here are all on our side?" He waved his hand toward the men who filled the hall.

"That darkie-lover could barely give a straight answer when crossed. I could see the jury lost interest in his story," Edward said in triumph.

"Now, don't start counting chickens. We've a long way to go here."

Asa listened as the attorneys briefed him and his sons on their thoughts about the case when a slight disturbance across the hall arrested their attention. A black man entered the atrium and eyed the crowd. At the sight of Edward McDougal, he lurched forward, walking with a slight limp.

Edward's face crinkled. "Who's that?"

The man stopped, opened his trench coat and produced a rifle.

"Guards!" Asa called out.

"You killed my wife!" the man shouted. "You killed her." His voice broke, and he trembled, tears coursing down his cheeks. He lifted the weapon and a shot cracked the air.

"Guards!" Asa's voice bellowed out as he tried to move out of the way of the rifle. He tripped and fell to the floor. Grunting in pain, he propped himself up on his elbow. A pair of lifeless eyes stared back at him.

Edward.

Blood seeped from beneath his form. Asa scampered back to avoid contact with the red river. Armed guards dropped to one knee and shots echoed in the atrium, ringing in Asa's ears.

"Kill him!" someone shouted. Local citizens drew their concealed weapons, aiming for the old man.

Asa's breath choked in his throat upon seeing that he, Jack, and Shane were right in the line of fire. Jack held up his hands, crying, "No!" but it was too late. More gunfire. Shane screamed, clutching his middle and falling to his knees. Asa dove to the tiled floor, slithering on his stomach like a snake to a nearby bench.

The assassin clutched his back, crying out in pain. Another bullet ripped through his left collarbone and out the front. He let out a gurgled sound. With his gun aimed at the ceiling, he fired a round before collapsing. Shards of the roof dropped onto the scene.

Another scream was heard as one of the McDougal attorneys fell in a heap, a victim of a stray bullet.

When the noise ceased, footsteps pounded the floor. Asa lifted his eyes, and tried to focus through the cloud of gun smoke. Police rushed into the building, their mouths dropping at the scene before them. Blood was spattered over more than just the floor, covering the walls, the people, the furniture. A couple of the officers removed their caps, and scratched their heads.

Asa inched from his crouched position behind a wooden bench. A cold sweat dripped from the strands of his hair, his body shaking with the shock of the attack. A fist went to his mouth, and he choked back a lump of something threatening to override his voluntary muscle response. The dead eyes of his son Edward still followed him even from across the hall. One of his high-priced attorneys, Jack Conner, managed to make his figure small against the opposite wall and his head awkwardly rotated as if testing his ability to move.

"Father," Chase called from near the body of Edward. He clutched his left arm, blood seeping through his fingers. Asa tore his eyes away. All he could see was his dead son's gaze, which he was certain would haunt him the rest of his days. A sudden jolt of anger struck Asa as he remembered why he was here. *Chase.*

A black man riddled with bullet holes lay sprawled almost in the center of the hall, a rifle a few feet away. A young man moaned as he tried to crawl across the floor, leaving a trail of blood behind him. Breathing heavily, he struggled to lift his face from the floor. His movements ceased.

"Shane!" Asa yelled for his son. Silence answered him. Asa's jellied knees prohibited him from standing, but after considerable effort, he managed to plod his way over to the body on the floor, the bitter smell of smoke from the gunfire bringing tears to his eyes. Blood siphoned from his face, and weakness brought him again to his knees. A few men turned Shane over and, seeing the large stomach wound, began placing handkerchiefs onto the gaping hole in an effort to stop the rest of Shane's life's blood from draining onto the floor.

"Is he…?"

"He's alive, mayor."

In the distance, sirens sounded. Shane McDougal was the first to receive medical attention. Asa climbed into the ambulance beside his son and shouted for the drivers to hurry to the hospital.

Chase was left alone.

****

Elie ran past the barn and toward the house, her sides aching as she forced her feet to move faster. *A shooting at the courthouse!* Edward McDougal was confirmed dead, Shane badly injured, and Chase had a bullet wound to the arm. An older black man had gone crazy, crying over his wife before shooting at the McDougals.

His wife! Elie gasped and halted at the kitchen's back door, her hand over her heart, feeling its rapid pounding against her ribcage. *It can't be. The old ragged man…what did the barber call him? Ray?* She slipped past the small kitchen table, shouting Eric's name.

"He's out back. Quit yellin'. And you know better than to run in the house! You are not ten years old no more, Elnora Brown!"

"Sorry, Miss Hattie," she called and waved as she passed. Elie made her way toward the back veranda, but before she could reach it, the door opened and Eric entered, a confused look on his face. She collapsed into his arms, her breathing hard. He lifted her chin as she struggled to catch her breath.

"Darling, what is it?" His voice filled with concern.

*Darling…*The word sounded like honey, and Elie had more than one sweet tooth.

She wanted to spend longer than a second daydreaming on how other endearments would sound coming from his lips, but the news of the shooting was more important. He pulled her out onto the veranda and they sat on a white wicker couch adorned with hunter green cushions.

Slowly, she repeated what her father had told her. There was no look of triumph on Eric's face. Instead, she saw his color drain as he sat back, absorbing the news. "Now, I'm sure the shooter is that man I saw earlier near the barber shop. I think his wife is in a coma."

"So there's a chance she could wake up?"

Elie shrugged. "The man sounded like he had no hope."

Eric stared out into the open field behind the house, a

pensive look on his face. "I've been spending all my energy on covering my father's duties at the bank and helping with his care that I haven't had time to be angry at the McDougals."

She slipped a hand in his. "So many have suffered at their hands," she said, her voice tinged in sadness.

"No doubt the Knights will avenge the McDougals."

Feeling the muscles in his hand tense, Elie gave him a gentle squeeze.

He smiled at the gesture. "Whatever happens, we'll face it together." Lifting her hand to his lips, he placed a tender kiss on it.

Miss Hattie cleared her throat, announcing she'd two steaming cups of hot chocolate for them. "It's all over the news…what happened down at the courthouse. They sayin' both Edward and Shane McDougal are dead."

"You said Shane as well?" Elie leaned forward.

"Mmm-hmm. Died at the hospital. Gunshot to the belly. Didn't have a chance." She excused herself and entered the house.

Elie put a hand to her chest and collapsed against the seat. Memories of their brief encounters flooded her mind. She immediately blocked that night before the Christmas pageant, but the afternoon at Wilson's stuck to her thoughts like a bur. It'd shocked her that Shane had harbored some romantic inclinations toward her. She never considered him as a suitor, yet she couldn't help but think he was different from his brothers—less culpable perhaps. What would have happened had he not been influenced by his elder siblings or his father? How could he have hated her people *and* been attracted to her?

Eric's keen gaze was on her. Did he guess her thoughts? She lifted the cup to her lips to hide the burn in her cheeks.

Narrowed eyes refused to look away. "What are you thinking about?"

Elie cleared her throat. "Shane approached me at Wilson's

some months back. He, um…I think he wanted to court me."

Eric spewed hot chocolate onto the veranda. "He did what?" His green eyes sparked in anger, the nostrils of his straight nose flaring.

"What if he wasn't like his brothers?"

"Elie!" He sat his cup on the nearby accent table and turned his stern gaze on her. "You don't seriously believe he didn't harbor those prejudices he lived out in every attack you saw him commit—every attack in which *you* were targeted."

"No, of course not, but I really think he liked me."

Eric's features softened, his gaze raking her face with unadulterated pleasure. "Of course he liked you. What man wouldn't?" He leaned forward, his lips taking hers.

He tasted like chocolate.

Slowly, he dragged his mouth away, his eyes smoldering with desire.

"What are you thinking about, Mr. Montgomery?"

Warm eyes reconnoitered her. A slow grin spread across his face.

Now how could I have ever considered anyone but him!

"I'm thinking about you."

She held his gaze and then set the hot chocolate down, lifting her weighty curls from her shoulders.

"Warm?" His eyes teased.

She let the curls drop. "How's your father?" she asked, ignoring the insinuation that he was the cause of her warmth.

Eric gave her a half-grin. "With Mrs. Hoover attending him, I doubt he feels any pain."

Elie laughed. "My father says she hums all day long."

"She does. She's in love."

Eric drew his fingers down her arm, drawing goose bumps to the surface. She was thankful her long sleeves hid them from his sight.

"I don't hear you humming," Eric said innocently.

"Perhaps I'm not in love." She stood but he wrapped his

arms around her waist and dragged her back and into his lap. Strong arms held her tightly against his firm chest.

"You want to repeat that? I didn't hear you." His eyes glinted a challenge.

"Eric—" He silenced her with a kiss. Despite the chilly January air seeping through the screens of the veranda, heat filled her as Eric's warm lips moved tenderly across her own.

"Elie…" he whispered against her lips, his hand reaching up to cradle the back of her head, pinning her pleasantly against his mouth.

"Ah-hem!" came the loud interruption. The cook's disapproving stare assessed them. Elie tried to wiggle out of Eric's embrace but failed, his hands locked around her waist.

"Your father is askin' for you, Mr. Eric."

He gave her a lopsided grin. "Thank you, Miss Hattie. The hot chocolate was excellent. Will we be having brownies later?" he asked in a somewhat childlike manner.

She jabbed a hand into the folds of her wide hips. "You will be gettin' no brownies."

Eric feigned shock. "Elie entrapped me!" His fingers pointed at his chest in innocence. "She jumped on my lap, and I was helpless. What's a man to do with such a beautiful woman?" He reached up to stroke Elie's hair.

Elie groaned and slapped him playfully across the face. She jumped up, moving quickly out of his reach. He rose, slowly rubbing the side of his face. "Thank you, Miss Hattie, I think I'll go see my father now."

Her stern look remained fixed. Eric produced his famous dimpled grin, and Elie watched as Miss Hattie's lips twitched. Though she tried to resist, Eric's smile undid her. His grin broadened at his triumph, and he planted a swift kiss on her cheek. As he went inside, she knocked the back of his wavy head.

"Ow!"

"Guess she's still a little mad about the two of us," Eric

whispered into Elie's ear as they climbed the staircase to Morgan's room.

Elie frowned. "I don't think she'll ever approve."

****

His office was trashed. Breathing heavily, sweat poured down the sides of his face as Asa leaned against his desk. Two sons gone. In his rage, he'd thrown anything he could get his hands on across the room. Two weeks ago yesterday, Shane had lost consciousness at the courthouse and never regained it, passing on right before he was to be wheeled into surgery. Asa didn't even have a chance to say goodbye.

Edward.

His eldest son had died instantly with a gunshot wound to the chest. Edward's cold eyes continued to plague him to the point he shook violently from the mental image. A telephone rang in the distance. He stood completely still. His secretary had been ordered to hold all calls unless it was his attorney or Chief Wilcox. The ringing ceased and he heard a soft knock at the door.

Ms. Graham quietly opened the door and entered. "Sir, Chief Wilcox is on the phone for—" A small gasp escaped her lips as her eyes slowly roamed the office: Papers strewn about. Glass and broken wood littered the floor. Everything out of place. Even the telephone dangled from the desk, and Asa's prized cherry leather chair was tipped over.

He cleared his throat. "Thank you, Ms. Graham, that will be all." He stooped to pick up the telephone and grunted as he lifted his weight. He put the receiver to his mouth and gave a low, slow greeting.

Chief Wilcox didn't even return the greeting. "Have you looked outside your office lately?"

Holding the telephone, he walked to the spacious window overlooking much of Main Street.

Picketers.

People of both races stood in front of the administration building, some holding signs with a message he couldn't read from his vantage point, and others shouting and waving fists in the air.

Asa's mouth dropped open in astonishment. "What's this?"

"People are demanding your resignation. Your sons, Asa…Morgan wasn't the first one shot."

Unable to speak, Asa could only listen as the police chief detailed the story of the attack on Ray, the man who'd shot his sons, and his wife Esther. A week before the courthouse shooting, Asa's sons had fired several rounds at Ray and his wife as they were walking to their home in an unpopulated area at the edge of town. Esther was comatose but died shortly after Ray took his revenge.

Asa's fury rose. "So?"

"So? *So?* It's no secret your sons are Klan members. Some of the townsfolk are sayin' you authorized your boys to set those fires in Selma!"

Asa's mind spun, unable to comprehend Chief Wilcox's meaning.

"Are you listening to me? You're now connected to the Klan, and all the violence your sons have done in town, including the shootin' of Morgan Montgomery. You're being blamed for all of it!"

A chill swept through Asa, his palm growing clammy around the phone. If that were the case, would that linkage go as far as the state capital? Since the shooting, Asa had received no word from Governor Wallace. His hope was the news of the incident would be contained to Freeman. With his connection to the Klan known, no doubt the negative publicity had reached the capital. It was only a matter of time until people started whispering about the governor. Asa McDougal prided himself as being a favorite of Governor Wallace. *I can't lose my position!*

"I'll handle it," Asa responded gruffly.

"What are you going to do?"

"Well, for starters, they're disturbing the peace, aren't they? Get your men out there and start cuffing people."

"Asa—"

"I mean it. Start making some arrests. I'll hold a press conference." He slammed the phone down and walked toward his office door. Yanking it open, he barked, "Ms. Graham!"

"Yes, sir!" She stood from behind her desk, just a few feet away from Asa's door. Frazzled, she smoothed her red wool skirt, erasing the startled expression from her face.

"Contact the press and let them know I'll be holding a brief conference on the steps of the administration building at noon."

"But sir, the protestors—"

"Do it! I'm sure by then they'll not be around." He stomped back into his office and picked up the phone to dial his speechwriter. He needed a dynamic address to quell this nonsense. His sons had brought shame to the family, but he was going to salvage whatever dignity was still attached to the McDougal name—and keep his job.

****

At noon, a mass of reporters gathered on the steps of the city's administration building awaiting the arrival of the mayor. A podium with a microphone was prepped, and protestors were nowhere in sight.

As soon as the building doors were opened and he stepped out, cameras flashed. Even before he reached the podium, reporters bombarded him with questions concerning the connection of his family to the black assassin killed at the courthouse, his personal membership with the KKK, Governor Wallace's opinion of his job performance since the slaughter at the courthouse, and whether or not a formal apology for the shooting of Morgan Montgomery would be issued.

That last question almost set him off. Now he understood why his sons were prone to react to everything with homicidal violence. He wanted to get his hands around the neck of the reporter who dared to ask whether he or any McDougal would apologize to a darkie-lovin' Montgomery. Morgan should be the one to apologize. *If he'd just helped his race like he was supposed to, none of this would have happened.* Edward and Shane would still be alive, Chase wouldn't be sitting in jail, and even Morgan wouldn't have been shot.

In his speech, he attempted to dispel any myths of his involvement in the Selma riot. The jury would exonerate his son Chase, and neither he nor his sons knew of Ray Burns before the courthouse shooting. One reporter asked whether the state governor had requested his resignation. Lifting his chin and scanning the crowd, he coolly replied, "I'm not leaving my position as mayor of Freeman."

No sooner had the press conference ended and he entered his office did Miss Graham's phone ring. She gave her usual cheerful greeting, but the change in her facial expression caused him to pause. She said nothing else and extended the phone. "It's the governor's office," she whispered.

Asa frowned. The press conference had been live. He took the phone from his secretary and, before he could greet Governor Wallace, he heard the words he was so sure he'd never hear. After the resounding click of the phone on the other end, he calmly handed the receiver back to Ms. Graham. She replaced the receiver and then turned concerned eyes toward her employer. He didn't enter his office. Shoulders slumped, he walked away without explanation.

He was fired.

Chapter Twenty-One

PROVEN FAITH

Spring brought rain that soaked the ground every afternoon and did on yet another gloomy April Saturday. Eric spent most of the day indoors in the front office, poring over banking documents his father was going to review on Monday. A few months prior, Eric had taken on the task of running the numbers on opening a second branch in Selma. Mark Greene was considering moving to the city to be closer to the residents the bank assisted there, and possibly provide more support for the civil rights movement. Morgan had once mentioned to Mark about expanding. However, Morgan was waiting for Eric to return home. That revelation bolstered his urgency to prepare the expansion plans.

Miss Hattie brought the mail in and Eric briefly scanned the pile. Elie's handwriting on the outside of an envelope had him snatching it from the stack and hastily slicing the top fold with a letter opener. She spent a lot of weekends at the university working on final projects and finishing her allotted tutoring hours, and during those times of distance, they exchanged many letters. It had been two weeks since he last saw her, and if he hadn't been working so hard on the second branch proposal, he'd have gone mad in her absence.

Eric had asked Emmett for Elie's hand in marriage and Emmett agreed, but stressed not to propose until after she graduated. Both her parents planned to watch their daughter walk across the graduation stage. Elie dreamed of being a teacher, and Eric wouldn't stand in her way.

Her final exams were in a couple of weeks, so she wrote of her decision to remain on campus for the weekend. He was beginning to understand—just slightly—the separation anxiety Morgan must have felt when Evelyn passed. Elie wasn't even his bride and yet, not being able to see and hold her caused excruciating loneliness.

Eric gathered the proposal papers and secured them with a paper clip. He was ready to present the plans to his father. Just outside the library, he paused at the slightly open door, hearing his father grumble to Madeline.

"This weather has ruined my plans for a picnic with you."

"That would have been lovely."

"You are lovely."

Eric rolled his eyes. *Father, that's how you woo?*

"Well, what do you want to do?"

Madeline's sharp intake of breath gave Eric chills. In a couple of months, Elie would have the same response.

"Madeline," his father whispered.

Eric strained to hear the rest of the proposal, but soon the elated cries of a woman in love drowned out any words.

Madeline was so different from his mother. It amazed him that a man could love two women completely opposite in nature. Where his mother was soft in her persuasion, Madeline was a firecracker. Morgan had always been tender with his mother, yet Madeline brought out a firmness he didn't know his father possessed. Eric could often hear what he thought was bickering until he could see with his own eyes that they were playing cat and mouse. After a heated discussion, Eric would see the two of them in a passionate embrace. His father was to marry a highly independent woman who could match him in almost anything.

Eric cocked his head, considering. His and Elie's relationship was extremely similar.

Eric tapped lightly on the door.

As he entered, Madeline turned, her cheeks wet with tears. "Oh, honey! Congratulate us." She held out her hand for him to see the ring.

Eric politely took her hand, having already viewed the ring when Morgan had asked for his son's permission to marry. He'd assured his father that his approval had come long ago. Eric kissed Madeline's hand and flashed a grin.

"You don't mind?"

He leaned in and kissed her cheek. "Not at all. Congratulations, and welcome to the family."

"I'm sorry, son. You had a proposal you wanted me to see?" Morgan stepped forward, his hand extended to receive the paperwork.

Eric glanced at the documents in his hands. "I can just leave it here for you to view later, if you want."

"Oh no, please, Morgan, go ahead with your work. I have some plans I need to attend to now." She grinned knowingly, and then hurried out of the room.

Eric handed the proposal to his father.

Morgan skimmed the first page. He met his son's gaze with brows raised. "Another branch? In Selma?"

Eric nodded, smiling. "Mark has offered to manage the new branch. He's reviewed the proposal, and is already making plans to move." Eric tried to read his father's response. "All we would need is your approval, of course, and your decision on the location."

"Can we afford—?"

"I've run the numbers. You'll find a prospectus is included."

With a concentrated look, Morgan seated himself behind his desk. He skimmed through a few more pages and looked up. "I'll let you know." His expression gave nothing away.

Eric nodded, grinning. His proposal was solid.

****

Character witnesses in the trial against Chase McDougal numbered close to one hundred. The community's courage to take a stand against the McDougals grew with the news that the federal government was set to pass the Civil Rights Act as early as the summer. Fear of speaking out against any white man, especially a Klansman, began to fade. In late April, a McDougal had finally seen justice.

Eric heard the news on television the morning after as he sat in the day room, munching on biscuits. "I wonder if his father plans to appeal," Eric said absent-mindedly.

"Heard his father wasn't at the trial. Ain't got no plans to visit his son in jail, neither," Miss Hattie responded.

Eric shot a glance to his father, who stood behind the plush sofa. He raised a brow. "Hasn't seen him…"

"His father done disowned him, is what they say."

"Miss Hattie is correct." Morgan came around to sit on the sofa, keeping his eyes on the television screen. "Asa blames Chase for the deaths of his other sons. Apparently, he can't stand the sight of the boy." Morgan's voice dropped with a touch of sadness and a hint of pity.

Eric scrunched his brows. *Is he feeling sorry for Asa or Chase?* Who would deserve it more? Eric rubbed the space between his brows as he tried to refocus on the news broadcast, a curdled knot growing in his stomach. He couldn't. The image of Chase sitting in jail alone, without any support, continued to gnaw at him. And it frustrated him that it did.

Morgan glanced sideways at his son. "It's affecting you, too, isn't it?"

Eric looked at his father without answering.

"Ironic, isn't it?"

"I've spent years nursing a grudge against God. Having one against someone like Chase seems pointless." By the grace of God, and the months of counsel he'd received from Emmett and even his father, he had released the weight of bitterness and anger that anchored his soul to the agony he'd been living with the past few years. His heart felt too light for him to ensnare it again in such dangerous emotions.

"I visited him last week."

Eric's eyes snapped to his father. "You did? Why didn't you tell me?"

"I didn't want you to be alarmed." Morgan looked off into the distance, as if seeing Chase in front of him. "He's rather lost and scared. Very pale—almost ill."

"What did he say to you?" came Miss Hattie's question.

"Nothing at first. He was surprised to see me, of course. I asked him how he was doing, and he mumbled something incomprehensible. When I asked him to repeat it, he just stared at the floor and wouldn't say anything else."

Eric leaned his elbows on his knees, listening intently.

"I told him I held no ill will toward him. I don't know if he heard me but, hopefully, what I said will somehow ease the anguish I know he's putting himself through."

Eric massaged the knuckles of one hand, pondering his father's visit. True, he and Chase had had several unpleasant encounters and weren't exactly friends, but his father set an example Eric was determined to emulate. After all, Chase had lost everything: his brothers, his father, the next twenty years of his life.

Now was the time to show compassion.

During his lunch hour one day the following week, Eric

visited Chase in the town lock-up before he was scheduled to depart to the state penitentiary to serve the rest of his sentence. When Chase was delivered to the visiting room, seeing Eric's face stopped him short.

His father was right. Chase had a sickly appearance. Sunken eyes, pallid skin—clothes hanging off a diminished form. Eric recalled the couple of times they'd come to blows. Now it seemed Chase didn't have the strength to lift his own arms.

Chase retreated a step, butting the guard behind him.

Eric held up his palms in a truce. "I'm not here to hurt you, Chase. I've come in peace."

The guard pushed Chase into the room and sat him down on the chair in front of Eric.

"Chase?"

A quick glance up.

"Look. I know we've had more than our share of differences, but I wanted to come here." Eric cleared his throat. "I know my father visited you last week."

Chase shifted in his chair, holding Eric's gaze.

"I want you to know that I'm not angry about what happened…with my father."

Silence.

"Believe me, I'm still wrestling with what you and your brothers did to Elie, but—"

"Why?"

"What?"

His eyes searched Eric's. "Your daddy's a good, honest man. I ain't surprised he came, but you? Why aren't you mad?" he asked in a hoarse whisper.

"If this had happened half a year ago, yeah, I'd be furious. In fact, I probably would have beaten Mr. Burns to the punch."

Chase's eyes sparked.

"You asked." Eric's gaze was even. "I'm sorry about

them…your brothers," Eric said softly. "Believe me, I've wanted justice to come to the three of you for what you did to Elie, but not in the way it came."

"Well, you got it, so you can leave."

The emptiness in Chase's eyes rooted Eric to his chair. Chase was a product of his father's hatred and, despite the solidarity the Klan displayed against blacks, Asa McDougal had left his son to swing in the wind alone. The thought sobered Eric. What if his father hadn't welcomed him home? He hadn't tried to murder anyone, but loyalty had a high price tag. Morgan Montgomery was willing to pay. Asa McDougal was not.

Chase leaned back, his brows furrowing. He scanned Eric's face and laughed before being seized by an uncontrollable cough. Eric reached over to pat Chase's back, but the second his hand touched him, Chase pulled back, the whites of his eyes gleaming.

"Sorry." Eric snatched back his hand. "Look, I know you don't believe me, and I don't owe you anything—but I'm here and, if you want to talk, I'll listen." Eric held his breath. Chase didn't react. The tick of the wall clock thundered. Eric folded his hands in his lap and relaxed into the back of the seat. Chase followed suit.

Tick. Tick. Tick.

Eric cleared his throat and rose.

"No," he said in a hushed reply.

Eric's brows rose, but Chase's head was bent down. Eric again took his seat.

Chase remained silent, his eyes averted.

Eric waited.

****

Eric visited the jailhouse every day until Chase was transferred to a new facility, where he'd spend the next twenty or so years of his life. He hadn't said anything else that first day, yet the two of them made progress before Chase's departure. Eric witnessed a profound sadness and loss in Chase and his heart had gone out to the man.

One day following a visit with Chase, Eric stepped into his father's office at the bank. His visits with Chase weighed on his mind, as did the knowledge Asa refused to visit *his* son—the one person Chase longed to see.

"Dad, I'm sorry for these last few years. I should have written more. I should have—"

His father waved a hand, laughing it off. "It was only a few years. Sometimes a man needs time to find his way…to know who he is."

Eric was grateful for the lack of criticism from his father, yet there was an unmistakable look in his eyes betraying the fear he'd felt during his son's absence. Eric was resolved to never see that look in his father's eyes again.

****

Eric and Elie walked in silence through the grass on the Montgomery estate toward the training fields. A gentle breeze offset the heat of the early summer sun. The spring rains had brought fresh life to the land, the green grass and wildflowers filling the air with an invigorating scent.

Elie felt warmth between her fingers, and glanced down to see Eric's fingers gliding gently between her own. Her lips tweaked upward as their eyes met.

Nearing the fence enclosing a training paddock, Eric slowed his pace, pulling her hand close until she faced him. He captured her other hand, his eyes growing warm and full of love as they took in her face. Her heart quickened. She'd recently graduated from college, but her parents had forbidden her to pledge herself to Eric until *after* her diploma was in hand. For weeks she'd been waiting for a sign from

Eric—any sign—that he'd propose.

"Elie." A slow grin spread across his chiseled features, tipping into two perfect dimples in each cheek. A short laugh bubbled up. "I have loved you since the moment you were born. There was nothing else so fascinating to me than to see you staring at me, grabbing my hand with your tiny fingers."

Elie's head flew back and laughter erupted. "You remember that! How can you—you were barely three years old!"

His eyes twinkled. "When you make an impression, you make an impression."

Heat flashed her cheeks, embarrassment muting her lips and creating a smile.

"You were mine then—my best friend." He drew her close, a hand catching a wisp of her hair floating near her cheek. His voice lowered, the timbre of his baritone sending pleasant shivers down her spine. "And you are mine now, and I am completely yours." He grinned lopsidedly. "It took me a long time to get here. And I've been a fool about a lot of things." He traced the fringe of her collar, dipping the tip of his finger just beneath the lace. "The years I've spent away have done nothing to add to my life in the way this past year has. What I've witnessed, the people I've come to know." He paused, searching her eyes. "The God I've remembered."

His hands came to the sides of her face as he leaned in, his breath warm against her cheeks. "Tell me you love me, Elie. Tell me you are free to love me as I love you." His smile crept up. "And want to love you," he whispered, his lips taking hers softly.

"I love you, Eric Montgomery," she breathed between kisses and wrapped her arms around his neck.

"Do you know how I've ached for you?" he asked against her lips.

She felt herself being lifted from the ground and twirled high in the air. She squealed and then grew quiet as she slowly descended into his embrace. Their lips met once again, her fingers threading his hair as his arms tightened around her.

She abruptly pulled away and saw a look of curiosity cross his face. Flashing him a mischievous smile, she darted away. Eric was quick on her heels as her laughter filled the air.

EPILOGUE

July 1964

Michael stared at the cigarette in his hand. He put the thin white smoke to his lips, inhaled, and then coughed—again. He flicked the nuisance away. He'd never get used to those things.

He pushed himself off the tree he was leaning against and began the short walk to the church. He'd accepted the position as an associate pastor of a small congregation in Selma shortly after graduation, and he had started immediately, eager to leave Freeman as soon as he could.

What's today?

He knew what today was. Elnora's wedding day. He angrily booted a small stone, watching it ricochet off a nearby tree until he had to duck or get struck in the head. Even though no one was around, embarrassment swelled within, and he yelled a curse.

Elnora.

What a fool he'd been. The one woman he'd believed his equal in heart, in spirit, and she was marrying a white man—a man who'd tossed away his faith. She'd told him Eric truly had a change of heart, but remembering how difficult she was to resist, he didn't doubt she'd helped persuade Eric with her charms.

Michael wiped the sweat off his forehead with the back of his hand, flinging droplets into the dirt. It was wrong of him to think of her in that way. Elnora had been innocent. But she'd made him believe she loved him, only to dump him for someone who wasn't even their kind.

Michael stomped up the steps to the church, yanked open the door, and stormed inside. A loud sniff caused him to halt his progress. In the shadows of the back pew sat a familiar woman with rich blonde hair. She dabbed her eyes with a tissue and stood. Light from the stained-glass window streamed over her, revealing red eyes and tear-stained cheeks.

What is she doing here?

"I'm sorry," she whispered. She edged out of the pew. "I thought the church was open."

Michael held up his hand. "No, wait. You don't have to go. Please," he gestured for her to return to her seat, "stay as long as you like. Your name, miss?"

"Amanda. Amanda Wilcox."

****

Late November 1964

Morgan watched as Madeline gripped the wall in their home, easing down the hallway at a painfully slow pace. One hand beneath her belly, she continued toward the kitchen and Miss Hattie's biscuits, their aroma seeping through to every part of the house all morning. When he couldn't stand to see her stubbornly struggle any further, he silently came up from behind, wrapped his arms around her, and nibbled on a pink earlobe.

"Why, Mrs. Montgomery, if you need something, allow me to get it for you," he breathed into her ear.

She giggled. "I'm quite capable of getting a biscuit by myself, thank you very much."

"And how long has this endeavor been going on?"

"Too long," she sighed wearily.

He laughed. Madeline blew out a breath to cool her hot forehead. Eight months pregnant with twins. So far the pregnancy had gone well, and he pampered her, attending to her every need.

The Civil Rights Act was passed in July. Celebrations all across the country were reported. Change was in the air, and people talked of their good fortune as if it were immediate. Some believed the violence and prejudices would end instantly, but they were wrong. In Jonesboro, Louisiana, the Klan continued to ride through the streets as a show of power.

Race relations hadn't measurably improved, but Morgan wasn't discouraged. After the removal of Asa McDougal from the office of mayor, a special election was held to fill the vacated seat chaired by an interim official. Morgan hadn't the faintest idea who wrote his name on the ballot, but apparently many voted in favor of him, and he was, to his shock, elected mayor of Freeman.

"Mayor Montgomery. Has a pleasant ring to it, if you ask me."

Morgan looked into the eyes of his teasing son one evening, convinced he was the mastermind. It made perfect sense. Eric could have spread the word around the community to vote for Morgan on Election Day, and it wasn't at all a stretch for the residents of Freeman to do so.

"Seems I have you to thank for this office."

Eric feigned an innocent look, but Madeline smiled proudly at her husband. "You know, Eric, you should be his campaign manager when he runs for governor. You do have a proven track record." She winked.

"Oh no, I've no desire for a career in politics." Morgan held up a hand, shaking his head in disapproval.

"Perhaps, not yet..."

Morgan kissed his wife gently on the lips. Settling back into the cushions of the couch in the den, he handed Madeline a biscuit from a silver tray held by Miss Hattie, who then offered the plate to Emmett and Jacqueline. Across from them sat his son and his new wife, who playfully curled a lock of blond hair.

Eric and Elie had married a couple of months after her graduation. They bought a small house between both sets of parents, and continued to work in Freeman.

Morgan chuckled. The honeymoon was still going on for them. He watched Eric whisper something in Elie's ear, and her giggle in response. Eric lifted her chin to guide her to his lips. Morgan sighed happily. Eric had fully taken over the responsibilities of the bank, now that Morgan was mayor. Elie was teaching to her heart's content, and both were helping set an example for racial unification in town.

Upon his swearing in, Morgan immediately set out to desegregate the city, creating policy memos for schools, public businesses, and establishments. He wanted Freeman to be a benchmark for the rest of the state of Alabama. *One day, I will see this division diminish to almost nothing,* he thought as he stared at his son and daughter-in-law, both too involved in each other to notice anything else.

"Hello? Mr. Montgomery?" A soft whisper floated over him and he turned to his glowing wife. "Where are you?"

"Right here, Mrs. Montgomery. With you." He bent to kiss her lips.

The End.

About the Author

K. Victoria Chase enjoys writing passionate, yet clean romance novels. She earned degrees in Criminal Justice and Diplomacy and worked as a federal law enforcement officer for several years before deciding to try her hand at writing a complete novel. Today, K. Victoria Chase is the published author of multiple titles in romantic suspense, contemporary romance, and paranormal romance.

Visit K. Victoria Chase at http://www.kvictoriachase.com

www.ingramcontent.com/pod-product-compliance
Lightning Source LLC
LaVergne TN
LVHW020707110826
845149LV00012B/2144

* 9 7 8 0 9 8 9 0 6 5 1 5 3 *